ELEPHANT IN THE DARK

CHRISTOPHER OTT

ELEPHANT IN THE DARK

Murder in the eye of the beholder

Christopher Ott

CHRISTOPHER OTT

Copyright © Christopher Ott, 2023

All rights reserved.

No part of this publication may be reproduced, distributed, or transmitted in any form or by any means, including photocopying, recording, or other electronic or mechanical methods, without the prior written permission of the publisher, except as permitted by copyright law. For permission requests, contact Christopher Ott at Christopherott@gmail.com.

The story, all names, characters, and incidents portrayed in this production are fictitious. No identification with actual persons (living or deceased), places, buildings, and products is intended or should be inferred.

Book Cover by Jacqueline Daniel

To Jacqui, Jude and Gwen

CHRISTOPHER OTT

Elephant in the Dark

One by one, we go in the dark and come out
saying how we experience the animal.
One of us happens to touch the trunk.
A water-pipe kind of creature.
Another, the ear.
A very strong, always moving
back and forth, fan-animal.
Another, the leg.
I find it still, like a column on a temple.
Another touches the curved back.
A leathery throne.
Another the cleverest, feels the tusk.
A rounded sword made of porcelain.
He is proud of his description.
Each of us touches one place
and understands the whole that way.
The palm and the fingers feeling in the dark
are how the senses explore the reality of the elephant.
If each of us held a candle there,
and if we went in together, we could see it.

Rumi

CHRISTOPHER OTT

ELEPHANT IN THE DARK

PROLOGUE

THE MARMALADE CAT has been staring at Detective Lanie Daniels for over ten minutes. It leaps down from the cafe's faded red-tiled roof, into the courtyard and noiselessly inches its way towards her like the sun stalking a shadow. It reaches her and before Lanie has a chance to stop the stray, it rubs the under part of its chin across her exposed left ankle. She shoos the pest away.

It's a typically crisp Melbourne Monday morning. The cafe's chimney eclipses the spring sun, casting Lanie in shadow. She's staring at her reflection in a pool of last night's rain, resting besides her scuffed RM Williams. She's wearing an appropriately worn-in black leather jacket, black jeans, and faded black t-shirt. Pangs of nostalgia bite as her dad's features stare back at her from the puddle: Malaysian, black hair, narrow-ish head and a full nose. He died when she was thirteen. Pancreatic cancer. She filled the void with things—lots and lots of things, which the insurance money paid for. And when they stopped bringing her joy, she stopped trying to fill the hole and instead fell into it.

As she types the cafe's WiFi password into her

phone, which she finds laminated and blu-tacked to a nearby wall, the waitress brings over her egg and bacon roll, along with an empty glass and old Hendricks bottle full of tap water. She thanks her, then deftly lifts the top of the brioche bun, douses the insides in sriracha sauce, returns the crown and takes a big bite. A mixture of hot sauce, egg yolk and oil drips out of the end and onto the custody papers she's reading for the millionth time. She has an eight year old son, Thomas, who she only sees once a month, because her ex-husband is an entitled prick who always gets his own way. The accident didn't help, either. Her phone rings and she picks it up.

"Daniels here," she answers. "Slow down. What's happened? Shit. I'll be there as soon as I can."

She takes a second and final bite of her roll, pours her still-boiling-hot coffee into a keep cup, and exits the cafe. As she leaves, the sun peeks above the roof and finally blankets the courtyard in warmth. The cat leaps onto the bench and tucks into her leftovers. That was her boss on the phone. Celeste Simone is dead.

ONE

LANIE WALKS OVER to her beat-up, paprika-red Ford Fiesta, parked half a metre from the sidewalk. She's holding off for as long as she can getting a new car. She likes her car. She calls him Frankie. After Frankie Lane, the country singer who sang Rawhide—and who Lanie suspects was her dad's inspiration for her own name. Not that Lanie likes country music. She hates it. But she does like the Billy Crystal movie City Slickers, which her dad rented for her whenever she was sick and he'd won a few bucks on the pokies. Frankie the Fiesta.

She jumps inside Frankie. More than half her worldly possessions are strewn across the backseat: a couple of sweat-stained t-shirts, a spare pair of inside-out black jeans and a few sport's bras she picked up for a bargain at Kmart. Among this embarrassment of riches is no less than three lost Chapsticks. Maybe four. And precisely $1.70 worth of recyclable empty Diet Coke bottles—a princely sum. It smells cold. And musky. But also familiar; cathartic. She pulls out from the curb; the radio crackles to life.

"Celeste Simone, famous social media influencer and

Melbourne export, has been found dead, in her bath in her hotel room, of a suspected drug overdose. She was back in her hometown attending the Melbourne Cup with her husband, famed futurist and owner of Umwelt Platforms, Jerome Pitt. More to come."

"Fuck," Lanie mumbles. "How did the media find out so quickly?" Of course she knew the answer. Ever since everyone started live-streaming every second of their lives on Umwelt Optic Lenses a couple of years back, there's not a lot that doesn't go unseen anymore. Who knows how many people were streaming Celeste's point of view when she died.

Live-streaming an influencer's point of view was the natural evolution from following them on social media, posting single frame images of their lives, to being put in their shoes at twenty-four frames per second, in real time. It started with Facebook Live, then Stories, then Twitch and TikToks and so on, but holding a phone or camera was clunky, so Umwelt took away the hardware. Now wannabe stars can buy a contact-lens that films and broadcasts their live point of view. As with most innovations, it was bankrolled by porn. Lonely perverts parted with their hard-earned cash, to virtually sleep with a deepfake version of anyone they chose in the first person. Of course it didn't take long for narcissistic influencers, like Celeste, to jump on board, letting their fanbase live vicariously through them. Society had reached peak voyeur.

Lanie rubs her front teeth with her tongue. The

mental mastication adds to the anxiety growing in her stomach. She pulls up to The Grand Theatre Hotel on Russell street in the CBD. For its namesake, it's a converted grand theatre; five-stars, extremely Instagrammable. The front is cordoned off, and journalists are gathered around the door, waiting to hear the official police statement. Lanie steps out of her car, jockeys her way through the frenzy of journalists, ducks under the yellow crime-scene tape, flashes her badge to no one in particular, and catches up with two very contrasting men inside.

"Detective Daniels, nice of you to finally join us," Captain Jon Bailey says. Jon looks stressed. He's a stoic yet kind man with thinning dark hair, and noticeably lighter skin on his upper lip where his moustache used to be. He shaved it last week for a kids' cancer charity—that's the kind of guy he is. She likes him, and he likes her. He's the closest thing to a father she's had in her adult life.

 Next to him is Jerome Pitt, who's normally winsome smile looks dulled. He's Celeste's husband—ex-husband. Jerome is a software engineer, entrepreneur and futurist, who founded Umwelt Platforms—an American multinational technology conglomerate based in San Francisco with the rest of them, which not only mass-produces Umwelt Lenses but also owns the accompanying namesake social media platform, which boasts over three million concurrent average streamers at any given moment. Forbes estimates his net worth to be around $US 31 billion, making him the 25th-richest person in the world. Not bad for a 41-year-old. He and Celeste have been, or had been, married for just over three years. Their faces splashed across the pages of all the gossip mags. One minute they're on the French Riviera, the next they're deep-sea diving in the Maldives. It was a modern day love-story. Him, a never-say-never tech genius out to change the world; her, the world's most influential influencer and content creator—famous for being famous.

Lanie couldn't tell if Jon was putting on a performance for Jerome, or just plain tired.

"I'd like you to meet Mr Pitt," he continues.

"Pleased to meet you Detective Daniels. I'm the one who asked for you to be on this job. Well, not you exactly, but someone like you. A detective, I mean." Jerome draws a deep breath. "I don't think this was an accident," he says matter-of-factly before applying lip balm to his cracked lips.

Lanie's eyes meet his, "I—"

Before she responds another man joins them.

"Ah, this is my head engineer and good friend, Mr Samuel Bateman," Jerome introduces him. "He's going to help you with your investigation. Anything you need, ask Sam."

Samuel Bateman is everything Jerome's not. Charmless, unconfident and unusually sweaty. His glasses conspire to highlight how close his eyes are set together. An unfortunate closeness that makes him objectively untrustworthy. But Lanie's not one to profile—most of the time. He's of an average height, and his brown hair is starting to grey.

Lanie shakes his hand too firmly, then turns to the captain. "Investigation?"

He doesn't respond. He knows her better than anyone, and her subtle change in posture betrays her intent to launch into a trademark tirade which he cuts off with a stern look—a we'll-talk-about-it-later look.

Samuel pulls his clammy hand away, which Lanie was still holding, and adjusts his glasses. "Pleased to meet you," he stammers.

"Pleasure's mine," Lanie replies, looking towards the Captain, who responds with a lopsided-smile before he and Jerome wander off. As they do, Lanie can hear the captain reassuring Jerome that she's the best 'man' for the job. *Now's not the time*. She lets it slide. Plus, if she's learned anything over the near decade she's worked with him, it's to leave the diplomacy to the captain. She has a job to do, and Celeste's body isn't getting any warmer.

"Oh and Lanie," the captain turns around, "don't forget to put on your camera." He taps the corner of his right eye. "You know the rules: all investigations must be filmed, and I don't especially want the coroner riding me because you forgot again."

Unlike the influencers who were using the latest Umwelt technology with the contact lenses, a lot of luddites like Lanie were still happy to use the more analogue alternatives, like old-fashioned body cams or in Lanie's case glasses. Hers were a pair of Ray-Ban Wayfarers, which she's had for years.

"Right," she turns to Bateman, "I need a list of all the people watching through Celeste's eyes at the time."

Samuel steps over to the front desk, to his laptop, and checks on its progress. "You will have it in twenty minutes," he finds his voice in the data.

"You know it'd make my job easier if you guys just handed over the footage, right?"

"There is no footage to hand over," Samuel scoffs nervously. "Celeste never saved her live streams. She hated watching herself back; seeing herself and hearing her own voice, so she'd stopped archiving her streams a long time ago. Plus it made her content more FOMO inducing, which got her more views. Anyway, even if she had saved them, data security has been the ethical cornerstone of Umwelt from the beginning. There's end-to-end encryption on the content that locks out everyone other than the owner from accessing the data. So, there's only one person who can access the footage anyway, and that's Celeste."

"What about people who were streaming, could they have recorded it?" Lanie knows the answer, but is more interested in how Sam responds than his actual response.

"No," Sam replies, rubbing his chin. "Umwelt doesn't let users take screenshots or screencasts to ensure the footage can't be reproduced or misused," he says as if he was presenting a well-rehearsed pitch to Umwelt's stakeholders. "Netflix has been doing it for over a decade to stop people pirating their shows—it's like that."

Lanie nods. "Okay," she says, keen to see upstairs. "Now, if you'd excuse me, I'm going to go look at the scene. Let me know when you have that list ready."

Sam blinks rapidly and looks back down at his screen. "No problem."

Lanie makes her way over to the elevators, presses the button and waits, shifting nervously from foot to foot for what feels like an eternity. She looks around. Police are milling about; journalists are still gathered out the front waiting, and a new crowd of people have begun to gather, snaking their way across the panel glass windows. *Not these pricks.* They're the Carters, so-called after Ken Carter, the photojournalist who became famous, or infamous, for his 'The Struggling Girl' photograph. The one with the vulture stalking the mal-nourished African girl, who'd collapsed on the way to a United Nations feeding centre. Instead of helping her, Carter waited for who knows how long, until the vulture was close enough for him to take the perfect Pulitzer prize winning photo. The Carters idolise him, making the utilitarian argument that the photo inspired millions of people to help, compared to Carter saving the one girl. *I wonder how many of them know he committed suicide months after he took it? They call themselves Carters, but they're really the vulture.* On more than one occasion, like their hero, they've chased the best 'shot' over helping a person.

"Detective Daniels," a voice calls out to her.

"Frank, how the fuck did you get in here?"

Frank Farmer is a Carter, but he's Lanie's Carter. He

comes in handy when Lanie needs some of the off-the-books kind of help.

Frank looks dishevelled, but that's no big surprise as he always looks that way. He's a little overweight, has scraggly greying hair, and is wearing a T-shirt with a Guy Fawkes mask screen-print.

"I have my ways," he answers easily. "What do you know?"

"I haven't even seen the body yet, Frank. But money talks, and Jerome Pitt wants us to investigate."

Frank nods. "Hmm, I don't know," he starts, "this feels wrong." Lanie looks up at him. He sips the remaining contents of his iced-latte, down to the cubes rattling in the bottom, and finishes his sentence battling a brain freeze. "Like, iced-coffee in winter wrong," he says, pressing his palm against his temple."

Lanie scoffs. "Yeah but you feel this way about every case."

"Yeah, I suppose that's true," he chuckles.

"Get out of here, Frank, before I see you."

"Goodbye detective," he says, turning towards a hotel worker sitting by herself, waiting to be interviewed. "You've got my number."

The elevator finally arrives. As Lanie steps forward to enter, she stops. She turns back to the group of Carters staring through the glass. Her eyes rest on a stranger, whose face is shadowed by a hooded jumper. It has a Nirvana screen print on the front.

"Hey Frank!" she calls out. Frank looks back at her from a few metres away. "Who's that?"

Frank looks in the direction Lanie's nodding. The hooded stranger is gone. "Who's who?"

Lanie's head darts back and forward, trying to spot them again, but they're gone. "Dammit, never mind."

Lanie shrugs it off, steps inside the lift and presses the button for the fifth floor. Just as she turns to inspect the blackheads on her nose in the elevator mirror, an arm pushes forcefully through the closing doors.

It's Jerome Pitt. He smiles at her. The elevator music plays—audible wallpaper, covering up the cracks of awkward silence.

TWO

"LET ME HELP you," Jerome says, as the elevator dings and the doors pull apart on the fifth floor.

"Help me, how?" She doesn't need his help beyond what he's legally obliged to do.

"I can help you get your son, Thomas, back."

Silence.

The doors close again. His words hang in the air along with the elevator. Lanie is frozen. She doesn't get caught off guard often. Ever, in fact. *Who the fuck does this guy think he is?*

"I know you lost custody of Thomas to your ex-husband, Brett." He lets the words marinate, taking a sip from his glass water bottle. "And I also know he used footage captured on his Umwelts. Our system triggers a notification anytime law enforcement is involved in a case, even ones as pedestrian as yours." He puts his hands in his pockets. "We can help each other out. I know you probably think this is just another OD, but there's more to it. I'm sure of it. Someone did this to Celeste—to me—and I want you to find out who. I need you to. Celeste is, was, the love of my life and I'm gonna make whoever did this pay, if it's the last thing I do." He draws in a deep breath.

Lanie looks into Jerome's eyes, studying him. He seems angry. *This may be the first time in his life he's felt helpless; out of control.*

"It's me. I'm being selfish," he bargains. "If I help you get your son back, you can focus on the case and help me find who did this to Celeste. You don't need to say anything right now. I can't make any promises but let me get in touch with my people; see what I can do." He reaches for the panel, opens the doors, takes a step backwards and makes an expansive gesture towards the hallway.

Lanie forces a smile and walks out, not taking her eyes off Jerome as if he were a magpie waiting to swoop. "We'll be in touch," he says as he presses the ground button.

The doors close; Lanie's left alone, staring at a blurry reflection of herself in the polished chrome doors. *What the hell was that.* She shakes off the encounter, turns a corner into a long hallway, then finally inhales—struck by the dour smell of death.

Lanie makes her way down the hallway, where a police officer's standing guard. The carpet is plush; with each step she sinks further into its deeply-dyed burgundy, birds of paradise motif. To her left there's a huge painting adorning the wall. Paint caked on, encrusted and extruding out of the canvas. It dominates the corridor. Lanie's seen something like it before in the National Gallery of Victoria. It has a visceral effect on her; hits her right in the gut—triggering studiously repressed memories of her childhood. She shakes it off and swallows the anxiety. *No point dwelling on it now. Celeste Simone is waiting.*

She reaches the room and nods to the guard.

"Good morning, detective," he sings out, elongating the 'o'. Lanie looks at him blankly.

"There's a dead body in there and you're saying good morning to me like you're in kindergarten," she says in a nasally voice, blocking her nose from the back of her throat, vetting the foul smell. He shrugs and taps the space in between his right temple and eye, reminding Lanie to put on her camera—no doubt at the captain's instructions. Lanie begrudgingly puts them on. He lifts the yellow tape so she can enter. A wave of rancid, stale air hits her. She swallows her gag reflex and surveys the scene.

The room is eclectic; industrial chic: concrete ceilings, wooden parquet flooring, and exposed cables. On her left, she immediately notices the 'do not disturb' hanger shoved into the room's power sleeve, rather than a key card. She steps further inside as the room opens up before her. An eight head Edison bulb chandelier pendant hangs above the bed like a pantomime octopus looking for a fist fight. A weathered ladder rests against the red-brick feature wall, adorned with miniature snake plants in small Aztec-patterned pots. There's a desk directly behind the bedhead, dividing the room from the bathroom. A black American Tourister bag sits on the desk, open with clothes spilling out. Lanie takes note of the king-sized bed. There're no less than six pillows of all shapes and sizes. The bed's made, but with two noticeable indents in the sheets.

"Have any of you sat on the bed?"

The investigators shake their heads, quietly offended.

She checks the mini bar. It's half empty. She cross-references it with the menu. It's missing two Coronas. The Nespresso coffee machine is switched on; there's no water in the reservoir. Beneath it, in the trash can, there are two disposable coffee cups; Sam's name is scribbled in sharpie on one of them, and the other says 'Abbie'. Lanie pulls out her phone and takes a photo. Next to the cups are also two used Nespresso coffee pods.

She wanders into the bathroom. A damp towel is hanging from the wall hanger. She pokes it. There's a blonde strand of hair clinging to it.

"I want this follicle bagged and tested," she calls out to the team in the main room. Celeste's make-up is scattered around the sink beneath a Hollywood vanity style mirror. A blue, white and pink box of Xanax is opened with two almost-empty blister packs hanging out. The tiny pieces of foil that fall off when a pill is pushed out litter the bathroom floor like chrome confetti. A tightly rolled up fifty dollar note rests next to a small, square, transparent plastic bag with a yellow smiley face on it, almost empty except for a white powder, clinging to its inside edges. Celeste's debit card and the remains of multiple lines of the white powder dust the counter top. Lanie can't tell what it is for sure, but it has all the hallmarks of cocaine, maybe MDMA. Lanie shakes her head, kissing her teeth. She steps back and takes in the scene. Everything is meticulously organised: the rectangle box of Xanax; the black, rectangle credit card and square bag of drugs—all unusually symmetrical. The white lights bordering the mirror are still on, burning brightly. Lanie looks up, and swiftly ducks out of the way of her tired reflection. She backs out of the bathroom, over to the freestanding black bathtub in the main room by the bay windows, which contains Celeste's submerged, lifeless body. A forensics guy is carefully examining the body.

"How's it going?" she asks.

"Another day in paradise," he says flatly, not bothering to look up as he checks his readings.

Lanie waits for him to finish.

He clears his throat. "Ah, detective Daniels, I'm surprised to see you here after the last case. You must have some days in lieu built up?"

"What can you tell me?" She ignores his small talk. Despite seeing this guy on most crime scenes, she always forgets his name. *Tod, Tom? It's definitely a T name.*

"There's not much to say about this one. Looks like she's taken a bath after ingesting toxic levels of cocaine, benzodiazepine and alcohol." He nods to the empty bottle of wine and then points to the bathroom and the empty packets of Xanax and now-confirmed cocaine. "It's odd but not unheard of," he begins, "but see how the body is at the bottom of the bath, rather than floating face down? Well this means she had stopped breathing before she submerged in the water."

"So, she didn't drown?"

"That's right. Based on what I saw in the bathroom, my guess is she probably died of a cardiac arrest as a result of a drug overdose while taking a bath, but then didn't slide into the water until after all the gases escaped her body, but," he swiftly caveats, "we can't be sure until further investigation."

Lanie nods, walks over to the sunken, bluish purple body in the bathtub—*it was an OD alright*—squats down, snaps on a pair of latex gloves, pushes her right hand through the surface of the warm water and delicately lifts her left ear back to identify a bloated tattoo of half a love heart; her and Jerome famously got together on their wedding day—like those necklaces you would share with your crush at school. Lanie also notices a nightclub stamp on her right arm, which hasn't been completely washed away yet. She can just make out the name: The Hunting Lodge.

Like the rest of the world, Lanie had seen Celeste before. From covers of glossy magazines to starring in advertisements for the latest high-end perfume, there was a time when Celeste was absolutely everywhere—you simply could not avoid her fame. Lanie always thought she looked like a young Grace

Kelly, or what Grace Kelly looked like when she was young—either way. But the empty body that lay before her right now hardly resembled the beautiful, blonde-haired, blue-eyed woman that graced news feeds and 'for you pages' the world over. *She looks different without a filter, and not just because of the bath.* "Such a waste," Lanie mumbles. "Who found her like this?"

"That would be the hotel concierge and Samuel Bateman. He works for her husband, I think."

"And he's the one who called the police?"

"Yep, I believe so. The call came from the hotel, but was made by Mr Bateman."

Lanie nods.

"Tod," one of his colleagues calls out. "We're about to do the bathroom now."

I knew it was Tod!

"Yep, I'll be right there," Tod replies. "Anything else I can help you with, detective?" He stands up and stretches his back, pushing his hands into the lumbar region, creating a symphony of satisfying cracks.

"Estimated time of death?"

"Approximately between 10 to 12 p.m. the night before last," he answers.

Lanie pulls out her phone and notes it down. "Only yesterday? Why does it look like she's been here for weeks?" She's exaggerating but not by much.

"You feel that heat when you walked in?"

"Yeah, what about it?"

"Well the heater was maxed out to a tropical 32

degrees, and this body has been—for lack of a better phrase—stewing in it for the last 30 hours."

Lanie adds it to her notes. As she's looking down at her phone, she notices a flash of blue at the foot of the bath. She gets down on one knee to take a closer look. Next to a crumpled-up mustard dress is a used, screwed-up, single-serve sachet of Equal brand artificial sweetener. She switches to her camera on her phone and takes a photo, before holstering it back into her pocket. "Would you get any prints off this?"

Tod cranes his neck and looks down on it. "The paper looks too porous, so it's unlikely, but I'll try."

Lanie nods. "I'm gonna need that tox report as soon as it comes back from the lab." She stands up and backs away to inspect the rest of the room.

As she takes in the scene, she can't help but notice the side-eye from the rest of the crew. She has a way of making people feel uncomfortable; always has. There's an involuntary sanctimony in her eyes. People mistake her introversion for arrogance and there's not much she can do about it. With her right hand, she delicately pulls back one side of the blackout curtains, and peeks out.

The city of Melbourne opens up before her, the soupy morning fog dissipates as the sun makes a memory of the night. Lanie looks down at a quintessential Melbourne rooftop bar. It's empty except a single, busied bartender closing-up for the night, smoking a vape, hosing down the floor mats. She turns away from the window, fighting the call of the void, and turns back towards the room, taking in her new perspective. There's a lounge with a coffee table opposite the bath on her right. A MacBook Air is plugged in and open on the table; Celeste Simone's name is obliviously bouncing around the screen. The charging light is a solid green. There's two empty Coronas, one tumbler glass, and one stemmed wine glass, both with dried red wine caked at the bottom—and an accompanying three quarters drunk bottle of St Henri Shiraz. Lanie gets down on one knee to inspect the tumbler, which is resting on top of a Who Magazine that has Celeste on the cover. *Narcissist*, Lanie thinks, before pulling out her phone again. She turns on the torch and flashes the light against the magazine; then the tumbler.

"I need these prints analysed," she calls out, before inspecting the wine glass, too. She rotates her phone around the bowl, failing to find any prints. "And, I want both these glasses tested for DNA."

Tod pokes his head out from the bathroom door. "You got it," he says.

"Lanie!" the Captain interrupts, calling to her from the doorway, as a member of the forensic squad shuffles past him. "Get over here. Bateman has the list you asked for."

Lanie looks up and walks over to him. "That was fast," she replies, as she follows Jon back down the hallway. "Jon, wait up!"

He stops; turns around and faces her.

"What am I even doing here? This is Melbourne. Girls get murdered walking home, or on their morning jogs. Fuck! In this city you just have to get off at the wrong tram stop at the wrong time. Is investigating a drug-addled influencer really the best use of our time—and taxpayer money? Plus, you know how I feel about these people."

Jon remains silent, forcing Lanie to continue.

"You know. These rich arseholes. They live in their own echo chamber, and don't give a shit about the rest of us."

"Lanie," Jon begins evenly, "just because you don't like them, doesn't mean their lives are worth any less than any others. Besides, it's a big deal. There'll be lots of eyes on this investigation, so I need my best person on the job." The flattery makes Lanie squirm. "And Mary's busy, so you'll have to do," he quickly follows up, letting her off the hook. "Anyway, this case will be good for you if you want that promotion. Do this for me. Interview one witness and if it looks like a dead end, then just say the word and I'll pull you from the case." Just as he turns away again to face the journalists waiting outside, he remembers something. "Oh, and Lanie... call your mum. She keeps texting me."

Lanie swallows. "I've been busy," she says defensively as she turns and leaves in a humph.

THREE

LANIE MAKES HER way back downstairs to find Samuel Bateman, choosing to take the stairs to avoid getting cornered by some skeevy billionaire again.

The foyer is still crawling with people. The night concierge's giving his formal statement to the police, while a maid sits nearby, waiting to give hers. The concierge is a young guy; he has short dark hair with a streak of red. He's still wearing his work uniform: a theatre costume.

Lanie walks over to him and interrupts the police officer mid-sentence. "Hey, did anyone else go up to her room after she got home the other night?"

The concierge looks up at the police officer, seeking his permission to answer. The officer forces a smile, flipping his notepad to a new page, by way of telling him it's okay.

"She came back alone."

"What was the time?"

"It was just past 11 p.m."

Lanie pulls out her own notebook and scribbles down the time, then nods for him to continue.

"I remember looking down at the time on the computer when she walked past. I was just telling the officer here that she seemed to be in good spirits; she said hello and waved as she went by."

"Okay thanks, Simon," Lanie says, reading his name badge. "If I have any more questions, I'll be in touch."

"Wait. One more thing," Simon says. "It's probably nothing, but at around two in the morning, I was standing out the front," he points to the entrance of the hotel, "having a cigarette, and someone left in an awful hurry. I couldn't make out who it was, though, because they were wearing a hoodie. And then—and this is the weird part—like ten minutes later, I thought there was a glitch in the Matrix or something because a second person in a hoodie walked out in the exact same way. I didn't think too much of it at the time, but now it seems a little suspicious—hindsight 20/20 and all."

"Interesting," Lanie ruminates. "Were they male or female?"

"Honestly, I couldn't tell. It happened so fast. And I was on my phone, so really wasn't paying that much attention."

"Okay, thanks Simon." Lanie turns to the cop. "You get all that down?"

He nods.

Lanie glances over at Sam. He's working on his laptop still. He doesn't look like he's going anywhere fast, so she steps over to the maid instead. A kindly old woman. Short with broad shoulders. She's sitting, waiting for her turn to be interviewed, clutching her handbag on her lap.

"Hi," Lanie says. "I'm Detective Daniels. What's your

name?"

The lady shuffles in her chair, straightening her back. "Margorie," she replies, with a hint of an Eastern European accent.

"You were the last person to see Celeste alive, is that right?"

The lady nods her head. "I think so."

Lanie takes in the lines shooting out from the corners of her eyes; the tremble of her hands; her posture. She's scared.

"What happened—what was she doing?"

"I, um. She had lost the key to her room, so I let her inside. Very sad. Ugly crying," she says, which probably makes more sense in her native tongue, but Lanie gets the gist. "Please don't tell my manager I let her in."

That's why she's scared. "I won't, Margorie," Lanie reassures her. "Did you see anyone else go into her room after you let her in?"

"I'm sorry, I didn't," Margorie replies, looking down, pulling on the straps of her handbag. "After I let her inside room, that was the last time I was on her floor that night."

Lanie kisses the front of her teeth. "Okay, Margorie. Thank you. Now just stay here and that police officer will get your formal statement. And, hey, don't worry about your manager. Mum's the word," she assures her before turning away to chase-up Sam about the list.

She strides over to him. "You got something for me, Mr Bateman?"

Sam looks up from his computer, sliding his glasses up the bridge of his nose with his forefinger. "Yes, I've got the audience list you asked for," he replies. "Here, take a look." He steps aside so Lanie can see his screen.

It's a long list, but not as long as Lanie was expecting. Celeste's popularity peaked years ago. Her dwindling audience should have come as no surprise—influencer years are akin to dog years. Regardless, the list was still too long for Lanie to process manually. "Is there any way to narrow down the audience?"

Sam shrugs his shoulders. "I mean, of course. We can vet the data any way you like: age, gender, pet-owner, favourite colour. Even their favourite internet porn, if you really want," he chuckles uneasily. "But, what were you thinking?"

Lanie pauses for a moment. "How about the people who were paying the most attention?" While this isn't the first time something like this has been captured on a live stream, usually it's just a family member or friend watching. In fact, women had started using it as a safety precaution; a mobile security camera. But, this is the first time it's happened to an influencer with a broad audience of complete strangers.

Sam scratches the back of his head, then slides his hand around to his mouth, rubbing his chin up and down, before a minor breakthrough. "Actually, there might be," he answers. "We've been beta testing a biometric measurement system for our advertising partners. "It, um," he stops. "Normally, you'd have to sign an NDA," he says nervously.

Lanie meets his eyes. "This could be a homicide, Mr. Bateman. I really don't give two shits about your IP."

Sam winces, then continues. "Okay. Right, well, it analyses a combination of eye tracking, skin conductance and heart rate of our audience to determine their engagement rate, which marketers use to A/B test their advertising so they can be sure they're running the most effective content. I could feed this list into the algorithm and cross reference it with dwell time. That should feedback with the viewers who not only watched for the longest amount of time, but who were also the most engaged." He inflects at the end.

"Do it," Lanie responds forcefully.

"Okay, but it may take an hour or two to chat to the right people to crunch the data. I'll email you the results as soon as I get them."

"Thanks—nice work," Lanie says. "One more thing. Jerome said you were friends with Celeste, right?"

"Yes, why?"

"Do you know who Abbie is?"

"Abbie Benson-Wheeler?" His feet start tapping a little faster. "She's an influencer like Celeste. I guess you could call them colleagues. She was out with us the night before Celeste, um, you know—"

"Died?" Lanie finishes his sentence.

"Yes, died," he says. "Why do you ask, detective?"

Lanie shrugs and turns to walk outside, leaving Sam alone at his computer, and with his question.

"Just email me those names as soon as you get that shortlist."

She takes the fire exit to her car, before digging out a lost Chapstick from the backseat and applying it liberally to her dry lips. It's brisk out. She zips up her leather jacket, puts a hand in each pocket, and rests her back against the car door, watching quietly as Captain Bailey makes his way to the front of the pack of journalists.

"Good morning. I'm Captain Bailey," he says in his best public-speaking voice. "Earlier today, at approximately 7 a.m., we received a call from The Grand Theatre Hotel," he nods backwards at the building behind him, "reporting that Ms Celeste Simone was found unconscious in her bathtub. Paramedics arrived on the scene at 7.12 a.m., and marked her legal time of death at 7:15 a.m. At this point in time, there's no signs of struggle or any indication of foul-play. However, due to the high-profile nature of the individual we will be conducting a full investigation. We are aware that Celeste was taking prescription medication for flying, which may have played a role in her subsequent drowning. We can also confirm that Celeste had turned off the auto archive feature on her Umwelt lenses, meaning that the live stream of her point of view, or POV, was not saved, however Mr Pitt is aiding us in putting together a list of people who were streaming her at the time, which we will shortlist and interview. That is all for now. Thank you all for your time."

As the captain steps back, Jerome steps forward, replacing him at the foot of the journalists. The captain looks uneasy—he hates surprises. Jerome still looks exhausted, but he's holding himself together with an easy charm—playing the role of heart-broken husband with aplomb, maybe genuinely.

"I just want to sincerely thank you all for coming out. Your support during this tragic time means everything to me and Celeste. I also want to take this moment to reassure the Umwelt community and the world that I will be doing everything in my power to uncover the truth, and I have offered every resource at my disposal to the Police to that end. I loved Celeste. She was and still is my world. Thank you," he says as he steps back down. Jon and Jerome turn their backs to the crowd and head back inside the hotel—a cacophony of questions court them through the entrance.

He's talking about her as if she were still alive, Lanie thinks as she finally hops into her car, pulling her hands out of her pockets and chucking the Chapstick onto the backseat. *And all that stuff about helping me with Thomas? Something's off.* She doesn't like him. He's too scripted; too performative. *Thank God this'll all be over in a couple days—most celebrity OD's are,* she continues. *A couple of days, and decades of conspiracy theories.*

FOUR

LANIE RENTS A spartan two-bedroom apartment in Preston, near the markets—in Melbourne's inner north, which only twenty years ago would've been considered the outer north. On the rare occasion she has guests over, she deflects and quotes Marie Kondo—discard everything that does not spark joy. But that's a lie. She just can't be bothered decorating. It's not on her list of priorities. The place boasts an open plan kitchen and living room, a relatively big balcony and two shoe-box-sized rooms. One for her and one for Thomas when he visits once a month.

Lanie takes the elevator up from the garage to her floor, turns right and arrives at her door. She fishes her keys out of her bag, unlocks the door and heads straight for the fridge, past the makeshift workspace, which she's set-up on the kitchen's island bench. Her stomach grumbles as she stares into the white void, remembering the abandoned egg and bacon roll from earlier. The fridge is empty barring a small bottle of Diet Coke, and a wilted bunch of broccolini held together by a purple rubber band. She grabs the Coke and places it next to her computer on the bench. She returns to the fridge and pulls out a loaf of frozen bread from the freezer, jimmies off two slices with a butter knife, and puts them in the microwave for thirty seconds. In the meantime, she takes a swig of the Coke—discovering the hard way that it's flat—and grabs the crunchy peanut butter from the pantry. The microwave finishes in a flurry of beeps. She grabs the soft bread, puts it on a plate and spreads it with peanut butter, shredding it to pieces. She scoffs down her excuse for a sandwich, sits down and turns on her laptop. Email notifications pop up in the lower right corner of her screen, stacking one above the other:

ChillTime. Want more out of your day?

Zenith. Your Zenith Energy invoice - customer numb...

Netflix. Top suggestions for Lanie

ING Bank. Your latest Orange One statement.

myaccount@vodafone.com. Account 8046 1829 500196 is ready...

Sea Shepherd. Together we're creating a wave of change.

Sam.Batemen@UmweltPlatforms. Celeste's active viewers.

Lanie clicks the email from Samuel Bateman: please find attached the names and contacts of the POVers. The temporary password is BR161982, regards

Samuel.

"Thanks Samuel", Lanie utters to her empty apartment, before dragging the file onto her desktop.

She unplugs her computer, grabs her phone, plus a notepad and pen and plonks herself on the couch. It's too quiet. She gets back up and shuffles over to her dad's record player. It's the one thing he left her, apart from the endless guilt. They used to listen to R&B music together—and it stuck. She thumbs through her collection, pulls out an Otis Redding record and puts it on. The record needle scratches as it starts. She hates herself for it: listening to music on vinyl. It's about as bougee as it gets, but she couldn't care less. She hates silence even more, so she's always finding ways to fill the apartment with a companionable clatter. She sits back down and just as she's about to open Sam's email her phone rings. It's Rebecca. She's an old family friend, who doubles as her lawyer.

"Hey Becs!"

"Hey Lanes!" a distant voice on the other end of the line replies. "How on God's green Earth do you know Jerome Pitt?" she asks, skipping the small talk.

"Jerome? Why?" Lanie begins. "I met him this morning. At the scene of his wife's death, actually."

"Yeah well, you must've left an impression, because he's got your custody case reopened."

"Re-opened? Already? How?" Lanie's surprised. Surprised that Jerome is a man of his word, more than anything.

"I haven't seen it myself, but apparently he has new evidence."

"Shit! I didn't think he was going to actually do anything," Lanie replies. "What's the evidence?"

"No idea, but it must be compelling for them to do a backflip like this—or, you know, he's just uber powerful, which he is. Lanes, listen to me. This could be good for you. Can you meet me at my office this Thursday, say 2 p.m.?"

"Yeah, of course. I'll be there." Lanie pauses for a moment, collecting her thoughts.

"Lanes, you there?"

"Yeah, I'm here, I just, I'd almost given up, and now this... Thanks Becs."

"Don't thank me. Thank Jerome. I just can't believe Jon is cool with you getting help from someone who's part of an investigation."

Silence.

"About that," Lanie begins. "Jon doesn't actually know yet. I honestly thought Jerome was full of shit."

"Ah, gotcha. Do you want me to hold off doing anything until you talk to him?"

Fuck. He's not gonna approve, and this could be my only chance of getting Thomas back. "All good. Carry on. Jon will be fine. I'll tell him next time I see him."

"Alright. Copy that! See you Thursday, Lanes!"

Yep, see you—"

"Oh, and also," Becca remembers something. "Call your mum. I keep getting these random messages from her."

Lanie kisses her teeth, tsking. "Not you, too!"

"That bastard. That beautiful fucking bastard," Lanie says, filling the apartment with the sporadic sound of guilty relief. She returns to her laptop and double clicks Sam's file. As it downloads she opens up another tab and through muscle memory types in the news site, killing time as the progress bar continues to slowly crawl across the screen. The file finally finishes downloading, and opens up with a shortlist of three names: Pimm Gilchrist, Redfern NSW. Paula Abbas, Brighton Vic, and Irene Burns North Adelaide SA. *Great, I guess I should pack my bags.* She dials the first number into her mobile phone. He picks up straight away.

"Hello, this is Pimm."

FIVE

YOU WOULDN'T CALL him her biggest fan, but he would. Pimm lives in Redfern in Sydney's inner west, and works for the government. Not in some flashy, hug-a-baby and smile role, but as a paper pusher for the Department of Roads and Transport —putting his degree in graphic design to good use. His job bores him, because it's boring. But at least he's getting paid too much, and he also gets to clock off at 5 p.m. every day. He has no choice. If he doesn't, his colleagues complain. Nobody at the office has time for an overachiever. And that suits Pimm just fine. It means his laziness is their fault; not his. Besides, the sooner he finishes work, the sooner he gets home to Celeste.

He lives life mostly inside his apartment, and head —sometimes Celeste's. Pimm's the kind of guy who's always thinking about the gap between how he sees himself, how he thinks people see him and how they actually see him. It always comes as an existential shock when the last two don't align. Maybe he's having an identity crisis. Maybe he should care less about what people think of him. Whatever it is, it's a weed he can't kill, no matter what meds the doctor prescribes.

He's been subscribed to Celeste's stream for almost three years. Three years and one hundred and nineteen days. It's his escape. His gift-shop exit from the listless production that is his life. He was a fan before everyone else, and will be after everyone else. Since her death two days ago, Pimm's been a little lost—lackadaisical. He's had to re-acquaint himself with the feeling of crippling loneliness. Yesterday he caught the train at peak hour, just to be close to someone—anyone.

Pimm's doorbell rings. He finds his phone wedged between two couch cushions and opens his off-brand Ring app to see who it is. It's the Melbourne detective who called him yesterday. She's not what he expected. She's half Asian, which her voice didn't give away on the phone at all. She's attractive in a no-fucks-given way. He unlocks the door from his phone. The lock clicks just as he reaches it. He pulls it open and is met by Lanie.

"Detective Daniels?" he asks despite knowing it's her.

"Mr Gilchrist, how are you? Can I come in?"

He takes half a step back, gesturing that she's welcome.

Lanie walks inside and scans her surroundings. The place is schmick: two story freestanding cottage. At least two bedrooms; probably two bathrooms, she guesses as she eyes the bottom of the staircase. There's a small astroturfed courtyard with an iron two-seater table next to a rusted Webber; modern subway-tiled kitchen, leading into an open plan living room, where she now stands on polished timber floorboards, surrounded by so much Tibetan art from Target that it leaves no doubt in her mind that he's involuntarily single.

Pimm is tall. At six foot something he dwarfs Lanie. His skin is quite fair, exacerbated by his reddish hair, which is showing signs of pattern baldness. He's wearing glasses with thick, dark blue frames. Under his left ear he has the same half heart tattoo as Celeste. *Big fan.* He's not attractive by any conventional measure, but his warm smile draws you in; makes you want to trust him. There's an absence in his eyes, and a strangled tone in his voice that gives away his nerves.

"Can I get you a drink? Glass of water? Coffee?" Pimm asks. "I got this new DeLonghi coffee machine," he says, punctuating *DeLonghi* by bringing his thumb and forefinger together and making a tick shape in the air, "because the baristas down the road are so inconsistent," he continues, before Lanie answers.

"Coffee would be great. Black, no sugar." Lanie sits down at the kitchen table and unpacks her black leather satchel—a gift for ten years of service. She pulls out a pen and paper and a manila folder with white edges of paper peeping out the side. She arranges them neatly on the table, with just a tinge of OCD. She pulls out her phone, opens the voice-recorder app, and places it on the table. As she waits for Pimm to sit with her, she watches a rainbow lorikeet hopping from foot to foot on the fence in his courtyard. Pimm finally joins her with two mugs: one flat white for himself, and a long black for Lanie. Steam curls from the lip of hers: a recycled Bonne Maman Apricot jam jar with a handle.

"Thanks," Lanie says, as she wraps her hands around it and blows at the steam, cooling it before taking a sip. She shifts her attention back to Pimm. "Like I said on the phone, our system found you were highly engaged while you were streaming Celeste on the day of her death. So, I need your account of what you saw—what she saw."

Pimm takes a seat next to Lanie, so he's sitting ninety degrees to her right. "Do you think it was suicide, because I can't believe she did it on purpose?"

Lanie looks up. "It's not my job to think anything—not yet, anyway. I'm just here to find out the truth, whatever that may be. Now if you could tell me what you saw that day, I'll be out of your hair before lunch." Lanie reaches for her phone and unlocks it to the awaiting voice record app. She presses the big, red button to start recording.

Pimm sips his homemade coffee and screws up his face. "Argh, I burnt the milk," he curses, before telling Lanie exactly what he saw through Celeste's eyes the day she died.

SIX

IT WAS SATURDAY morning. Celeste had just flown in from San Francisco. She got off the plane, walked down the aerobridge and out into the duty-free store. She groggily poked around the rows of oversized booze and Toblerones—the kind that prop up the last-minute-gift economy. She grabbed a bottle of Sailor Jerry spiced rum—Jerome's favourite—in one hand and a bottle of red wine for herself in the other, which he hates. She tossed up between the two. The decision would've been easier if she wasn't reeling from the sixteen-hour over-nighter. She put the rum back neatly where she found it and took the bottle of red up to the counter. The shop assistant asked to see her ticket as she scanned the wine. Celeste stared at her blankly before reaching into her bag. She was old and had that pack-a-day croak in her voice. She had platinum blonde hair with dark roots coming through. Celeste fished the ticket stub out of her Chanel passport holder and flashed it at the woman. She thanked Celeste in a broad Aussie accent that dragged her back to Earth.

"Home sweet home," Celeste said under her breath. She looked up at the wave of travellers. The small head-start she'd enjoyed from being let out first had all but gone. The cattle-class flooded past, eagerly making their way to their happy families. She thanked the lady as she forced the wine into her bag, squashing it down into her neck pillow. She stepped into the current of people and got swept to the back of the passport scanner line. She scanned her passport, grabbed her suitcase from the carousel, went through customs and left through the arrival gate.

Jerome wasn't there. Instead Celeste was met by a man in a wrinkled, buy-one-get-one-free suit, holding up a tablet with her name written in a sans serif font. He had the look of an ex-football player. Celeste made her way over to him, past the growing crowd of adoring fans. But not fans of hers. Fans of Abbie Benson-Wheeler's. She's an influencer like Celeste and was well on track to taking Celeste's crown as the most followed human on earth. Celeste was totally fine with it. She knew she couldn't stay on top forever.

Celeste stepped over to the man in the wrinkled-suit and dropped her handbag at his feet.

He recognised her immediately. "Miss Simone?"

"Yep, that's me," she replied curtly.

"Mr Pitt told me to tell you he's sorry he couldn't make it. He's at work, so he sent me to pick you up."

"Typical," Celeste murmured.

"I'm Gary," he introduced himself.

Celeste forced a smile. She was distracted by Abbie's army of fans. "Excuse me Gary," she said. "I'll be right back." Instead of suffering the ignominy of Abbie's popularity, Celeste went to the bathroom. Just because she could wrap her head around Abbie's inevitable rise, doesn't mean she had to tolerate it. When she returned she found Gary waiting where she left him, holding onto her luggage. She hadn't packed much: just a small overnight bag. The mobile kind you drag around with a handle you can pull out. American Tourister sent it over a few weeks earlier for her to review and share with her followers.

Gary grabbed the bag and led her out the entrance to his car. Celeste let him help; not that she needed it. She'd been live-streaming HIIT work-outs for years.

Gary chucked her bag into the boot and opened the back door for her. She slid in and gave him a grateful nod.

As they pulled out Celeste saw Abbie getting into a car as well. It was brand-new; impossible to make out the model, on account of it being inundated with fans, but it was blue.

Celeste used the drive to the hotel to catch up on her messages. After replying to every single one of them, and sending her mum the requisite 'I've arrived safely' text, she—

Pimm coughs. "One minute," he says as he clears his throat before standing up to top up his glass of water. Lanie swishes the granules of coffee at the bottom of her mug, peering intently, briefly thinking about her own mum. *I gotta call her.* Pimm sits back down and continues.

Celeste sipped at the free bottle of water, chewed on a single-serve Mentos; then mindlessly started doom scrolling social media, before catching herself, and opting to stare out the window instead. Not out at the growing city of Melbourne, but at her own reflection. She passed the 'Is Don. Is Good' silos on the freeway—the ones painted to look like an enormous packet of salami—winded her way through the CBD, dodging trams crawling along at an aggressively slow pace, and then pulled up to The Grand Theatre Hotel on Russell street.

The car door clicked open from the outside as she was met by Jerome's business partner, hanger-on-erer and bottom-feeder: Samuel Bateman.

"Miss Simone," he said, in a put-on, formal way, holding out his hand, pretending to be the hotel concierge.

"Sam," she replied, playing along to be polite. She took his hand and pulled herself up out of the car.

He gave her a hello kiss on both cheeks, holding for just that little bit too long. "Where's my hug?" he says, leaning in for an uncomfortable embrace—the kind that makes onlookers shudder. In this case Gary, who was now standing beside them clutching Celeste's bag, looking everywhere but at the two of them.

"Thanks Gaz," she said as if they were old friends, making his day—he just stood there for a moment, basking in the lightness of Celeste's familiarity.

"Let me help you check in," Sam offered, while he grabbed the bag from Gary, gesturing towards the hotel entrance. They walked through the large, automatic doors and into the plush lobby.

"Welcome to The Grand Theatre Hotel," the doorman greeted them.

On the left was a small cafe. It was morning peak hour, and even non-guests were walking in off the street to get their morning caffeine fix. The steamer hissed above the noise of the crowd like an old locomotive.

Shabby chic lounges peppered the right-hand side, punctuated by an eclectic mix of colourful velvet cushions. The lobby was filling up with other guests, visiting for the Melbourne Cup, like Celeste.

Sam lined up to check-in to the hotel for Celeste, while she grabbed coffees from the cafe. Celeste rejoined Sam just as he stepped up to the front desk.

The concierge looked up from his screen to greet them. "Miss Simone! It's a pleasure to have you back with us at The Grand Theatre." He needed to dial it down. Coincidentally, he and the rest of the hotel staff were dressed in old theatre costumes. Not theatre-theatre costumes, but the uniforms the ushers and ticket-takers used to wear: a double-breasted red jacket with gold buttons, and black pants with a gold stripe and of course a matching usher hat—like the monkey from Aladdin. "As requested, you're on level five, room twenty-seven in one of our luxury suites. Here's your key card." He held out a small bespeckled, off-white envelope.

"And please don't hesitate to call if you need absolutely anything from us—anything at all. Enjoy your stay."

Sam grabbed the envelope. "Can you please send up extra towels?" he asked. "Celeste goes through them like you wouldn't believe."

The concierge looked over at Celeste, who was looking up the stairs to the breakfast buffet, then turned back to Sam. "Of course, sir."

Celeste and Sam made their way up the elevator to her room on the fifth floor. They walked down a long corridor, past an enormous painting of a burning, bullet-riddled battleship, cutting its way through the ocean. Sam put his hand around Celeste's waist, pulling her out of the way of an oncoming room service lady, who was walking in the opposite direction, wheeling her cart.

"Morning," Sam said. She ignored him.

Celeste and Sam reached the room. Sam pulled out the key card, unlocked the door and held it open for Celeste. Celeste walked inside and immediately jumped on the bed, while Sam cased the place. He stepped right past the bath in the main room and up to the huge windows that overlooked the city. He stopped for a moment to enjoy the view, then grabbed the blinds, swinging them back and forwards, testing how much they blocked-out the light, before joining Celeste on the bed.

"Your skin looks amazing by the way. You're glowing—even after being on a plane all night," he said, as he pulled out his phone and buried his head in his emails.

"You always know exactly what to say, Sam." Celeste smiled. "So where's Jerome, really?"

Sam looked up from his phone. He scoffed. "You know where."

Lanie taps her pen against the wooden table. "So, where was he?"

Pimm reaches behind his head with both hands and slowly rolls his neck, ironing out the knots. "Celeste often jokes that his work's his mistress, so I'd say he was working."

"And," Lanie checks her notes, "how come Celeste and Jerome weren't staying in the same room—is that normal?"

Pimm frowned. "Huh? No, yeah. They never stayed in the same room. Jerome keeps weird hours because of his work, plus he needs his own space to meditate. He's part owner of ChillTime, the meditation app."

"Same hotel at least?" Lanie leans forward.

"Nope. Celeste chooses her own hotels. I think Jerome was staying in the Hilton or some other chain."

Lanie looks over Pimm's shoulder for a moment. "And how would you describe their relationship, then? Were they happy?"

"Oh, yes," Pimm says, as if there was no doubt. "They had the ideal arrangement. There was no forced intimacy; they gave each other all the space each needed. It may sound weird, but the truth is they were actually just brave enough to do what was right for them—what they wanted; not what was expected by society's standards," Pimm continues.

Lanie twists her pen around her thumb and forefinger. "Okay," she says. "And where does Sam fit into all this? Is it common for him and Celeste to be alone together?"

Pimm sips his coffee. "More and more." He chews his top lip . "He loved her, you know?"

"Who did, Sam?"

"Yeah, but Celeste friend-zoned him."

Lanie scribbles Sam's name down.

"Okay," Lanie says again, encouraging him to elaborate.

"He was your classic 'nice guy'," Pimm says using air quotes. "He was always simping on her."

"Simping?"

"Yeah, you know, like, sucking-up to her. Always complimenting her and saying stupid shit like Jane Austen was his favourite author, because it was hers. I mean, seriously!? Austen is no better than any wish-fulfilling, Disney princess movie," Pimm says —clearly carrying baggage on the topic. He sits back down.

"Okay," Lanie says yet again, nodding for him to continue.

It was a long flight; Celeste was tired. "Thanks for helping me with my bag, Sam. And for helping me check-in," she said. "I don't know what I'd do without you sometimes." Sam relished her gratitude. "But if I don't get my beauty sleep, I'll be cooked tonight."

Sam took the hint and stood up to leave. "Oh, I almost forgot," he said, "check your wardrobe."

Celeste shot him a quizzical look before getting up off the bed and checking it out. She flung open the wardrobe. It was bursting with new dresses by all the hottest designers. Each one of them hoping Celeste would wear their design.

"Seeya tonight!" Sam said as he left. "Oh, and one last thing," he doubled back for a second time, one foot out the door, "Abbie's coming too."

There was a strained pause.

"Awesome," Lanie replied.

"Thought you'd be thrilled." Sam chuckles. "See you tonight." Sam made a quick exit, escaping before Celeste concocted another one of her famous excuses to get out of coming so she could sit in her hotel room, overordering room service and watching the free movies.

Celeste slumped back onto the bed, grabbed one of the pillows, hugged it like a plush toy, and fell asleep within minutes. She forgot to turn off her Umwelts, so treated her fans to an exclusive live-stream of the back of her eyelids.

"Does that happen a lot?" Lanie interrupts.
"Not really. Not never, but pretty rarely. I'd say it's from the pills she took for the flight."
"The Xanax?"
"Yeah, how'd you know?" Pimm replies, moments before realising it was a silly question. "Never mind,"

he says as he rubs his chin where stubble should be.

Lanie clears her throat. "Is it possible that she did it on purpose?"

"Why would she do it on purpose?"

"I don't know, maybe she felt safer with them on. Plenty of other women—non-celebrities—leave them on all the time for safety."

Pimm scratches the back of his head. "I guess, maybe. She sometimes joked that people were out to get her," he says, grimacing, hearing it through the detective's ears. "But, it was always just a joke, you know? Like, she wasn't being serious."

"Hmmm," Lanie starts. She rubs her left cheek. "Did she ever say who?"

"Nah, honestly, it was just a throwaway line. She was always just kidding."

"Okay." Lanie inhales and nods for him to continue.

Celeste stirred a few hours later; then got up and made her way over to the Nespresso machine to make a coffee. She searched high and low but couldn't find the pods anywhere, so resorted to a glass of tap water. She stepped over to the window and sipped it standing atop the city. Her eyes wandered over to a nearby rooftop bar, opening for lunch. The mere sight made her stomach groan a deep baritone rumble. She hadn't eaten since the plane, and you could hardly call that food: a grotesquely dense bread roll and powdered scrambled eggs. She'd been so busy she'd forgotten to eat—she was famished. She ordered room service:

some coffee pods and a tuna on rye with salad. Not tinned tuna but an actual fillet of tuna.

Ten minutes later, there was a knock at the door. Celeste opened it to the same room-service lady from the hallway from earlier. She was old, with a storied face, which Celeste stared at for a while, working out what she would've looked like when she was younger. Beautiful.

Celeste ate her lunch, put her plate back on the tray and placed it outside her door, before making her way over to the wardrobe and pulling out the colourful haul of dresses. She laid them on the bed, then sent out a notification to her fans, before addressing them through the mirror in her room.

"Hey guys, I need your help deciding what to wear tonight, and for the Melbourne Cup on Tuesday. So, what I'm gonna do is try on all these incredible dresses, which these very talented designers have so kindly lent me, while you guys vote on which one you like the best. And remember, you can buy any of the dresses for yourself, just follow the links. Okay, let's do it!" she said before trying on all the outfits. There were heaps of designs and colours to choose from: red, purple, yellow and even a totally extra mirror ball option. With the help of the Simoners—that's what her fans call themselves—she picked the yellow dress for dinner, and the iconic mirror ball one for the races on Tuesday. It was a vibe.

Celeste always involved her fans with these things. It not only engaged them, but it also insulated her from the vitriol of the fashion bloggers, tabloids and even Jerome, who could sometimes be her harshest critic. By outsourcing these choices to her followers, she made them a convenient scapegoat when she got it wrong. Not that she ever did, because she literally looked good in anything.

Celeste scooped up the dresses and hung them back up in the wardrobe. Except the yellow one, which she slung over a chair for later. She turned back to the mirror, kicked up her heel, slanted her neck slightly and made a peace sign.

"Seeya lovelies! I need some Celeste time before Jerome gets here," she said, before ending her livestream.

Lanie's phone rings. "Do you mind?" She raises one finger, shushing Pimm's answer anyway. She mouths a thank you and makes her way out to the courtyard to take the call. It's Captain Bailey. By the time she makes it outside it stops ringing. She calls him back. He picks up immediately.

"What's up?" she asks. "Yep, interviewing the first witness now." As she's talking she notices the front door isn't the only place Pimm's set-up a security camera. There's one in the courtyard, too. She looks back through the streaky glass doors into the living room to discover another one was in the corner concave of the ceiling. *This guy's serious about his home-security.* "Don't worry Jon." She shifts her focus back to the captain. "If I uncover anything suspicious, you'll be the first to know." She finishes her call and walks back inside to find Pimm's brought out a small flourless, orange and poppy seed tea cake for them to share.

He slices it into four equal wedges, carefully places one of the wedges onto a small plate and slides it towards Lanie's folders on the table.

Lanie had a ham and cheese toasted sandwich at the airport when it was still dark this morning, so she's more than a bit peckish. She leans over and helps herself to the slice. It's delicious.

"Okay, so, where were we?"

It was around 6 p.m. when Celeste started live streaming again. Jerome was there to pick her up for dinner. He looked nice. He was wearing tan chinos, a blue shirt, light-green sports jacket and Clarks moccasins. Celeste was already dressed in the yellow dress she picked out earlier. Jerome grabbed a beer from the mini-bar and poured Celeste a glass of red wine—the one she bought duty-free. He couldn't find any wine glasses, so he used a tumbler instead, which worked great as a wine glass, anyway.

"Go with the boots," he suggested, as he saw Celeste struggling to choose between them and her high heels. Celeste didn't disagree. She grabbed her boots and put them near the door before joining Jerome on the couch.

"Here, quick," she said, putting her wine down on the table, pulling out her phone and taking a selfie of the two of them to post on Instagram. "Thanks for sending a driver this morning," she said while posting it.

Jerome didn't reply. He was distracted, airing her wine. "Abbie says she saw you at the airport," he said.

"Did she now?" Celeste replied. "She should've come and said hi."

Jerome smiled as he rolled Celeste's wine glass around, letting it breathe, before handing it to her.

She joined him on the couch, grabbed the wine and took a sip. Celeste closed her eyes to savour the taste. When she opened them again Jerome had a surprise for her. He was holding out a teal-coloured box. He handed it to her. She took it eagerly, pulled the ribbon and lifted the lid to find a stunning pair of white-gold earrings.

She stared at them for a moment. "I love them," she finally said.

"Thought you would—Abbie told me these ones are popular right now. Put them on, let me see."

She took out her mum's pearl earrings and swapped them out for the new pair.

"They really do look good on you." He walked over to the mini-bar to grab another beer, topped up Celeste's glass and sat back down on the couch. "What'd you get up to this afternoon; I tried calling a few times, but you didn't pick up?"

"You know what I was doing. I was trying on dresses for Tuesday."

"No, I mean after that. You were offline for hours."

"After that, I was doing nothing. Just hanging around here, waiting for you. Why?" Celeste got up and went to the bathroom.

"No reason." He took a shallow sip of his beer, and

pulled out his phone.

When Celeste eventually finished in the bathroom, Jerome was standing ready to leave. "Let's go," he said.

Celeste put on her boots and they left. They made their way downstairs to the lobby, where the dinner crowd was beginning to gather.

"You wanna walk—the restaurant's just around the corner?" Jerome asked.

Celeste agreed. She was wearing boots, so she didn't mind. The doorman put his hands out to trigger the automatic sliding doors, and then held them in the doorway so it stayed open.

The two of them stepped out onto Russell street, turned right, walked for five minutes, then turned left onto Flinders Lane and walked until they reached a fancy Thai restaurant. The kind that doesn't have a pun in its name. And based on the crowd waiting outside, was also the kind that didn't take bookings.

"C'mon," Jerome said, nodding towards the greeter —a beautiful Thai woman.

"My name's Jerome Pitt. I'm meeting Mr Marco Vellis," he said in his cavalier way.

"Of course, Mr Pitt," she said, paying no attention to the pissed-off couple who had been waiting in the cold for God knows how long. "Right this way, sir." She opened the door and lead them through the restaurant to a big round table in the back corner where the others were already waiting. They were the last to arrive.

Abbie was there, sporting newly dyed blonde hair; looking even more like Celeste than usual—there's a rumour that Abbie had some work done before she got famous to look like Celeste, and if that was her aim, then she nailed the assignment. She was even wearing a yellow dress, which she would have known Celeste was going to wear, because she'd promoted it all afternoon on her live stream.

Sam was there as well, but had changed clothes since Celeste had seen him earlier: blue chinos and a white shirt. And another guy was there, too, who Celeste had never met before.

"This is Marco Vellis," Jerome introduced him. Marco stood up and pecked Celeste on both cheeks. "Marco's the promoter. He's the one who brought us over for the Melbourne Cup."

Celeste smiled as she studied him. He was your typical second-gen Aussie—show-muscles bulging through a short-sleeved, two-sizes too small, floral-print shirt. He'd pegged his skinny-legged black jeans—exposing his age and ankles in equal measure—and was wearing light brown, weaved leather loafers with no socks.

Marco ordered a round of drinks: jugs of mojitos and Coronas for the table. Sam ordered himself a red. It was better for his diabetes. Five minutes later the drinks were delivered to their table.

Celeste stirred her mojito, creating a hurricane in a high-ball with the metal straw she carried with her. She took a sip and savoured the soft tickle of the brown sugar granules sliding around her tongue, before being dragged back to reality by Marco's incessant chatter.

He was trying to talk Jerome into going-in on a racehorse with him. Celeste was not a fan of the idea. Not even a little, so she stood up and absolutely torched Marco, who you'd feel sorry for, if his face wasn't so punchable.

"What do you even know about horses?" Celeste began. "It's a hellish sport!" She turned to Jerome for support that was not forthcoming. "I can't believe kids get a day off of school to watch these majestic creatures get kicked over and over. It's brutal; barbaric. Humans, no, men," she stared at Marco, "are the real animals!"

There was a moment's pause. No one at the table knew how to respond to Celeste's unexpected outburst. Marco especially, who would yeet himself out of there if he could.

"I'll drink to that!" Abbie said buoyantly, hoisting her San Pellegrino into the air. "To something we can all agree on: men being animals." Their glasses met cheerily in the centre of the table.

Crisis averted.

Dinner was served. Celeste was probably just hangry. The more she ate, the less abrasive she became.

"How was your flight this morning, ladies?" Marco asked.

"I loved it so much!" Abbie gushed. "It's not every day you get to fly first class," she added. "They even give you these cute pyjamas to wear! Thank you so much for bringing us over, Marco."

Celeste forced a tight-lipped smile. "Yes, thank you," she added with less than half the gusto of Abbie.

"Celeste doesn't love flying," Sam qualified.

Celeste's nostrils flared. She shot him daggers. "I don't need you to speak for me, Sam."

Sam looked down. "Sorry, I didn't mean to." He fastidiously lined up his cutlery.

There was a strained silence.

Abbie covered her mouth and coughed lightly. "You shouldn't let her talk to you like that," she whispered to Sam, thinking Celeste was out of earshot.

Celeste was about to say something but didn't waste her energy. Once the plates were cleared, Marco ordered coffees for everyone. "I've called ahead to The Hunting Lodge; got them to save us a table upstairs," he said. "It's a cocktail bar around the corner, not far from here—I know the owner." Everyone was keen.

Marco took care of the bill and they all stood up and exited out the door they entered, past the line which had only gotten longer, and over to Marco's driver, who was waiting out the front. It was Gary, from the airport.

"We've got to stop meeting like this," Celeste said, smiling her infectious smile.

"Good to see you again Miss Simone. I've—"

"Get out Gary," Marco barked, as if he was talking to a pet dog rather than a human being. "I'm driving. I'll leave the car out the front of The Lodge for you to pick up."

Celeste and Abbie were mortified.

"What a dick," Celeste mouthed.

Abbie nodded in silent agreement.

"I'm happy to walk," Celeste said, turning to Jerome for support.

"Me too—I'll walk with you!" Sam jumped in.

Gary pats his stomach self-deprecatingly. "It's fine, Miss Simone, it's only around the corner, and I could use the walk." He reached into the car and pulled out a crumpled grey cardigan and half-drunk water bottle.

"Wonderful! It's agreed," Marco said. He jumped in the driver's seat and pressed the ignition button. The car roared to life as he revved it like a pimply teenage boy. Jerome joined him in the front. "Women in the back," Marco jested as Sam crawled in the back with Celeste and Abbie.

Gary was right. The Hunting Lodge was literally around the corner. They arrived within minutes, crawled out the car and skipped the line, walking past a throng of resentful faces, yet again. It was dark inside, with lots of hidden nooks.

Muddy cloud rap was blasting from the speakers, orchestrating the crowd's collective heart-beat.

They made their way up the stairwell to the top floor, to a corner roped off for them. There were full bottles of Grey Goose and Courvoisier on the table. Marco cracked open the cognac and poured a glass for everyone. Abbie turned to Celeste and asked if she would go to the bathroom with her. Celeste nodded. They stood up and went off together. As they reached the door, Celeste triggered a commercial to play. It was for the Grey Goose they were drinking.

They emerged from the bathroom and headed back to their table together. Celeste came out a different person. They both did. They were more relaxed; more comfortable around each other.

"Hey Marco," Celeste called out. He looked up from across the table. "Sorry about earlier," she said. "I think I was just a bit hangry, and tired. I only flew in this morning, you know? What is with those dense bread rolls on aeroplanes, anyway, right?"

He smiled. "Water off a duck's back, sweetheart."

Celeste joined Marco at the bar in time for a round of shots. She threw one back. It zigzagged down her throat and went straight to her head. With the help of Sam, she grabbed a glass of water and made her way back to the roped off area and sat down on the outdoor lounge.

It was windy; her hair was flying all over her face. She saw Jerome's light green sport's jacket hanging over a chair, took it and wrapped it around herself. She sipped her glass of water, drew a couple of deep breaths and slowly grounded herself.

"You alright Cel?" Sam asked, sitting just close enough to lightly brush her with every subtle movement.

"I'll be right," she said, shuffling sideways. "Have you seen Jerome?" She looked up to find Sam's attention had turned to a stain on his white shirt.

"Last I saw him, he was downstairs with Abbie."

"Just perfect." Celeste rolled her eyes.

"Hey, stay right here," Sam said as he stood up. "I'm just going to go get some soda water for this stain. I'll be right back."

As soon as Sam disappeared into the crowd, Celeste jumped up and pushed her way back inside to go find Jerome and Abbie.

The bar was made up of five floors—a forest of faux plastic plants created an infinite number of hiding places.

Celeste spotted Marco at the bar, where she'd left him. "Marco, have you seen Jerome?"

He shrugged and returned to the swath of barely legal girls, wearing what may as well be their underwear, hanging off his arms.

Celeste searched the place systematically. She started at the bottom, where they entered and made her way up one floor at a time, spelunking each and every nook. She found what she was looking for on the third floor. Jerome and Abbie were tucked away in a corner, chatting very closely—too close for Celeste.

Celeste willed her hands to stop shaking as she stormed over to them, her mind raced along with her feet, pushing through hordes of innocent bystanders; knocking their drinks out of their hands—she didn't care. Jerome looked up, saw her coming and took a quick, guilty half-step back from Abbie. As she reached them, Jerome's brain scrambled to invent a story.

"Celeste, there you are," he said. "Abbie and I were

just talking—"

"How could you do this to me!?" Celeste fumed, at a pitch that cut through the music.

"Do what?" He was rocking backwards and forward on the balls of his feet, pretending everything was okay.

"And you!" Celeste turned to Abbie.

"I knew I couldn't trust you. You bitch!"

Abbie looked everywhere but at Celeste.

Jerome grabbed Celeste by the arm and pulled her away from Abbie; trying his best to reason with her.

"Celeste, calm down, will you!?" Celeste shrugged his hand off of her.

"What's your problem? We were just talking for God's sake."

"Just talking?" She pinched the back of her neck and clenched her jaw. "I didn't know Abbie's ears were in her fucking mouth, Jerome! You know what!? Nah, whatever. I'm out—we're done!" She marched towards the exit.

"Wait!" Sam just found them. "I'll walk you back to the hotel." He seized the opportunity to be her knight in shining armour.

"Leave me alone, Sam. You're just as bad as him—worse, at least Jerome knows who he is! You don't want to be my friend, do you? You want more from me just like everyone else; I don't owe you anything. Get out of my way!" She shoved past him.

Sam took a step to go after her, but Jerome stopped him. "Let her go. It's all a big show for her fans, anyway."

Celeste ran down the stairwell, barrelling out the club, bumping into all and sundry. She was devastated. She stumbled past a group of people rubber-necking her public break-down, live-streaming their POVs all over the web, when all of a sudden, a busker's singing voice floated above the crowd—an audible oasis from the drama.

"Those boots were made for walking," he sang in a baritone pitch in Celeste's direction. "And that's just what they'll do." He shifted his gaze to Celeste's boots. The ones Jerome had insisted she wear.

Celeste slowed down and came to a complete stop in front of him, sitting against a derelict shopfront.

"Because one of these days these boots are gonna walk all over you," he finished, furiously strumming his electric guitar plugged into a small amp, plastered in stickers of bands you'd never heard of.

The single point of focus helped Celeste catch her breath. She nodded gratefully, before patting the pockets of Jerome's green sports jacket, searching for change. There was none, but she had a better idea. She took the jacket off and handed it to him. "Here, take this."

He couldn't believe it.

Celeste winked at him and strutted off towards the hotel, grinning a conspiratorial grin.

The busker's voice followed her as she walked away. "Yeah, and one of these days those boots are gonna walk all over you…"

The hotel was just around the corner. It took Celeste no time to get there. The doorman must've knocked off for the night, and Celeste timed her run through the lobby perfectly, making a beeline to the elevator, as the concierge went into the back room—

"Wait. Sorry," Lanie interjects. "Are you saying that the concierge didn't see Celeste when she got home, because he's told me otherwise?"

"Hmmm, he may have seen her, but she definitely didn't see him."

"You're positive?"

"Yep. Hundred percent."

Lanie flicks back a few pages of her notebook. "And what time was it when Celeste got home?"

Pimm leans back and tilts his head. "I'd say it was around ten o'clock, I think—I could be wrong."

"Okay," Lanie says as she jots down the time under the eleven o'clock time the concierge had given her, before urging Pimm to continue.

The elevator arrived with a dulcet ding. Celeste got in, caught it up to her floor, spilled out into the hallway and drunkenly bounced from wall to wall to her room.

She got to her door, stopped and searched her clutch for the key card. It wasn't there. She leaned against the door, gently resting her forehead against the hard, cold wooden surface, steeling herself for a trip back downstairs.

"Are you okay?" the room-service lady from earlier asked in a kindly voice, pushing her trolley packed with fresh linens over to her.

Celeste swallowed back tears.

"It's okay, love. I can open the door for you."

"Thank you," Celeste said in between sobs, as the woman opened the door with her card, then folded and wedged a 'do not disturb' sign from her cart into the empty card slot so the power would turn on.

"Thank you," Celeste said again, wiping her face. "I'm good now."

The room service lady gave her a warm smile and pottered off down the hallway.

Celeste stepped inside, immediately hung the room's 'do not disturb' sign on the door, then turned back inside and made her way over to the small table near the big windows, where she poured a glass of red wine into the same tumbler glass Jerome had used earlier. She took a long sip, then walked over to the heater and turned it up, before going over to the windows and shutting the blinds. She walked back into the middle of the room and turned to the mirror to say goodnight to her fans.

"Well, it's been a day! Thank you all for streaming. I can always count on you to be here for me. It's been real! Love you all!" she said before turning towards the bathroom and switching off her live stream.

SEVEN

"AND THAT'S IT. That was the very last thing I saw through Celeste's eyes," Pimm says.

Lanie takes a sympathetic breath and a sip of water, before clearing her throat with a perfunctory cough. "So, she went back to the hotel alone?" she finally asks.

"Well, alone with all of us."

"Sure, but not with anyone in real life, right?"

"No, no one in real life," he concedes. "I thought she was just exhausted. It was a big day for her. If I'd known she was going to pass out in the bath, I would've told someone, I swear."

"It's not your fault, Mr Gilchrist," Lanie reassures him. "I've just got a couple more questions for you: you're sure Celeste used the same tumbler glass she drank from earlier? She didn't use a new one?"

Pimm rubs his chin. "Pretty sure."

"Pretty sure?" Lanie echoes, grabbing her phone from the table, opening her photo app and confirming there were definitely two used glasses in the room when she was there yesterday morning.

"What's that," Pimm asks, craning his neck to see the photo. "Is that the glass?"

"Yeah, it is," Lanie replies. "Why?"

"I just remembered something." He pulls out his phone. "When Jerome was there before dinner, Celeste took a selfie of them and posted it on her Instagram." He brings up the post. "Look, see in the background on the table? It's the tumbler." Pimm takes a screenshot of the post and Bluetooths it to Lanie, before opening up his photos app. "And when she got back to her hotel I took a picture of the glass on my screen, because I liked it and was going to buy a set. Here take a look—check the metadata, it's legit." He hands Lanie his phone.

Lanie holds the phone next to the post Sam had just sent her. *It was the same tumbler, alright, which means someone else used the stemmed wine glass, after she'd logged-off.* "Shit," Lanie blurts out. *Hopefully Tod's able to find a DNA sample.* "Can you send me this photo?" She hands Pimm back his phone.

"Yeah, sure thing."

"Actually, one more thing," Lanie adds as he sends it to her. "What time does it say you took that photo?"

Pimm taps into the photo's metadata. "It says 10:07 p.m." He looks up at Lanie. "Oh, right, so yeah, I was right. She did get back to the hotel around ten o'clock."

Lanie navigates back to the voice recorder app on her phone and presses stop. "You've been extremely helpful, Pimm." She stands up and hurriedly packs her notepad and folders into her satchel.

Pimm gets up and takes the plates over to the sink. "If you think of anything else, let me know—you've got my number."

Pimm walks her to the front door. "I will. Goodbye Detective Daniels."

The warm Sydney day grabs Lanie by the hand and drags her outside. The sun beats down on her all-black ensemble. Her flight home doesn't leave for four hours so she's got time to kill. She takes off her leather jacket, tucks it neatly over her satchel, hanging off her shoulder, and strolls in the direction of the nearest pub. Lanie's been to Sydney many times, so knows a place nearby called The Lord Franklin.

She briskly pulls out her mobile and writes the Captain a message:

Strike 1: Extra glass in the room. Strike 2: Huge discrepancy of when she got back to the hotel. Strike 3: Don't trust Jerome or Sam. Something's up. I'm in.

Her brain starts organising the information she gathered from Pimm like an excel spreadsheet, tabulating names and events into neat columns in her mind. She crosses the street to avoid a junky pacing back and forward, slapping his forehead, remonstrating with himself—the commission flats are only a few blocks away. She saunters past the Prince Charles Park, where pasty English backpackers dot the grass, sunbaking. The basketball courts are buzzing with Chinese exchange students playing pick-up games, and the tennis courts are packed with pimply teens and their aggressive eastern European parent-coaches with toxic delusions of grandeur—all to the inimitable backdrop of the Sydney skyline dominated by the Centrepoint tower. Lanie's deep in thought over Pimm's point of view, wondering how objective anything he said was. *He's really not a big fan of Samuel Bateman.*

She reaches the pub, pushes through the suicide doors and takes a moment to let her eyes adjust to the dim light, before making her way past a stained-glass window of a cheeseburger, and up to the counter. The place smells of a mix of ladies' perfume and Weet-Bix—they brew their own beer on site. She orders a pint of lemon lime and bitters and sits at the front bar by herself.

It's busy for a Tuesday afternoon. There's a febrile energy about the place. A twenty-something guy joins her at the bar to order drinks. He's wearing a grey suit with a matching vest. There're creases in his shirt that give away it's brand new.

"Two Hawke's Lagers, a house champers and three pickle backs," he orders over the hubbub. He glances over at Lanie, smiles and tilts his head, led by his eyebrows, by way of hello.

Lanie looks him up and down. *This kid's more confident than he should be.* Lanie holds his stare, forcing him to retreat. He swiftly pays for his drinks and then goes running back to his friends with his tail between his legs.

She takes a moment to look around. All the guys are in suits, and the girls are in fancy dresses. *This bar used to be cool.* The bartender makes a sudden movement. Lanie looks over at him, watching him pull out a TV remote control from the top drawer beneath the cash register. He points it towards the big Samsung flat-screen over Lanie's shoulder, and switches it on. *Shit!* Lanie forgot, it's Melbourne Cup day.

Jerome's face appears in ultra-high definition on the TV—you can count the pores on his nose. There's a blonde-haired, blue-eyed woman a step behind and by his side in a gaudy silver shiny dress that changes colours where the sun catches it.

"Jesus, he really has a type, doesn't he," she mutters. "Can you turn that up for me?" she asks the bartender.

He shrugs and turns it up; then serves the next man-baby in an off-the-rack suit.

Lanie shifts her attention to the TV.

"Celeste was suffering from depression. I didn't know how bad it had gotten. I knew she took beta-blockers or benzodiazepines for flying, but never realised she'd begun taking them all the time. It's a tragedy, and we can't let it happen to anyone else. That's why I'll personally match any donation Celeste's followers make to Beyond Blue. But enough of that. I've been kindly asked by Marco here to help judge the Melbourne Cup fashion parade. So, I'll stop bringing down the mood." His eyes show all the compassion of a dead shark.

"Poor guy," a young woman standing next to Lanie at the bar says. "It's brave of him to turn up, after what happened."

Lanie's face creases into a frown as she briefly stares at the woman, then back at the TV. She looks down at her hands to discover she's torn her beer coaster into a confetti of red and yellow squares. Her hands continue to fidget while she ruminates over the case, simultaneously rubbing her tongue across her front teeth in a slow left to right motion.

She knows that in the majority of cases where the spouse is murdered, it's the partner. With the proliferation of true crime content, everyone knows that by now. But Lanie also knows that the easiest way to get away with it is by accidental bath drowning—she's seen it before. She fights off the urge of the obvious when suddenly she feels the crowd around her hush in unison and take in a collective breath as if it were a single organism.

The race is about to start. Lanie has zero interest in horse-racing, and detests betting for reasons, so she turns her back on the crowd and faces the bar.

"And they're off and racing," the announcer calls in that unmistakable cadence. The crowd heaves backwards into Lanie, who has to pick up her drink to avoid knocking it over. There's a nervous quiet before the call gets increasingly more frenetic. Staccato cheers begin to ring out go, go, go, go! The crowd clamours, waving betting tickets in the air.

"And it's Sparrow to the Heart by a nose!" The crowd cheers and curses in equal measure, before dispersing. Within ten minutes the bar is empty, minus the bartenders busily cleaning-up the aftermath.

Crazy how fast the race goes when you don't give a shit. Lanie straightens her bar stool and orders another drink—a Diet Coke this time.

Now that there's some quiet, Lanie pulls out her phone to do some desk—or more accurately 'bar'—research. She types Samuel Bateman's name into a Google search. The first result is a Wikipedia article. *Good place to start.* She clicks it with her thumb before gourmandising the article.

Samuel Bateman (born August 11, 1996) is an American electronics engineer, programmer, and technology entrepreneur. He is most known for his oft-forgotten role in co-founding Umwelt Platforms, which today is the world's largest optic lens hardware company and streaming, social media platform by revenue and the largest company in the world by market capitalisation. Through their work at Umwelt in the late tweens, he and Umwelt co-founder Jerome Pitt are widely recognized as the two pioneers of the optic POV revolution.

Lanie skips the boring bits: what school he went to, his first love, and that he was deep into live action role-playing, and thumbs down to the part about the founding of Umwelt.

As the company was about to boom, tragedy struck for Bateman. His mum was diagnosed with lung cancer. At the time the cancer drugs cost an average of $10,000 per month. Sam needed money to cover the bills, so he *approached Jerome. At this stage they were still a start-up. The potential was evident, but you can't quantify potential. Jerome borrowed money from his parents, who themselves came from generational wealth, and bought out Sam's share, to help him pay for his mum's treatment. Within a month a Silicon Valley investor bought-in and the company's value skyrocketed. Jerome became a multi-millionaire overnight. But the same thing could not be said for Bateman. Having sold his share to Jerome, he made nothing out of the deal. With his new fortune, Jerome paid for Sam's mum's treatment, as well as made sure Sam remained the lead engineer at the company. Over time, Jerome's legend grew as Sam's part in the Umwelt story diminished. No one remembers the quiet introvert. No one except the hard-core nerds, who, to this day, see him as a God—his minimalist, software-intensive engineering was ground breaking.*

So, she thinks, *Sam's more than just Jerome's lackey. He's a self-made man. Or, at least he would have been under different circumstances. Something's going on here, and I'm going to find out what.* She settles her tab, before walking out the side-door and calling for an Uber.

Lanie pulls up to the T2 drop-off at the Sydney Airport. The Uber driver's a friendly South African. She was only forced to hear one cautionary tale about a brother-in-law who got mugged at a traffic light, or 'robot' as he called it, which was a pleasant change from the usual one hundred. She thanks him, hops out, and waves goodbye through the tinted window.

She makes her way through the automatic doors, anxiously double checking her email on her phone for her boarding pass. She finds it and walks over to the check-in kiosks. She knows she doesn't need a paper ticket, but she likes to print one anyway. So many things can go wrong at the airport, printing a tangible, tactile ticket helps her hold onto some control—or, at least, the illusion of some. The kiosk spits out her boarding pass and she joins the back of the security line. It was short and moving fast. Lanie reaches the front of the line and turns to her left—knowing most people are right-handed and most right-handed people turn right—and joins the shortest lane. She leans over, grabs a tray and puts it down on the sliding surface. She pulls out her laptop from her satchel and drops that in first, followed by her keys and phone. She unbuckles her belt and adds it to the tray, too, before topping it with her empty bag and leather jacket. She slides the tray towards the security guy, who takes a quick glance at the pile. He pulls out another tray and moves her jacket to that one.

"Any aerosols?" he asks, for the millionth time today.

Lanie shakes her head and walks through the metal scanner. It flashes green. Security waves her through. Just as she takes a step forward an alarm squeals from behind the counter, accompanied by a red flashing light. Lanie looks more annoyed than worried. She knows what comes next.

"I need you to follow me," an out-of-breath, portly security guard demands, smugly resting his hands on the layer of fat suspended on his belt, which he's put a few extra notches in with a hammer and nail.

"Let me guess," Lanie says. "Dezunka Jurić?"

"Congratulations! You know your own name," he scoffs.

Lanie's jaw clenches. "If you just let me get my bag, I can show you my badge."

"Badge? Looks like we've got a cop here," he chortles to the other guard behind the camera. "This way please, officer."

Lanie gives up arguing, turns on her heels and just as she's about to be escorted away a clear, commanding voice rings out across the crowd.

"What's going on here?" It's a federal police officer. She's taller than Lanie and has reddish hair and a pale complexion. The security guard and Lanie grind to a halt.

"Lanie Daniels, is that you?" she asks knowing it is.

"Hey Martha," Lanie responds, sheepishly.

"Again?"

Lanie grimaces.

"She's fine. Let her go," Martha orders the guard.

He hesitates, but swiftly remembers it's above his pay grade to care, so does as he's asked.

Lanie grabs her satchel, digs around for her badge, pulls it out and thrusts it in the guards' faces. "See!" she says with pointless satisfaction. But they've already moved on. Lanie grabs her stuff and does likewise. It's not the first time this has happened and it won't be the last.

At university she had her identity stolen from her Messenger account. Someone had set up a profile with the same name as one of her friends and asked her to fill out a form for an assignment they were both working on. Lanie gave them everything they needed to steal her identity. It wasn't until weeks later when she was flying to Bali, she got stopped at security—like just now. She was frog-marched to the holding rooms and interrogated for eighteen hours for a slew of seriously bad stuff—from run-of-the-mill credit fraud to human-trafficking in Bulgaria. She could deal with the tables bolted to the floor, microwave dinners, and even the endless inane questions, but to be dragged out of line and gratuitously patted down in front of strangers and friends alike, was mortifying. Needless to say her holiday was cancelled, and the ramifications still reverberate to this day—this very day it turns out.

"You really need to get that fixed," Martha says. Martha and Lanie have done this dance at least three times in the last year—enough times to form an unorthodox friendship. Lanie loops her belt around the waist of her jeans.

"Maybe I just love that free mac and cheese dinner you've got back there in the holding area?" Lanie coughs. "But seriously every time I call them, they put me on hold for hours, tell me it won't happen again, and then it always does."

Martha turns to face Lanie. "No wonder I never see

you on social media—it's really done a number on you."

"I hate it."

"You don't hate it, you're just scared of it."

Lanie's eyes narrow. "Is there a difference?"

"Ha, but seriously, sort this out. One of these days I won't be here."

"Yeah, right. You love work more than me!"

"Speaking of which, got to get back to it. See you next time Dzunka," she says smirking.

Lanie heads downstairs to find out which gate her flight leaves from. The airport is starting to fill up with day-trippers like herself arriving to fly home. She takes the stairs over the escalator, wanting to get a few extra steps in before sitting down for the next hour and a half on the plane. She gets to the bottom and looks up at the boarding information on the TV.

"Shit," she mumbles. 'Final call' is flashing in red next to her flight. She planned on picking up something for her son, Thomas, and grabbing a bite on the way through, but with the drama at the security gate, now she's late. She only has time to do one or the other.

She hurriedly puts on her jacket, threads her satchel across her body, and scrambles to her gate via the newsagent where she picks up a plush, glittery-eyed Ibis. She gets to the gate and joins the back of the line just as it reaches the front. She reaches into her back pocket, searching for the printed boarding pass. It's gone.

"Of course it is!" she curses. She checks her other

jean pockets and it's not there either. She tries her left jacket pocket, then her right, and then finally the inner breast pocket. She reaches in and it's not there. It's completely gone.

"Tickets please?" the hostess at the gate asks.

Lanie pulls out her phone, hastily thumbs through her emails and finds the boarding pass. She smiles a relieved smile, flashes it in front of the scanner, and boards the plane. No worries.

EIGHT

LANIE GETS HOME to her apartment around ten o'clock. It's windy. The plane had to fly around in circles before it was given clearance to land. Lucky Melbourne airport is out in the sticks and there's no curfew, otherwise they would've turned the plane around and flown back to Sydney. She chucks her bag down next to the kitchen bench, uses the opposite foot to kick off each boot, and, through muscle memory, turns on the TV. The background noise helps her forget she's alone. The remote has been stuck on ABC News for months now. Some talking heads are just finishing up discussing Celeste's death, before moving onto the next segment:

"Deepfake technology has been outlawed by the Australian Government, with an anti-impersonation bill passed today," the news reporter reads.

Lanie's phone went flat on the flight thanks to the flying around in circles thing, so she plugs it into the charger in the kitchen and places it on the bench.

The doorbell rings. *It's a bit late for a house call.* She forces down her paranoia; shuffles over to the bottom drawer, unlocks it and pulls out her holstered, police-issued .40 calibre Smith & Wesson semi-automatic pistol. She hates guns. Hates everything about them, but not as much as feeling helpless. She steps over to the intercom and answers it. The video screen blinks to life and a black and white image of Jerome Pitt appears. He's downstairs.

"Detective Daniels? Can I come up?"

Lanie breathes a sigh of relief and unlocks the door, which makes a big click sound by way of an answer. She quickly returns to the kitchen, puts the gun back in its place, pivots towards the sink and splashes cold water on her face, washing away the adrenalin.

A minute later Jerome's at her front door. At the precise moment he's about to knock, Lanie opens it. His hand is cocked back, suspended in the air. "Hi," he says as his hand swings forward like a pendulum, the momentum pushing him through the door and awkwardly into Lanie. "Sorry," he says as he regains his balance and straightens his shirt. He's still in his suit—the one Lanie saw him wearing on TV earlier, but he's lost the jacket and loosened the tie. "Sorry for the house call, but I thought we should talk. I won't be long, promise; I've got to get to an after party downtown. I hate them, but it's for work."

There's a strained silence as Lanie studies him. "I'd ask how you know where I live, but I suspect having access to everyone's data is the answer," she says. "What are you doing here, Mr Pitt?"

Jerome surveys the apartment, then Lanie. "You look exhausted."

Lanie couldn't care less what he thinks she looks like. "Save the judging for your fashion parade, Mr Pitt."

Jerome winces. "You saw that?"

Lanie nods as she moves over to the fridge, looking for something to drink. It's still empty, barring the shrivelled broccolini. She turns to the sink, grabs a cup from the dish rack and pours herself a glass of tap water, not offering Jerome one.

"Not my finest hour, but I still have commitments. No matter how frivolous they feel now." He sits down on one of the stools at the kitchen bench. He runs his hand through his hair, scrunching it into a ball. "I hear your custody case is getting re-heard?"

Lanie turns and meets his eyes. He's grinning. Not a swinging-dick grin like she was expecting. But a sincere smile. "Um, yeah, I've been meaning to thank you for that," she says sheepishly.

"It was nothing," he replies. "I'm just happy to help bring some justice to this world. What did Jon say when you told him?"

Lanie scrambles. "Look, I'm guessing you're not paying me this very unusual, after hours visit to talk about the custody of my son?"

"That's true, detective," he inhales. "Listen, I just wanted to tell you to stop your investigation. I was wrong; you were right. I was in denial because it felt like my own failure, but Celeste is—I mean was—suffering from severe depression, which led to some very serious substance abuse. Benzos, apparently. I had to look it up. It's Xanax. Sam told me. And he said Celeste made him promise not to tell anyone. He feels responsible, but that's ridiculous. It's my fault. I blame myself. I should've been there for her; been a better husband." He looks down at his hands. His two thumbs make rapid circles around each other. "I just get so lost in my work. If I wasn't so wrapped up in it; if I was around more, I would've noticed earlier. I could've gotten her help." His eyes are pink. "I just wish she told me. I don't know why she didn't just tell me!" He rubs the back of his neck. "When another friend of ours, Abbie, was suffering through her own demons, she told us. And we got her help. The doc gave her antidepressants and they helped. If only Celeste told me!" He buries his face in his hands.

Lanie's never had a good bedside manner, but she shuffles across to the other side of the bench and clumsily puts her hand on his shoulder. "It's only natural for the people left behind to blame themselves," she awkwardly quotes the handbook.

He looks up at her. "I'm sorry, I just don't want her reputation ruined by this investigation—you understand, right? It was brash of me to get you involved so quick. It's a major flaw of mine—Celeste would always tell me that I'm a control freak. I try to control everything, even when I'm wrong— especially when I'm wrong. I've been this way since forever. It's just not fair on Celeste. I don't know if I could live with myself if the media drags her name through the mud, telling the world about her drug problem, because I was angry and needed someone to blame!" He wipes his eyes with the palms of his hands. "I'm sorry. I, um, I should go. I didn't mean to burden you with all this."

Lanie pulls back her hand. "It's okay Mr Pitt."

Jerome takes a deep breath and collects himself.

"In fact, I may have found some evidence that you were right—I think someone else was in the room with her when she died."

Jerome sits up a little straighter. "You what!?" he says. His whole demeanour changes. "Aren't you listening?" He leans forward. "There is no case. I want this over. It was an accident. She OD'd."

Lanie walks back behind the kitchen bench, putting space between them.

"I asked for the investigation, and now I'm asking for it to end."

"It doesn't quite work like that Mr Pitt. Once a case is open, only we choose when to close it. Standard procedure. Dotting i's and crossing t's kind of thing."

Jerome drops his head and draws a deep breath. "I understand. But I, at least, want you to get it over and done with as soon as possible. Can you do that for me, detective?"

Silence hangs in the air.

"So, you mentioned Abbie?" Lanie moves on.

"Yeah, what about her?" Jerome looks up.

"You're friends?"

Jerome checks the time on his phone. "She was more of a business associate, I guess—she was going to be the next big thing."

"What do you mean 'was'?" Lanie's eyes narrow.

"I'm sure you've heard by now," Jerome starts, "the

night Celeste died, we got in a big fight. Celeste and me, I mean. She thought Abbie and I were having an affair. Paranoia from the pills, I guess. And—and I don't want to talk ill of the dead—but Celeste went hard at Abbie in front of everyone. It was grim." He scratches his collar bone. "Anyway, the next morning I got a message from Abbie telling me she was taking a break from Umwelt. Here, let me show you." Jerome pulls out his phone from his jacket pocket, navigates to his messages and puts it down on the bench in front of Lanie.

Hi J. I'm shook from last night. I need space. Don't contact me... I'll reach out when I'm ready xxx

Lanie reads it and winces. "Can I get her number?"
"Of course—go for it."
Lanie grabs her phone from the charger and saves Abbie's number. "Was there anything I should know about you two—you and Abbie? Was Celeste's outburst warranted? Were you cheating on her with Abbie?"
Jerome pulls his phone towards himself and fidgets with it in his hands. "Nothing was going on between us." He clears his throat. "We were just friends," he adds, although that's not what his body language was saying. Either way, Lanie has her answer.
"Sorry Mr Pitt, I had to ask."
Jerome smiles, puts his phone back in his pocket and steps in the direction of the door. "Of course. Thank you for everything, again, detective. It'll be good to put this whole thing to bed and let the

healing begin."

"Wait. Mr Pitt," Lanie says. "One more thing while you're here—saves me from chasing you up this week."

"What is it?" Jerome turns back towards her.

"Samuel Bateman?" she inflects, "what do you know about his and Celeste's relationship?"

Jerome walks back into the room and sits back down on the bar stool. "What? Why? They were friends," he says, bemused. "He's my oldest friend and she is," he stops and scratches his nose. "I did it again, didn't I? I should say was. She was my wife."

"That's okay Mr Pitt. But was that all? They were just friends?"

Jerome leans his hip against the kitchen bench. "Samuel Bateman?" he asks. "You're talking about my friend Samuel Bateman?"

Lanie's left eye twitches.

"Surely Sam's not a person of interest, detective—he's hardly interesting!" He laughs uneasily.

Lanie doesn't see the funny side.

He clears his throat.

"Okay, don't get me wrong, but that would never happen. She's way out of his league. She needed a man who could protect her." There's a conceit in his voice.

"A man like you?"

"No!" he exclaims, before doubling down. "Actually, yes exactly like me—she was my wife afterall!" He fixes his shirt as he regains his composure. "Anyway, I've known Sam for years and never seen him with a woman—like with-with a woman. Between you and me, I think he's asexual. Trust me, they were just friends," he says. "Now, like I said, I've got an after party to attend. I really must go."

Jerome turns back around, walks out the door and leaves the building the way he came in: through the hallway, down the lift and out the front automatic door.

Lanie makes her way over to the bedroom window. She peeks out the timber venetian blinds to see Jerome's brand-new, blue Tesla parked on the street. From her viewpoint Lanie watches him walk out the sliding doors and over to his car.

A passers-by Cavoodle barks incessantly at Jerome. He ignores it and jumps in the front seat of his car.

He looks up to Lanie's apartment; their eyes meet. Lanie smiles, then turns back inside and grabs her phone from the bench. She goes to dial Abbie's number but thinks better of it because of the time. She writes her a message instead.

Hi Abbie. Detective Lanie Daniels here. I'm investigating the Celeste Simone case. Can you please call me back on this number when you get this? Thanks.

NINE

IT'S WEDNESDAY MORNING. Lanie pays her mum a surprise visit at the nursing home—as much a surprise to herself as her mum. This is the first time she's seen her since she moved in, eight whole months ago.

She steps through the automatic sliding doors. A bouquet of disinfectant and adult diapers needle her nostrils. She pushes on towards the front desk, to a lady sitting behind the counter on an old, beige computer. The kind of computer that would play 'Where in the World is Carmen San Diego'. The lady's name is Fiona. It says so on her name badge, which is decorated with tiny sunflower stickers.

"How can I help you?" She looks like she's one of the residents, but isn't.

"I'm here to see Susanne Daniels," Lanie replies.

The lady's eyes light up.

"That's marvellous," she says, almost giddy. "It's been so long since Susanne has had a visitor. How do you know her?"

Lanie rubs the back of her neck. "I'm her daughter," she says, as if it wasn't obvious, which it wasn't on account of Lanie looking more like her Malay dad, and not her mum who is roast-pork-every-Sunday white as they come.

The nurse looks up from her screen. "Lanie!? Oh Susanne has told us so much about you," she says excitedly. "She's going to be thrilled you're here." Guilt stabs at Lanie's chest.

"I've been busy," she says, defending herself from the phantom accusation.

"We know. Susanne never stops talking about you. She's so proud," Fiona says cheerfully, while slowly copying over the room number from the screen to a torn-off piece of paper.

Lanie feels guilty. She wants to be judged, and judged harshly. That's what she deserves. The opposite hurts worse than any criticism.

"So," Fiona's voice interrupts Lanie's self-pity, "if you walk through this door," she points over Lanie's shoulder, "turn right and then left, then right and right again, then follow the corridor until you reach room 233. That's your mum's. She should be there."

Lanie pulls her hands from her jacket pockets to accept the piece of paper from the lady. "Cheers," she says, trying her best to sound casual; nonchalant.

"Oh, and keep an eye out for Raymond," Fiona says in earnest, as Lanie turns away.

Lanie winds her way through the nursing-home's endless corridors. Every step closer to her mum's room heaps on the guilt. Lavender potpourri drifts out of one of the rooms, staining the smell of ammonia. A physiotherapist is aiding an old man in loose-fitting, blue, flannel pyjamas, glacially hobbling on a second-hand walking frame. The man stares at Lanie as she walks by, his hand unashamedly reaching for his crotch. His carer slaps his hands away and apologises profusely. Lanie stops herself from retching and pushes forward. She side-steps the lunch lady, blindly wheeling her loaded cart, full of white-bread, ham and cheese sandwiches, out of a room.

"Sorry love," she says, but Lanie's already well past her. She slows down as she closes in on her mum's room.

"231, 232 and 233… here it is," she murmurs. The door's shut. Lanie gently knocks on it. The minimal force creaks it open. "Hello?" she calls out as she pokes her head through the doorway.

"Lanie?" her mum responds from a floral-patterned recliner by the window.

"Hi mum," Lanie says, fighting the flight instinct, which feels like a far more appealing option than withstanding the flooding reservoir of remorse.

The two women couldn't be any more different. Chalk and cheese. Apples and oranges. Where Lanie is quiet and weighed down by her thoughts, Susanne is the life of the party; light-as-a-feather. She's confident and could not give fewer fucks. Both women identify as feminists, yet they go about it in totally different ways. Susanne embraces her femininity. She loves jewellery and make-up and isn't offended by a man opening the door for her, whereas Lanie is more Destiny's Child Independent Woman. Not that she'd ever admit to liking Destiny's

Child—that would be way off-brand.

Mrs Daniels makes a curling gesture with her free hand, urging Lanie to come over. "Come give your old mum a hug. It's bloody great to see you," she says with her trademark squeaky voice.

Lanie's defences crumble. She forgets herself, rushes over and gives her mum a big hug. An unfakeable hug. As Lanie leans over and wraps her arms around her fragile frame, she glimpses the garden through the window. Sparrows dance among unfurling violet daffodils, accompanied by free, fluttering butterflies. Spring has sprung.

"Let's get out of here—this place gives me the creeps," Lanie says, squirting sanitizer into her hands and rubbing them together.

"Ah, you've met Raymond then, that filthy old bugger?"

Lanie grimaces as she helps her mum up out of the recliner.

Susanne Daniels is doing alright for an old chook. She had a few spills a year or so ago, which meant she couldn't live by herself anymore. And there was no way Lanie was going to let her live with her. The two women's relationship had been strained for as long as Lanie could remember. After her dad passed away from cancer, her mum completely abdicated herself of any maternal responsibility. Naturally, Lanie acted out. In hindsight she could've been a better daughter, and, in classic Lanie style, she did feel the weight of responsibility for years afterwards. Until one day she simply said *fuck it*, and stopped blaming herself. She was a kid; how could she have known better? Her mum was meant to be the grown-up. This revelation did wonders for their relationship. Susanne was living with her own demons, feeling guilty about burdening Lanie with guilt. When this break-through happened in one of their many screaming matches, the two women knew they both cared deeply for each other, and always would. Even if Lanie didn't see her for the last eight months.

She drags her mum's right arm around her shoulders and hoists her into her nearby wheelchair. Lanie got the wheelchair for a bargain price on Gumtree, leaving no doubt in her mind the previous owner had carked it. It's not the fanciest model—doesn't have all the bells and whistles—but it does the trick. It rolls in a straight line, most of the time. She grabs a mauve coloured cardigan from the wardrobe, tucks it into the back pocket and wheels her mum out the place at breakneck speed, exiting the way she came in, past the lunch lady, past Raymond and finally past dear old Fiona at the counter.

"Adios Fi-Fi!" Susanne hollers as they fang past.

Lanie takes her for coffee at the cafe inside the nearby local shopping centre. The kind that seems to be from a bygone era, replicated in every suburb, featuring a supermarket, butcher, bottle shop, key-cutters, tobacconist and run-down cafe, like the one they're sitting in right now, that serves their coffee at boiling-point, because all their clientele are over sixty and have long lost their taste buds.

The amicable clatter of coffee cups, along with the short sharp hisses of the milk steamer, put the two women at ease. It's cosy. The table and chairs are a uniform orangey-beige colour. Two big drink fridges sit on the outside of the counter, containing small bottles of juices, soft drinks, and chocolate milks in fruit boxes. Prints of Monet's Garden in bulging beige plastic frames hang lopsided on the paint-cracked walls.

The only other customer is a young mum with her baby and young child, getting out of the house to break up the gruelling monotony of stay-at-home parenting. She's feeding the baby from a squeezy pack. Lanie can just make out the meal: sweet potato, carrot and barley. *Delicious*. Meanwhile the other child is pulling at the mum's free arm asking for money to play on the ride-on Wiggles car, which is actually a boat, sitting in the middle of the mall, between the cafe and supermarket.

Both Lanie and Susanne stare, entranced at the cliched scene.

"Sisters?" The waiter interrupts, with a cheeky grin.

Lanie looks up from her menu. He's handsome. Too handsome for this dump.

"What's your name? Are you single?" Susanne asks candidly. "My daughter here needs a good," she pauses, choosing her next words carefully, "night out."

Lanie would care more if she wasn't used to her

mum's batshit craziness.

"I am, and my name's Piero, but I'm afraid your daughter is way out of my league." He clasps his hands together, shaking them up and down, while winking at Lanie. "Now, what can I get for you two lovely ladies?"

"A long black for me, extra hot and..." Susanne turns to Lanie.

"A long... same for me," Lanie says. *Shit! I'm turning into her—but without the sass.*

"No problem." He walks away to clear a nearby table, reaching over to wipe the sugar granules on the way back to the kitchen. The two ladies brazenly admire his... work ethic.

"You need to go out more," Susanne says.

"Trust me mum, if you saw what happens to women that go out more," she makes air quotes with her hands for extra emphasis, "like I do, you'd stay home, too."

Susanne screws up her face and scoffs. "What kind of talk is that?" she says. "Dentists still eat chocolate, don't they?"

"Not quite the same thing, mum."

Susanne shrugs and moves on. "How's my beautiful grandson? You know Brett brought him over for a visit last month?"

Lanie's eyes gloss over. *Fuck! I need to tell Jon about Jerome helping with Thomas' custody case.*

"Don't tell me you're still bitter?' Susanne asks, reading Lanie's tortured face.

Lanie looks up. "He took Thomas from me, mum!"

she trembles, involuntarily scratching her shoulder. "And even if the court hadn't ordered Thomas to stay with him, he'd probably want to, anyway. He has everything. He makes me feel," she searches for the right word, "useless." Lanie lowers her eyes.

"Two long blacks, extra hot," the waiter interrupts. He puts the coffees down, one in front of each woman, and walks back to the kitchen. The coffees have tiny, bite-sized white-chocolate-chip and macadamia cookies accompanying them.

Susanne dips hers in her coffee and swallows it whole. "He," she finally responds, "doesn't make you feel anything." She levels her eyes at Lanie's. "There's only one person who controls how you feel, and that's you. Don't let it get to you."

Lanie crosses her arms. "Like you didn't let dad's gambling get to you?" You guys didn't talk for years before he died."

Susanne stirs her coffee and taps her teaspoon on the lip of the mug. "You're right, I never liked his gambling. Did you ever stop to think why we had toasted cheese sandwiches for dinner three nights a week? But I never stopped loving your father, and we didn't stop talking. Our relationship had grown beyond words a long time before he got cancer."

Lanie shifts her weight on the rigid cafe seat.

"Anyway, this isn't about me. It's about you. And Brett and Thomas."

Lanie slumps in her chair.

"God, you haven't changed one iota," Susanne continues. "I remember at school you used to get so down on yourself when your friends did better than you on tests, even when you did well. Remember little Carly Davis, with that bitch of a mother I had to get along with for you two girls? Candice! That was her name. Do you remember those hideous nails of hers—she looked like Morticia Adams!"

Lanie coughs up a chuckle, welcoming the moment of levity.

"Lanie, you've always had an unhealthy habit of comparing yourself to others, letting them live rent free in your head." She leans forward. "Look at me," she says. "Brett's, or anyone else's, successes are not your failures." Susanne pauses, letting it sink in. "He was born with a silver spoon. Why would you even compare yourself to that? What have I always said: comparisons are odious. Thomas loves you for you—and he always will. You're his mum; that's something Brett can never take from you."

Lanie sips her coffee, trying to hide behind the mug.

"You've created this tough exterior," she points to Lanie's greasy, ponytailed hair, "because you don't want people to think you care."

Lanie's face flinches slightly as she reaches for her hair, brushing it with a clawed hand, feigning offence.

"But I know you do!" Susanne continues. "And I know you're angry. And I know that your anger is eating you up inside." She kisses the small crucifix around her neck.

Lanie holds back an eye-roll.

"Don't waste your energy comparing yourself to

him and don't waste your energy hating him. It doesn't affect him one little bit, only you. He's moved on." Susanne leans back in her chair. "Anyway, it's easy to hate. And since when do we..." she slams her open palm on her chest, then reaches over the table to poke her bony finger straight into Lanie's chest, where her heart would be. "When do we Daniels women ever do things the easy way?" Susanne unceremoniously dips the same finger in her coffee, then thrusts it skyward. "Piero, I need you to microwave my coffee; it's cold!"

"You've been practising?" Lanie jests, tugging at her right ear.

"I've had eight months," Susanne answers with a maternal wink, brimming with forgiveness. The kind that doesn't need or expect an apology.

Piero comes over and wraps his hand around the mug. "But this is still boiling hot?" he says as a half-question, half-statement.

Susanne gives him a lascivious smile, then wraps her hands around his like the scene from Ghosts, except she's Patrick Swayze and he's Demi Moore. "Mmm, you're right but it can always be hotter." She bats her eyelids, making both him and Lanie squirm.

"Yes, mam," he says, pulling his hand away, taking the coffee with him to zap it in the microwave.

He returns moments later. "Here you go." He places the piping hot coffee down.

Susanne takes a sip and it scolds her tongue. "Perfect," she says, making the chef-kiss sign with her thumb and forefinger. "So what are you working on, can you tell me?" She grins a conspiratorial grin.

Lanie leans back. "The Celeste Simone case."

"I thought it was an accident. Didn't she pass out in the bath from too many drugs?" Susanne's big into her gossip mags, so has obviously been following the case.

"So did I, but the more I look into it the less likely that's the case—some things just don't add up."

"It was the husband, wasn't it?" Susanne quips. "I've watched enough crime shows to know it's always the husband."

Lanie rubs her eyes. "Everyone's a detective these days, aren't they? Anyway, let's talk about something other than work, can we?" she says while absently shifting sugar granules around the table with her forefinger.

"Sure," Susanne says. "There is something I've been meaning to tell you…"

"Oh, yeah? What's that?"

"I, um, I went to the doctors the other day, and…" Lanie's looking at Susanne urging her to spit it out. "And, I put your name down as my emergency contact. I hope that's okay."

"Oh, is that all?"

Susanne nods.

"Well, of course it is mum," she says. "Jesus, I thought you were gonna say something serious then."

"Oh, no. That's it."

"Okay," Lanie shrugs before the two women sit there comfortably; quietly finishing their coffee.

The waiter returns and collects their empty mugs, leaving behind an origami swan made from a brown serviette in front of Lanie. She notices writing on it, so picks it up and unfolds it. It's got his number scribbled down in blue biro. He walks back over to the counter looking down bashfully when their eyes meet.

Susanne smirks.

"Don't say it!" Lanie gives her a look.

"Shit, I got to go. I've got to interview a witness." She checks her watch. "C'mon, I'll drive you back to the home—I'm sure creepy Raymond's missing you." Lanie stands up, walks around the table—gracefully in case Piero is watching—does a quick three-point turn with Susanne's wheelchair and heads out the cafe back to the car.

"Where are you headed?"

"Brighton," Lanie replies.

"Oh, Briiighton," her mum says, with a lilt mocking the way the well-heeled locals say it.

Lanie smiles, and tries it on for size. "Briiiiiighton." The joke felt good rolling around her mouth.

TEN

PAULA'S NOT SURE whether it's the best ramen in Brighton because it tastes good, or because it costs a lot. Maybe it's both. Maybe it tastes so good because not everyone can afford it. It's around two in the afternoon. She's home by herself, again, while her husband is at work. He's an anaesthetist at the Windsor Hospital. It's a high-pressure job, and he works long hours, leaving Paula home alone a lot.

The doorbell rings. It's the DoorDash driver. She answers it, grabs the paper bag and carries it outside to the big, concrete table in her backyard. It's just Paula now. Paula and her vegan ramen.

She's pretty well off. What she wanted, she could have, unless it was her independence. Her family shipped her off to Australia from Dubai to be with her husband, and now she only has one maid, and has to wash her own clothes—and his. Not that she minds. Sometimes it makes her happy to be busy.

Paula is a Muslim like the majority of Christians are Christians, or Hindus Hindus. She does all the big stuff, like Ramadan and Eid, but otherwise it's not a day-to-day thing. It's just something she inherited; something she goes along with, without much thought. Unfortunately, her and her husband are not fully aligned on this.

She's a romantic. She watched too many Disney movies as a girl, so was always looking for her frog-into-prince happily-ever-after, until her family arranged her marriage, and she was forced to grow up.

She pedantically lays out the plastic cutlery and ramen in front of her, slides over her laptop, switches it on, logs into her Umwelt account and connects to a random live stream which the algorithm recommends.

Her screen morphs into a bustling teppanyaki restaurant. It looks familiar. She's been there before in real life. It's Tango Teppanyaki on Chapel Street. She takes in the scene: a large stainless-steel exhaust fan hangs from the ceiling, devouring a tangerine flame. The seat next to her is empty but with a letterman jacket hanging draped over the back support. The walls are made up of long caramel-coloured wooden planks, interspersed with traditional Japanese paintings of farming villages. Despite it being the middle of the day, it's dark inside. Dim flickering lanterns dangle from the exposed wooden beams overhead. The wooden bench where she's sitting, wraps itself around a sizzling hotplate with a chubby Japanese chef in an oversized red chef's hat at its centre. Beads of sweat trickle down his cheeks, dissipating into steam as they hit the hibachi grill. He cracks five eggs, then chases them around the surface of the hotplate with his spatula, until they're a cloudy yellow. He folds the eggs into themselves, creating a long flat cylinder, before chopping them into bite-sized pieces and slinging them into everyone's mouths.

Since Celeste passed, Paula's been left watching random streams of whatever Umwelt serves up to her. It beats eating lunch alone.

As they were getting to the mains, a notification pops up in the right-hand corner of her screen. Someone's at the door. It's the detective who called her yesterday—she insisted that Paula could be helpful. She slaps her computer shut, heads towards the door, quickly fixes her terracotta coloured hijab at the mirror with a couple of pointless dabs, and opens the hefty, solid-oak door.

The two women stare at each other for a second. Paula waits for Lanie to talk first, so she does.

"I'm Detective Daniels," Lanie finds her voice. "We spoke yesterday."

"Yes, yes. Please, come in," Paula replies. They walk through a big open lobby area, past the downstairs kitchen and living room and out onto the alfresco dining area, where they take a seat at the concrete table next to the lap pool. On the table is the noodle soup. The warm smell makes Lanie's stomach yearn. Above them is a gaudy crystal chandelier. The kind you see literally nowhere; maybe in Bollywood movies. If Lanie is moved by the wanton display of wealth, she doesn't show it.

"Thanks for seeing me at such short notice, Paula," Lanie starts. "I'm investigating Celeste Simone's death, and I think you may be able to help me piece together exactly what happened the day she died."

She does the same well-rehearsed preamble as yesterday: pulls out pen, paper and mobile phone, pressing play on the voice recorder app, ready to capture Paula's interpretation of events.

"If you could just tell me what you saw through Celeste's eyes, starting with when she flew into Melbourne."

Before Paula begins, she gets up and pours herself and Lanie a glass of sparkling water from a long jug filled with fresh lemon and clapped sprigs of mint. She sits back down. "So I just talk?"

"Yep, go right ahead."

ELEVEN

IT WAS SATURDAY morning. Celeste's plane touched down at the Melbourne International Airport a little earlier than scheduled. She waited for everyone else to disembark first. Partly because she wanted to avoid the crowd, partly because she wanted to avoid Abbie Benson-Wheeler—an emerging influencer who modelled herself on Celeste—who she'd spotted sitting a few rows up.

She sat patiently, scrolling through her phone until she was the last one in first class. It had been over a month since she'd last been with Jerome, so she couldn't wait to see him. She grabbed her Louis Vuitton tote and launched herself down the empty aisle to the door.

She stepped out onto the air bridge, walked down the hallway, out the gate and straight into the duty free store. She shopped around before settling on a nice bottle of St Henri Shiraz for her and Jerome to share.

She took it up to the counter, bought it from a salt-of-the-earth shop-assistant, shoved the bottle into her bag, then made her way out of customs to find Jerome.

She walked past a crowd of people, who were swamping Abbie.

People always said Abbie and Celeste looked alike. Now it was undeniable, owing to Abbie's new hair colour. Something had compelled her to dye her hair blonde like Celeste's. The combination of that; the blue eyes, and the same upturned nose, resulted in them looking uncannily similar. But, the hair was just another thing, in a long line of things that Abbie copied from Celeste.

When Abbie first started out, she would travel the world streaming from the exact same spots as Celeste. She put it down to coincidence, but it wasn't.

Celeste pushed past Abbie's fans and found that Jerome had sent a driver to pick her up, because he was stuck at work—he's a hard worker.

Celeste walked up to the man holding a sign with her name on it and introduced herself—not that she had to.

His name was Gary. He was big. He grabbed Celeste's luggage from her and walked her out to his car. It was nice, but not as nice as Abbie's.

Lanie clears her throat and leans forward. "Why do you follow Celeste, if you don't mind me asking?"

Paula places her spoon down onto the table. "Celeste was in her prime when I moved to Australia, and I was going through a really hard time, not knowing anyone. And being Muslim didn't help. Outside this house I was—or still am—too Muslim, but inside I'm not Muslim enough. Celeste was my escape from my life. I could stream hers, pretend it was mine and feel normal. I could wear what I want; brush shoulders with the people I want—it was magical. So, I don't know, I guess I feel like she was always there for me."

"Okay." Lanie scratches her neck. "Go on."

On the ride from the airport to the hotel Celeste messaged her mother, informing her she'd arrived safely. It's something she does after every flight. Every flight, except one. There was one time she didn't, and her mother was worried sick. But it wasn't Celeste's fault. Her phone died, so she couldn't contact her until she got to the hotel. The problem was, she was in Bombay and it was peak hour, so she didn't actually get to the hotel until hours after she landed. Her mother understood, eventually.

She finally arrived at her hotel in the city: The Grand Theatre, where Samuel Bateman was waiting.

Samuel's Jerome's best friend. Over the years Samuel and Celeste had become close friends, too. Whenever Jerome couldn't make it to an event: dinner or cocktail party, Samuel would go in his place, which meant Samuel and Celeste were out together a lot. He grabbed her bags and carried them inside for her. They walked in through the big, main entrance.

The door woman was dressed in an old-fashioned theatre costume. "Welcome to The Grand Theatre

Hotel," she said.

It was really busy. Celeste wasn't the only one staying there for the Melbourne Cup. A lot of other women were in the foyer, holding onto their silk, designer garment bags. In front of them was stairs that lead to a restaurant. At the bottom of the stairs on the left—or stage-right—there was an oak bookshelf, filled with dusty, old books, and to their left was a busy little cafe.

"You go line up and check-in, while I'll grab us coffees," Celeste said. "It's been too long since I've had a proper cuppa. That American, percolated crap is slowly killing me."

"Okay, but make mine a green tea, please," Samuel said as Celeste turned towards the cafe.

Celeste lined up for their drinks and ordered them from the barista, a short-haired, tall woman, wearing a crisp black shirt, black jeans and branded apron. "One flat white, and a green tea, please."

"Name?"

Celeste paused before answering. "Abbie."

Her order didn't take long. "Flat white; green tea for Abbie!" The barista called out only minutes later. "Abbie!?" she called out again, before Celeste remembered that that was her.

"Yep!" Celeste raised her hand before collecting them from her. With a cup in each hand, she made her way back to Samuel, who had only just reached the front of the line to check-in.

Lanie rubs her eyes with both hands. "Well that's

one mystery solved."

"Huh? What do you mean?" Paula looks up from her soup.

Lanie brings her hands together. "When I was investigating her room, there was a disposable coffee cup in the bin and it had Abbie's name on it."

Paula nods vigorously with wide eyes. "Was there? Yeah, Celeste always gave out fake names like that. It helped her stay incognito."

Lanie sips her mint water.

Paula continues.

Celeste handed Samuel his tea and they walked up to the desk.

"Miss Celeste Simone! It's a pleasure to have you back with us at The Grand Theatre," the man behind the desk said. His energy was infectious. He checked her in, handed over the room key card to Samuel and gave them quick directions to the room. "Take the elevators behind me up to level five, and walk to the end of the corridor."

They grabbed the card, walked around the front desk and caught the elevator up to the fifth floor. They stepped out of the elevator and made their way down the hallway to Celeste's room.

"Morning," Samuel said to the maid as they crossed paths under an enormous, obscene painting of a woman's naked body with outstretched arms.

She ignored him—rude.

They reached the room; Samuel unlocked the door with a tap of the key card, took a step backwards and gestured for Celeste to walk through. She did; the room opened up to a chic, designer suite.

Paula stops to take a sip of her soup and looks up. "I booked a weekend there in the same room."
Lanie cocks her head. "Jesus, that's a bit morbid, isn't it?" She leans back in her seat, crossing her arms.
"Oh no, I booked before she died!" Paula's mortified. "I wonder what it means for my booking? Not that that's important. I don't want to stay in that place anymore, anyway. It's probably haunted."
Lanie waits to see if she's joking. She's not. "Call the hotel. I'm sure they'll understand." She looks up at the gaudy chandelier again. "Or just let it go…" Paula misses Lanie's snide quip—or chooses to ignore it—and continues.

The room was gorgeous. Jerome knew her so well. Celeste explored every corner of the suite, showing it off to her fans streaming at home. The bed was enormous with lots of pillows. There were giant west-facing windows that overlooked the city. The bathroom was glamorous, like something from a Hollywood movie. Big lights bordered the mirror. She turned around, grabbed the room-service menu and jumped on the bed.
She looked up to find Samuel wondering around the room, holding his phone heavenwards trying to get reception. Celeste watched on smiling, as his phone led him past the bath to the windows, where he found a single bar of service—when he held it just

right.

"The Wi-Fi password is on the tray on the mini-bar." Celeste smirked.

"Why didn't you... never mind." Samuel let go of the blind he was holding in his free hand, walked over and grabbed it. He joined Celeste on the bed and typed in the password. "Much better," he said, before diving head first into his emails.

"Where's Jerome really, though?"

"Where do you think?" Sam looked up from his phone.

"Well," Celeste sighed. "If there was ever a doubt who he loved more, I think we have our answer."

"Oh, there's never been any doubt, has there?"

They both chuckle uneasily.

Celeste was tired. It had been a long morning, and an even longer flight. Samuel left so Celeste could take a nap, but not before pointing out the wardrobe of designer dresses for her to try on, as well as inform her that Abbie was coming to dinner.

"Awesome!" Celeste grimaced.

Samuel left and Celeste crashed out on the bed, not bothering to take off her make-up or turn off her live stream.

"What was Abbie and Celeste's relationship like?" Lanie asks. "Were they friends?"

Paula scoffs. "Ha! Maybe for the cameras, but not IRL." She dabs the back of her hijab with a flat hand, revealing a strand of blonde hair. Lanie does a double take. She leans forward and finds confirmation in a few loose blonde-with-dark-root locks clinging to Paula's left shoulder.

"Like I said," Paula continues, thinking Lanie's just trying to get comfy. "Abbie was a copy-cat. She mimicked everything Celeste did, but never credited her. But you know what they say," she straightens her back, "imitation is the highest form of flattery. She wanted Celeste's life. And she was getting it too: the sponsors, the followers, the fame. She was getting it all—"

"Including Jerome?"

"Ha," Paula scoffs. "She wishes! Celeste and Jerome were soul mates."

Lanie strokes her chin as she shifts her weight in her seat. "So, Abbie was jealous of Celeste, then?"

"Oh, yes, absolutely."

"Hmm…" Lanie makes a note in her book. "Okay, go on."

Celeste slept for a few hours, before finally getting up and stumbling over to the coffee machine. It was one of those George Clooney ones with the pods, which Celeste couldn't find anywhere. She poured herself a glass of water from the sink in the bathroom, then walked over to the blinds and swung them open. She drank the tap water while looking out the window, down onto a rooftop bar, which was opening for lunch. She was hungry—she hadn't eaten anything since the plane. She picked up the room's phone and ordered a tuna sandwich from room service—and coffee pods.

While she waited, she stepped over to the wardrobe to take a quick look at the dresses. She pulled open the door and was greeted by a burst of colour. She smiled, then closed the wardrobe, saving the enviable task of trying them on for after lunch. She walked back to the bed, where she sat scrolling on her phone, waiting for her food and better mood to arrive.

"Room service," a warm voice sang out, accompanied by a knock knock knock.

Celeste hurried over to the door and opened it. It was the same woman that ignored Samuel in the hallway earlier. She wheeled in a cart with a shiny, silver cloche on it. The kind you only ever see at nice hotels and reality TV shows. The old lady wheeled it in and left it by the mini-bar.

"Thank you," Celeste said as she signed the receipt. She lifted the polished lid off the cloche to find her tuna sandwich.

After lunch Celeste tried on the dresses. The greatest designers in the world were all vying for her to wear their design to the Melbourne Cup on Tuesday, knowing whatever one she chose would become an instant classic. Instead of choosing one by herself, Celeste turned to the mirror and asked her fans for help.

"Hey guys," she said. "I need your help deciding what dress to wear tonight, and for the Melbourne Cup on Tuesday. So, what I'm going to do is try on all these amazing dresses, which these incredible designers have kindly sent me, while you guys vote on which two you like the best. And remember, you can buy any of the dresses for yourself, just follow the links. Okay let's do it!"

Celeste did the right thing by each designer, giving them all a little publicity.

She narrowed the options down to four of her favourites, then turned to her chat. "So, guys! I have a quartet of incredible dresses here; it's impossible for me to separate them, so I need your help." She walked into the bathroom—her stream cut to an advert—then came back out again, wearing the first option.

"There's this sultry raspberry pink mini dress by Camilla and Marc." She pirouetted, forcing one of the spaghetti straps to dribble down her shoulder. "Don't vote until you see them all!" Emojis prematurely started filling the screen before she returned to the bathroom with the next dress draped over her arm, triggering another ad break to play while she changed.

She came out in the new dress.

"Or how about this one?" It was a mustard one-shoulder midi from Alice McCall. Celeste playfully strutted around the room, like a little girl playing dress-ups. She went into the bathroom; then back out again.

"And what do we have here?" She took the label between her forefinger and thumb and read out the designer's name. "By the one and only Toni Maticevski we have a..." she studied it, trying to work out the colour, "mauve ruffle dress." She looked up at the mirror. "What do you reckon, fam? Is this the dress for dinner tonight, or the races on Tuesday?" Hundreds of smiley face emojis and love hearts floated up on the right side of the screen. "C'mon! What did I say? Don't vote yet, I've got one more to try on. A wild card!"

Celeste cut to another ad before she came back wearing the final dress: a Manning Cartell one-sleeved, mirror foiled jersey dress.

"Introducing Celeste Simone, the human disco ball!" she announced. "I low-key adore this dress, guys! But, this is where I need your help. What dress should I wear for dinner tonight? Hit the smiley face emoji for the Camilla and Marc mini dress. The love heart for the Alice McCall midi; lips emoji for Toni Maticevski and, you guessed it, the mirror ball for the Manning Cartell."

Emojis floated up the right-hand side of the feed, from bottom to top. "Looks like the love hearts have it, and I will be wearing Alice McCall for dinner. Great choice, everyone. Same deal for the cup, minus the Alice McCall of course—can't wear the same dress twice, obvs!" Emojis filled up the screen again. This time it was much tighter, but there was a clear winner yet again. "You guys are wild!" she said. "Looks like I'm going as a disco ball. Awesome choice, though—retweet! Mwah! Seeya later lovelies. I need some Celeste time before Jerome gets here." She kicked up a heel, made the peace sign and logged out.

"I ended up buying the Alice McCall dress, too," Paula says.

Lanie cocks her eyebrow.

Paula gets up off her chair, walks inside and back out again, holding the mustard dress. "It arrived yesterday. Do you want to see it?" She holds it up.

Lanie fidgets with her pen, swinging it back and forth like a pendulum between her middle and forefinger. She looks up at the dress in Paula's hand. *She's already worn it.* Lanie notices a little stain on the front. "That's okay. I've seen it," she says, thinking back to the crumpled dress at the foot of the bath.

Paula's eyes widen. "Oh, right. Sorry. Where was I then..."

When Celeste's live stream came back on a few hours later, Jerome was there to pick her up for dinner. She was already dressed and ready to go, which would have been a huge relief to Jerome, as he normally had to wait for her.

Jerome was a very uncomplicated man. He just wanted to love and be loved. When he was in love he was happy. Simple. And he loved his family. In fact, he always wanted one of his own, a son especially —an heir to the Umwelt throne. He'd make an excellent father, too, with so much love to give. Him and Celeste had been trying for a while, but it just never happened for them.

"You look stunning, as always," he gushed, as he took a Corona out of the fridge. Celeste's long golden hair was tied up in a low chignon. Her makeup was perfect. It accentuated her features, rather than failing at recreating them like so many other influencers—like Abbie. Celeste was still young—her youth did most of the work, anyway. She finished off the look with a smattering of lip gloss, which caught the light just right.

"I bought wine coming through the airport. It's in the duty free bag next to the mini bar."

Jerome spotted it, walked over and searched for a wine glass. He couldn't find one, so went with a water glass instead. He popped open the bottle with a corkscrew he found in the mini-bar, poured the wine, and shuffled over to Celeste, who was putting on the finishing touches to her outfit. She was tossing up between heels or boots when Jerome handed her the glass of wine.

"Go with the boots," he said thoughtfully, so Celeste did. She put the heels back in the wardrobe and rested the boots by the door to put on when they left.

Jerome always helped her choose what to wear. It was adorable. He was so in tune with her, plus he had great taste.

Celeste joined Jerome on the small sofa, placing her glass of wine down on the table just in front of her laptop, before taking a selfie of the two of them. "Thanks for sending a driver this morning," she said, as she posted the photo.

Jerome nodded agreeably. The two of them sat there by the big window, watching the sun slowly set off the adjacent building.

"Abbie said she saw you at the airport?" Jerome inquired.

"Did she?" Celeste raised her eyebrows. "I must've missed her. Pity! She should've come and said hi."

Jerome picked up her wine and brought it up to his nose. "She said she saw you standing alone, but couldn't get past all her fans to see if you were okay."

"She said that, did she? Well, you tell her that I was trying to keep a low profile, because, unlike her, I don't need my fans' validation 24/7."

Jerome winced. He sipped his beer with one hand and swirled Celeste's red wine around with the other, while explaining how 'airing' works—he's very knowledgeable about wine. He passed it back to her. Celeste took a sip and shut her eyes to enjoy the taste.

When she opened them again, Jerome had a surprise for her. He was holding a jewellery box. It was teal, so Tiffany. He passed it to Celeste and she grabbed it, eager to find out what was inside. She opened it and was dazzled by an adorable pair of white-gold earrings—so romantic.

"I love them, Jerome."

"Thought you would. Abbie helped me pick them out," he replied. "Go on, put them on, let me see."

Celeste tried them on for him and they looked stunning. "They really do look good on you," Jerome said.

Celeste stood up and did a little twirl, cupping her ears to show them off, putting on a private show for Jerome.

Paula stops, stands up and walks back into the kitchen. She pulls a couple of tissues out of the tissue box and dabs her eyes. "It's the ramen. It's hot."

"It's fine, don't worry about it." Lanie scratches her forearm. "Did they talk about anything else on the couch?"

Paula places the tissues in the bin. "Yeah, I think Celeste was a little upset. She didn't want Abbie there—Jerome and her hadn't seen each other in ages," she says, returning to the table and continuing.

Jerome stood up and walked over to the mini-bar to get another beer, topped up Celeste's wine and sat back down on the couch. In the meantime, Celeste had made her way over to the mirror in the room to fix her hair one last time.

"What were you doing this afternoon—I tried calling; I was worried about you?"

"You know what I was doing. I was trying on dresses."

"No, I meant after that. You were offline for hours."

"I was just hanging around here, waiting for you. Why?"

"No reason—I couldn't get a hold of Sam, either? Was he here with you?" His voice followed Celeste into the bathroom, where she went to put the finishing touches on her make-up.

"Sam left here just before I had that nap," she said. "I've got no idea what he was doing this afternoon. Why don't you ask him—he's your friend?"

As Celeste walked back into the room, she caught Jerome anxiously checking his watch.

"Alright, alright, just making conversation." He finished his beer. "It's time to go, anyway."

Celeste did likewise with her wine, slapping her empty glass down on the table, next to her laptop. They scampered over to the door, Celeste pulled on her boots and spilled out into the hallway, while Jerome grabbed the key card from the wall, put it in his breast pocket, and joined her in the corridor.

They made their way down the hallway and took the elevator downstairs to the lobby.

"The restaurant's just around the corner, so we can walk," Jerome said.

Celeste was glad she went with the boots.

They walked to a Thai restaurant a few blocks away. When they got there, they walked straight up to the maître d'—a Thai woman wearing too much make-up and leaving too little to the imagination. It's Melbourne, so normally there are no reservations—unless, of course, you're Jerome Pitt.

"Follow me," The maître d' said, before leading them through the restaurant. It was busy. The percussion of porcelain plates was only drowned out by the clatter of conversation. They finally got to their table where the rest of their party were already seated.

Abbie stood up and pecked Celeste on both cheeks. "Love the dress," she said, looking down at the similar mustard coloured dress she was wearing. "Are those new earrings, too?" she asked, unaware Jerome had told Celeste that she'd helped him choose them.

Celeste clenched her jaw. She noticed the light reflected off something shiny on Abbie's wrist. Abbie was wearing Tiffany as well: a bracelet, which also looked brand new.

Samuel said hello from across the table, waving short sharp waves as Jerome introduced Celeste to a guy she'd never met before: Marco Vellis.

He was the promoter that brought them over for the Melbourne Cup. Marco was very handsome: he clearly worked-out, he was a good-dresser, and had a fresh haircut. You could tell he looked after himself. And he was charming, too—full of exciting stories. He was sitting next to Abbie, who was sitting next to Samuel, next to Celeste, next to Jerome. Abbie wasn't impressed about sitting in between Marco and Samuel, so she asked Jerome to swap, which meant Jerome was no longer sitting next to Celeste, which may have been Abbie's plan all along.

Marco had been to the restaurant before, so he ordered for everyone. The entrees took a long time to come out and the drinks added up, especially for Celeste, who was already tipsy from the two glasses of wine she had back at the hotel. Alcohol and an empty stomach don't mix, but especially for Celeste. She gets a bit fiery after a few, and that night was no exception. After a lot of mojitos and a little encouragement from Abbie, she hopped onto her animal-rights soapbox—her most recent cause.

"What do you even know about horses?" she shouted at Marco across the table, who was in the middle of talking Jerome into buying a racehorse with him. Jerome looked everywhere but at her. "It's a hellish sport," Celeste ranted. "I'm embarrassed my hometown gives kids a day off of school to watch horses get brutally kicked in their ribs by vertically challenged men! It's barbaric. You, men, are the real animals!"

Before she could say any more, Abbie butted in, wearing a big, devious smile. "I'll drink to that!" She winked at Jerome, as she hoisted her glass into the air. "To men being animals."

Lanie massages her jaw. "Sounds like you think Abbie set her up?"

"I wouldn't go that far," Paula replies, "but Abbie knew, like the rest of us, that Celeste gets triggered easily when she drinks. A little nudge was all it would've taken to set her off."

Lanie makes a note in her notepad and underlines it, before looking up at Paula and nodding.

The waitress finally brought out their dinner. The food was colourful, like Celeste's speech. Abbie fawned over Celeste. She told her she was her inspiration. It was all very sweet, like the desserts that followed. They finished eating, Marco settled the bill, tipping generously, and they all left together.

Marco's car was waiting outside with the same driver that picked up Celeste from the airport. There weren't enough seats for everyone so Marco volunteered to drive. Jerome rode in the front with him. The other three got in the back. The trip was short; they really could've walked.

They pulled up at The Hunting Lodge.

Marco had organised a VIP area for them upstairs—he knew everybody. Like the restaurant, they walked straight through, past the line. They all got a stamp on their arms, and then made their way up to a roped off area on the fifth floor. The bar looked like something out of Alice in Wonderland. Plush animal busts hung from the walls. Fake plastic ferns draped from the ceiling, winding around brass chandeliers. Palm trees sprouted haphazardly from the scuffed wooden floors. Blue velvet lounges lined the walls, while pink lighting dripped from the cornicing. It was a lot.

Celeste and Abbie went to the bathroom together—as girls do—where they must've really connected, because when they came back out, they were best friends.

Celeste's mood had done a full backflip. "Sorry about before!" she shouted to Marco over the music.

"Huh?" He cupped his ear with his hand.

"Sorry for the thing earlier!"

Marco still couldn't hear her, but he could make out her meaning. "Forget about it!" He passed her a bright green shot.

Celeste threw it back with a jerk. She felt its effects immediately. She dug her fingernails into the bar top to stop herself from falling, inching around it until she found the water jug.

Samuel came over as she was attempting to pour

herself a glass. He helped her with the water then half-carried her back to their private area outside.

She was shivering, so she wrapped Jerome's jacket around her shoulders.

"You alright, Cel?"

Celeste nodded her head. "Yep, I'll be right." The minutes passed slowly as they sat there silently, before Celeste jumped up, breaking the spell. "Where's Jerome!?" It'd been hours since she'd seen him. She took a long sip of water and scrambled to collect her thoughts. "Have you seen him?" she asked, more calmly this time.

Samuel was dabbing a stain on his white shirt. "Last I saw him, he was downstairs with Abbie."

Celeste sat up straight. "Of course he was!"

"Cel, stay here. I'm just going to go get something for this stain."

Celeste looked at Samuel for a long moment as he walked towards the bar, then shot up and launched herself into the crowd.

After almost twenty frantic minutes of looking, Celeste found Jerome in a dark corner on the third floor, standing under an artificial palm tree next to Abbie.

Celeste pushed her way through the crowd, launching herself at them. "How could you do this to me!?" she shrieked. It had been a long day. She wasn't herself. She was exhausted.

"Do what?" Jerome's voice cracked.

"And you!" she screamed, turning to Abbie. "I knew I couldn't trust you. You bitch!"

The uncensored rawness shook Abbie. She raised her arms to ward off the riptide of rage rolling in waves towards her. She was the proverbial deer in headlights. And by headlights: Umwelts. Everyone could see it. Not just at The Hunting Lodge, which had gathered a crowd of onlookers, but on both Abbie's and Celeste's live streams. It was mortifying. She froze-up. Just stood there and copped it, tears streaming down her face, until Jerome stepped in.

He pulled Celeste to the side by her arm. Her eyes were red. He tried reassuring her nothing was happening, but she couldn't hear him over her anguish. She was inconsolable. After blasting Jerome, she turned around and stormed out.

"Wait!" Samuel called after her, who had finally found them. "Let me walk you back to the hotel."

Celeste was mad. So mad she even said some nasty words to Samuel.

He went to chase her but Jerome blocked him. "Let her go. It's all a big show for her followers, anyway."

Lanie leans back in her seat. The chair legs screech against the concrete floor as she flirts with the space in between landing and falling. "Was there something going on between Jerome and Abbie?"

"Of course not!" Paula screws up her nose. "That's ridiculous—It just doesn't make sense. Why would Jerome ruin what he had with Celeste for Abbie? It was Celeste's insecurities. That's all. She gets jealous. It's what made her so human; so relatable," Paula says, trying to convince herself. "Why?" Paula continues. "Do you think it's Abbie's fault that Celeste overdosed?"

Lanie instinctively rubs her tongue against her front teeth, ignoring the question. "And what did Abbie do after the confrontation. Did she stay with the guys?"

"Abbie? She went home, or, you know, back to the Hilton where she was staying, then stopped live-streaming."

"The Hilton?" Lanie inquires, flicking back to Pimm's notes. "The same Hilton where Jerome was staying?"

"No. The smaller one on Flinders Lane, which, now that you mention it, is weird, as she normally stays at The Grand Theatre, like Celeste."

"Okay, but how do you know that?" Lanie asks. "If you were streaming Celeste, how do you know Abbie went back to her hotel?"

Paula scratches her collarbone. "After Celeste left the club, I opened up another window with Abbie's live stream to see how she reacted—lots of people did—and she reacted by going back to her hotel, like I said."

Lanie runs her hand through her hair.

Paula draws a deep breath; then continues.

Celeste was devastated. She ran down the stairs and out the club to her hotel. She was stumbling down Bourke street when a busker started serenading her with the Nancy Sinatra song: These Boots Were Made for Walking. She stopped, stepped over to him and caught her breath, wiping her eyes with the sleeves of Jerome's jacket. The busker was dirty; dishevelled. His hair was oily and disgusting. He was wearing ripped—and not the fashionable kind—black jeans, ratty boots and a dark hoodie with a graphic on the front—

"Was it a Nirvana hoodie?" Lanie interjects, remembering the stranger loitering outside The Grand Theatre Hotel the morning of Celeste's death.
"What do you mean? Like, Buddhism?"
Lanie coughs out a sharp laugh. "No, Nirvana are—were—a band. One of their albums, its CD cover has an image of a naked baby swimming towards money. Is that what was on the busker's jumper? Here, let me show you." Lanie reaches for her phone on the table, opens up a browser and searches for the cover art. It comes up instantaneously, and she shows it to Paula.
"Hmm, I'm really not sure," Paula says. "Maybe—it could've been," she adds.
Lanie winces, kissing her teeth. "Okay, no problem," she mutters. "Sorry, keep going." Lanie places her phone back down on the table between them, double checking it's still recording.

The small performance gave Celeste a chance to compose herself. She reached into her jacket pockets, searching for money to give to him. She couldn't find any, but had another idea. It was a cold night and her hotel was only up the road. So, she gave him Jerome's jacket—his favourite jacket.

The busker couldn't believe it. He tucked his hair behind his ears again and took it eagerly.

Celeste winked, waved goodbye, crossed her arms, and ran to the hotel.

"Hang on! She gave him Jerome's jacket!?" Lanie flicks back a few pages of her notes.

"Yeah. Hell hath no fury and all that."

"No, not that," Lanie says, finding her page. "The door key. You said you saw Jerome put Celeste's door key into his jacket pocket." Lanie points at where the breast pocket would be if she was wearing it.

Paula's eyes widen.

"Shit!" Lanie says, leaping to her feet and dialling the captain's number.

He answers. "Lanie?"

"Jon! I've got something big. I need you to find a busker, male..." Lanie holds her hand over the receiver and turns back to Paula. "What did he look like, again?"

"I don't know. Like if you were going to cast a busker in a movie, that's what he looked like."

Lanie grimaces. "C'mon think, Paula!"

"Okay. Um, he was white, and he had medium length, brown hair, and he was wearing the black hoodie," she says. "Does that help?"

Lanie nods. "The concierge said he saw someone leaving the hotel in a hurry wearing a hoodie, and there was that stranger out the front the next day! This might be our guy," Lanie says to Jon on the phone, before turning back to Paula. "Do you remember what time it was, and tell me again where exactly?"

"It was the corner of Bourke and Russel at around 10 o'clock."

"You get all that Jon?" Lanie asks. "Check the CCTV on the corner of Russel and Bourke street near The Hunting Lodge, around 10 p.m."

"Copy that," Jon's muffled voice on the other end of the line says. "Good work, Lanie."

"Okay, tell me when you find out. Bye." Lanie turns back to Paula. "Alright, let's wrap this up."

Celeste reached The Grand Theatre within minutes, ducking and weaving past the chaotic nightlife. She entered through the big glass doors, and straight past the night-shift concierge, who'd just ducked into the room behind the desk. She kept her head down as she crossed the foyer; reached the elevators and caught them up to her floor, where she zig-zagged down the hallway to her room. She finally got to her door, reached into her bag, and realised she didn't have the key card.

Luckily the same room service lady from earlier was still working, and she passed by at that serendipitous moment, and remembered her.

She unlocked the door.

Celeste thanked her, relieved that she didn't have to go back downstairs and talk to the guy at the desk.

She walked inside and kicked off her boots, before making her way over to the small table near the bath and pouring herself a glass of wine. She took a long sip, then walked back to the thermostat near the door and turned the heater up to maximum—she would've been cold from giving the jacket to the busker.

After that, she turned to the mirror to say goodnight to her fans. "Well, it's been another big day in the life of Celeste Simone. Thank you all for streaming it. I'm just so grateful I can count on you to always be here for me. It's been real! Love you all!" Then she switched off her live stream for the very last time.

TWELVE

LANIE PRESSES THE stop button on the app on her phone, then starts gathering her things. "That'll do, thank you Paula."

Paula stands up and walks her to the door. "Nice to meet you," she says. "I hope that was helpful—sounds like the busker had something to do with it."

"Yeah, we'll find out soon enough," Lanie replies, walking out the house. Paula stands at the door as Lanie makes her way over to her parked car. In the driveway she crosses paths with a short man, sporting a tangerine beard. He's wearing a patterned traditional shirt and a pair of mocha-coloured Birkenstocks.

"Who are you?" he barks.

"My name's Detective Lanie Daniels."

His eyes widen.

"I'm here—"

"Detective!?" he interjects before Lanie can finish. "What are you doing at my house?" His knee jerk hostility gives away a hard-earned distrust of authority.

His house? This must be Paula's husband. "It's okay, Mr Abbas, I've just been chatting to your wife about the Celeste Simone case.

"Oh, that slut?" His body language relaxes, contrasting against the harshness of his language. "Serves her right, what happened! I've been telling Paula to stop wasting her time with that rubbish for years. It fills her brain with all sorts of delusions." His head bobbles from side to side.

Paula appears in the doorway. "Just leave it," she calls out.

Lanie uses the distraction to make her escape. "Nice to meet you, sir," she says. "And thanks again, Paula. You've got my number, call me if you need anything." There was something in her tone that gave the impression the offer transcended the case.

She hops into her car and chucks her things on the passenger seat. Lanie's not quite ready to pat herself on the back for cracking the case with the busker—her default pessimism has drowned out the initial dopamine hit. In truth, she doesn't know what to think.

She turns off the 'do not disturb' setting on her phone, which she'd put on before interviewing Paula. Her phone makes a string of notification sounds. There's an email from Tod Cheeseman from forensics. He's got the toxicity report back. Lanie swipes up and opens the email.

Det. Daniels,

Sorry for the radio silence, but I only just got the preliminary results of the tox report ten minutes ago. I've attached the doc but basically, I was right the first time. We found cocaine, Xanax and Mirtazapine—an antidepressant prescription medicine—in her system, which led to a cardiac arrest. While coke and Xanax are not an entirely safe mix, it's very likely it was the addition of the Mirtazapine that led to the heart attack. Finding it came as a surprise as there wasn't any evidence she was taking them among her belongings or in her medical records. Unfortunately, that's not the only thing we found. We also uncovered that Celeste was in her first trimester of pregnancy.

Also, I couldn't lift any prints off the sugar sachet, and we found no DNA on the wine glass. Sorry. Call me if you want to discuss anything further.

Regards,
Tod Cheeseman

"What the actual fuck," Lanie says. "This just keeps getting worse." She coaxes Frankie to life; puts him into drive and exits the Edward-scissor-hand-esque horseshoe driveway, one hand overlapping the other on the steering wheel. "I think it's time to pay this Marco Vellis guy a visit."

She calls Mary at the station.

"Yes, Mary. It's Lanie. I'm gonna need you to find me an address."

THIRTEEN

IT'S LATE MORNING on Thursday. The sky is dark. Rain is bucketing down. Lanie finds a park on a rooftop behind the Prahran markets. She sits for five and then ten minutes, waiting for the rain to ease up. It doesn't. She zips up her jacket, jumps out, hoists her prized satchel over her head and dashes the three hundred metres up Chapel street to Marco's office. She finds the place between a reggae bar, belting out Peter Tosh, and a thrift store with bags of used clothes and cigarette smelling plush toys resting by the door. She pats the water off her jacket and walks in. A bell rings as the door slaps it forward. The girl at the front desk looks up reactively and sizes her up without hesitation.

"Marco!" she calls out in a thick western suburbs accent, not taking her eyes off Lanie, "the pigs are here again."

Lanie can hear some rustling around in the back room before a barrel-chested man comes pacing through the door, preceded by the distinct smell of bourbon and brylcreem.

"What do you want?" Marco asks flatly. "I told you guys last time, I never said those Grand Final seats were at the stadium. They should've read the small print—it has nothing to do with me," he says with a wry smile that gives away that it had everything to do with him.

"I'm not here about that," Lanie says sharply. "I believe you were with Celeste Simone the night of her death?"

His smile straightens. "Yeah, so what?"

Lanie looks around at the office. The way the empty desks are lined up it looks like it used to be a travel agency. Damaged boxes of promotional keyrings, lanyards and rubber wristbands are stuffed in every nook. Promotional posters take up every inch of the wall and the place is caked in dust, probably from when it was a travel agency.

"I have two witnesses telling me you and Celeste Simone got in an argument at dinner on the night of her murder. I was hoping you could add some clarity?" That seems to sober his bravado.

Marco gestures for her to sit down. She shuffles over to the closest desk, while he picks up a pile of flyers and stores them deeper inside the shop, before walking back to her and sitting down.

"Detective…" he waits for her to introduce herself.

"Daniels."

"Detective Daniel," he replies, intentionally leaving off the 's'. "I have a—how do I put this—a unique personality. Celeste is not the first person to have a go at me and she won't be the last. Jesus, my own mother can't stand me half the time." He curls his bicep and rotates his wrist.

"It's true!" the girl behind the front desk adds, looking up from her phone.

"What I'm trying to say is if I went around being offended by everyone I offended, well there wouldn't be much time left in the day for anything else. That bitch was a controlling nutcase, anyway—I don't know what Jerome even saw in her, but for you to think I'd kill her is a joke."

Every micro-expression told Lanie he was telling the truth. "I believe you," she says. "But I am interested to know why, when I called it a murder just now, that you didn't blink, when as far as Joe public know, it was an accident?"

Marco crosses his arms. "If you call it a murder then it's a murder. Who am I to correct an officer of the law," he says. "This has nothing to do with me. It's not my fault I got stuck in the middle of their weird love triangle." Marco shifts his weight in his seat. "Although, quick math, it's more of a love square, I suppose, because there's four of them—a ménage à quatre if you will." He laughs while interlocking his fingers. Lanie isn't laughing. "Look, I had dinner with them, took them out for a couple of drinks and never saw 'em again."

"Except at the Melbourne Cup, right?" Lanie's eyes narrow.

Marco leans forward. "Oh, yeah, except a few days later at The Cup. That cheap malaka, Jerome, was trying to get out of it, can you believe it?"

Lanie looks up from her notepad. "Can I believe that a husband didn't want to work days after his wife passed away? Yes, I can."

Marco chortles. "Ha! You make a very good point, Detective Daniel," he says, not pronouncing the 's' again."

Lanie ignores him. "And the cocaine?" Lanie cocks her head. "I suppose you have no idea where Celeste got it from?"

Marco guffaws. "Coke?" he says on cue. "If I knew she was carrying the devil's dandruff, I would've asked her for some!" he says, laughing. "Just kidding. I don't touch the stuff. It's cut to hell with shit knows what, probably washing powder for all I know—prescription meds if you're lucky. And it's stupidly expensive—I could buy a fucking PlayStation 5 for the same price of a bag." He meets Lanie's eyes as he makes his point. "Or, I mean, so I've been told," he quickly corrects himself, straightening his pink polo shirt, pulling down the sleeve over his bicep. "But, I guess it explains why she had those insane mood swings." He picks up his phone to write a message.

Lanie coughs to get his attention. "Did you want to elaborate, Mr Vellis?"

"Sorry, that was important." He blinks rapidly. "She went all psycho-bitch at Jerome for talking with Abbie without her permission. And if you're saying she was on the bags, and she got it here in Melbourne, well, there's no doubt whatever it was cut with triggered her paranoia. I've seen it a million times with chicks." Lanie inhales, as Marco continues to editorialise. "She was a bloody hypocrite if you ask me. She led that poor bastard,

Sam, on all night, just to make Jerome jealous, and then all he does—Jerome—is innocently chat to Abbie and she goes apeshit. Women, amirite, detective. You'd know what I'm talking about," he says, looking down at her boots. Lanie ignores the sophomoric implication and continues.

"And what did you, Jerome and Sam do after the big argument?"

"Mr Jerome Pitt and I went back to my apartment in South Bank with some tasty young girls—legal, of course—and partied."

"Ignore him, detective—he's a pig!" the girl at the front desk chimes in.

Lanie rubs her right eye. "And Sam too?"

"Nah, that pussy left us after the club—he wouldn't shut up about Celeste, so I, for one, was happy that he didn't come—he was killing my vibe."

"Really?" Lanie asks. "Yeah, he's not really my cup of tea—"

"No, I mean 'really' you guys parted ways after The Hunting Lodge?"

"Oh yeah, just ask my driver, Gary. He'll verify it for you—I can give you his number, if you want it? It was just me, Jerome and a few random babes. Actually, if you find those girls, tell them I want my shirt back!" Lanie stares at him. "What?" he says. "I really liked that shirt. Anyway, that was it. I swear. Would I lie to you, detective?" His phone vibrates on the desk between them. Gary is calling—Lanie can see his name on the screen. It's still ringing as he looks up at Lanie. "Sorry detective, unless you have a warrant, I think we're done here."

Lanie clenches her jaw. "Nope, we're done. Thank you for your time Mr Vellis." She gets up, turns towards the door and leaves. Marco answers the phone as she does. "Gary, meet me round back."

It's almost two o'clock and Lanie still hasn't eaten lunch. She finds a cafe nearby and steps inside out of the rain. The place is an old car garage, decked out with Goodwill couches and Americana bric-a-brac.

She orders a coffee and chilli egg wrap on the way past the counter and finds a table in a dark corner out the back. Minutes later the waitress tails her with her coffee and a bottle of tap water in an old, transparent teal Bombay Sapphire bottle. While she's waiting for the wrap, Lanie picks up her phone and dials Abbie's number; she hasn't replied to Tuesday night's text yet, which has been sat on 'unseen' the entire time. The phone rings and rings, before going through to Abbie's message bank. Lanie leaves her a voicemail.

"Hey, Abbie, Detective Daniels here again. I'm still waiting to hear back from you. Please give me a call when you get this. Or, if you'd prefer, text me back with a time for me to call you—that will work, too. Thanks."

Why doesn't anyone pick up their bloody phones anymore! She places the phone down on the table in front of her and flicks through a newspaper someone has left behind. She thumbs through the first few pages, which feature the Melbourne Cup results, followed by the usual wowser piece, feigning outrage over drunk people acting drunk. *Big surprise!* She smiles at the images: guys and girls are splayed out on the grass in pools of their own vomit; grass-stains all over their best going-out clothes. She takes a sip of her long black and turns the page. On page four, she finds what she's looking for. It's a feature piece on Celeste's death.

Beauty in the Eyes of the Beholders

From holidays to handbags, as the world's most famous influencer Celeste Simone would regularly receive things for free, but in the end, she paid the ultimate price.

The world's foremost streamer, Celeste Simone, was found dead in the bathtub of her hotel room on Monday morning, most likely the result of a drug overdose.

Sources close to her reveal Celeste was suffering silently from clinical depression. Ironically, the same ailment she was providing an escape from, for her multitude of fans.

"We live in a perpetual state of comparison. It's not healthy," said Abbie Benson-Wheeler, months earlier, when talking about her own mental health battle.

A longitudinal study conducted by Berkeley University, found that social media is the biggest contributing factor to depression in the 21st century.

And Celeste Simone was in the eye—pun not intended—of the storm.

With the bombardment of perfectly edited lives, it's impossible to avoid the affliction known as 'compare despair'—the gateway to depression.

When our sense of worth is derived from a comparison to others' hyper-curated highlight reels, our happiness becomes a variable outside of our control.

The cycle of comparison fed on Celeste's insecurities. This was her killer. And we must not let her death be in vain. It may be time we close our eyes to Umwelt...

The waitress comes over with Lanie's wrap and places it down in front of her. Lanie goes through her ritual: opens it, squirts in the Sriracha hot sauce then neatly tucks it back together—all the while not taking her eyes off the article.

We're fucked. A sense of dread becomes her. "Shit! Thomas!" Her phone rings on cue. It's Becca. "Fuck, fuck, fuck! How could I forget." She frantically grabs her bag and dashes out of the cafe, finally answering the phone on the way out. "I know I know. I'm on my way."

FOURTEEN

LANIE DRIVES TO Becca's office in Fitzroy to find out more about next week's custody hearing. The traffic is unusually light so she's only fifteen minutes late.

Becca's office is on Brunswick street, near the Crown and Anchor pub, which has sat there for over a hundred years, quietly watching the suburb gentrify into vogue, minus the commission flats.

Lanie parallel parks on the side of the road, hops out, walks over to the parking machine to find the street code, then inputs it into her parking app. She grabs her jacket from the backseat and walks over to a nondescript door. She buzzes up. The lock makes a heavy clunk sound, which Lanie interprets as her invite to come in. She pushes the door open and is greeted by the bottom of a staircase. It smells like wet dog and Plaster of Paris. She trudges up the stairs, blocking her nose from the back of her throat. The stairwell leads to a single door at the top. It's solid oak. Screwed into it is an engraved brass sign: O'Malley Legal. She knocks and lets herself in. Had she not been there before, she would be surprised. Beyond the door is an ultra-modern office of exposed brick, glass and right angles.

Natural light filters through the ceiling, reflecting off the transparent meeting room walls, brilliantly illuminating the open plan layout. It's a corporate law firm, but Becca's been handling Lanie's case as a personal favour. To Lanie's left is the front desk with three white Eames chairs, lined up against the wall.

Lanie approaches the receptionist, who's busy on a call. She motions with her free hand for Lanie to take a seat. She sits and pulls out her phone to message Becca, but before she even unlocks it, Becca comes bounding around the corner.

"Lanes! Finally! Come on, let's get outta here; grab a coffee."

Lanie gets up and follows Becca back down the stairs, holding her breath once again.

Out on the street the two friends hug.

"Good to see you," Becca says.

"Always," Lanie responds. Lanie's always been the cooler of the two—in her opinion.

"C'mon, this way." Becca heads in the direction of the pub.

"I thought you said coffee?" They've been mates since forever. Ducking out for a sneaky vino fits Becca's MO perfectly. When they were kids Becca would ride her push bike over with a bag of Starburst lollies she swiped from her dad's stash on the top shelf of the pantry, spoiling both their dinners. A day-drink is just the adult version of that, after all.

Becca stops and makes a quick U-turn like a catwalk model. "Espresso martini has coffee in it, right?"

Lanie sighs knowingly, then follows her.

The pub is an eclectic gem. One of those if-walls-could-talk places, which they did, graffitied in black Sharpie markers.

Becca heads straight to the bar with Lanie in tow. "An espresso martini," she orders. "And a..." she turns to Lanie.

"Do you have herbal tea?" Lanie asks unconfidently.

"Yeah," the bartender, a tattooed-from-head-to-toe native, nods as he puts down the empty pint glass he's polishing and reaches for the menu. He turns it around in his hands. "We've got: Ginger and Lemon, Green, English Breakfast and," he double checks the list, "Fruitilicious?"

Lanie's feeling adventurous. "Fruitalicious," she orders, her intonation rising at the end as if she's asking a question.

"Easy," he says, more to Becca than Lanie, holding his gaze just a moment too long. Long enough that Lanie doesn't need to be a detective to see her friend has caught his eye. "Grab a seat, I'll bring 'em over."

Becca taps her card to pay and the two of them shuffle over to a round high-table with bar stools. Becca's phone rings. "Just give me a second, then I'll turn it off," she says as she takes the call.

Lanie looks over at her friend. She's always been pretty, but she wears her thirties especially well. Even better than the power suit she's got on. She has short, pixie, chestnut hair, dark eyes, and freckles. She's taller than Lanie—but who isn't? They don't have anything in common except their friendship. In truth, if they met as adults, they probably wouldn't be friends. Their mum's met at mother's group, and now these two polar opposites have a friendship that transcends validation or even rationalisation. It just is, and always will be. It's the most constant thing in Lanie's life, and she's grateful for it, even if she is a bit lax on showing gratitude.

Becca wanders back over to the table as she finishes her call. "It's so you can make a dildo out of your own dick and go fuck yourself," she says as she hangs up. Lanie stares at her, waiting for an explanation. "What!? I sent Mike—you remember Mike—one of those Clone A Willy kits, so he can…" she doesn't need to finish. "You get it."

Lanie doesn't say a word. She doesn't need to.

"Talking about dicks, what's Jerome Pitt like in real life?" Becca asks, wanting the tea.

Lanie places her jacket on the chair and sits down. "He's interesting."

"That's it? Interesting? The world's most interesting man is interesting?" Becca responds incredulously. "Hey, if you don't want to tell me, that's fine—"

"What do you want me to say?" Lanie bites. He's a stereotypical rich, white dude with a knight in shining tin foil complex, thinking all the helpless, defenceless women around him need saving."

"Savage," Becca responds, playfully pursing her lips.

The bartender walks over with a tray. He lays down a coaster in front of Becca, followed by her espresso martini and a small wooden bowl of popcorn with some kind of spicy paprika seasoning.

"But he did actually help you get your case reheard," Becca adds, as she takes the orange-peel garnish and rubs it around the lip of her martini glass.

"Yeah I suppose he did," Lanie concedes.

The bartender returns and sets a small white porcelain pot of steaming Fruitalicious tea in front of her. "Thank you." Lanie catches him looking at Becca again. "Just shoot your shot, dude!" she encourages.

"Huh? What?" he replies. His tattoos belie his inhibition. Lanie's put him on the spot. "I like your hair," he blurts out. His whole body slumps. "That was shit," he berates himself. "Let me go again."

Lanie and Becca let him suffer in silence, holding onto their smiles.

"We should grab a drink some time?"

"Hmmm, better," Becca responds. "Let me see how good this espresso martini is first." She gives him a playful wink.

He nods, holds the empty drink tray against his chest and heads back to the bar. "Let me know."

"Poor bastard," Lanie says, pouring herself a cup of tea and blowing away the curls of steam to cool it down. "He has no idea the trouble he's in."

Becca grins a cheeky grin. "Anyway, c'mon spill the tea about Jerome."

"I guess him and his associate Sam have both been helpful-ish—"

"Who's Sam? Is he hot?"

"Ha! Gross. The guy's so beta, you'd hate him. Or

maybe you'd love him—I can't keep up. But, there's just something about him and Jerome I can't put my finger on. They're hiding something. I don't know if I trust them."

Becca pinches the muscles between her neck and shoulder. "Yeah, but you don't trust anybody."

"Haha, very true."

"Have you spoken to your mum yet?" Becca changes topics.

"I have actually," Lanie gloats. "I saw her yesterday. She's still bat shit crazy!" She blows on her tea again.

"So, do you know when the treatment starts?"

"What treatment?" Lanie's heart skips a beat.

"For the cancer?"

Lanie's back stiffens. The mere mention of the word cancer transports her back to when she was twelve:

She's in her room on her bed, reading the newly released Harry Potter and the Order of the Phoenix. She'd lined up at Borders, dressed up as Hermione, with her dad until midnight the night before. There's a knock at the door and her mum and dad walk in. The look on their faces—it's seared into her memory. They sit down on her bed and tell her that her dad has cancer. Two weeks later he died, along with a part of Lanie.

Lanie reminds herself to breathe. "Oh, the cancer, um, the treatment is," she stammers. "I think it's um…"

Becca's eyes widen in terror. "Shit! she didn't tell you, did she?"

Lanie stares up at Becca with equal parts horror and

guilt. She's trembling.

"Lanes, I am so sorry. I thought... that's why she wanted to see you so bad. Shit." Becca moves around the table and puts her arm around Lanie to comfort her. "It's okay, she'll be okay. They've caught it early. It's going to be fine. She's a fighter, your mum. She raised you, didn't she!? Besides, only the good die young, so aunt Susanne is fine."

Lanie snorts and chokes up a laugh. Her heart rate slowly returns to normal. "Why didn't she tell me?" Lanie asks indignantly. She was angry at her mum for a fleeting moment, before that anger morphed into guilt and then into sadness at herself for feeling angry in the first place.

Becca drags her stool over and rests her hand on Lanie's leg. "I guess she didn't know how. Having to tell your kid that news once is enough for several lifetimes. Twice would be, I don't know... unimaginable."

Lanie takes a sip of her now-lukewarm tea. *Yuck.* She stops herself from spitting it out. She needs a hard drink, but she can't, for Thomas. *Oh God, how am I going to tell Thomas about this.*

Becca gets up. "Where's the toilet?' she asks by way of letting Lanie know where she's going. It's to the left of the bar, but she already knows that.

Lanie sits there in shock. She puts her hands in her pockets and absently feels around at its contents: Chapstick, keys, and a serviette—from the waiter from earlier. She'd forgotten about him. She pulls it out and unfolds it. His name's Piero. *He looks like a Piero*, she nods in agreement with herself. *Do I look like a Lanie? What does a Lanie even look like —probably not half Asian.* She smiles a tight-lipped smile. She buries the napkin back in her pocket and searches for her phone. It's missing. "Becs!" she says with a tinge of panic to Becca who's half way back from the bathroom. "Give me your phone, I've lost mine and I need to call it."

Becca gets back to the table, fishes her phone out of her bag, opens it with her fingerprint and hands it to Lanie.

Lanie calls herself. "It's ringing," she says as they listen out for it. "It's not here." Lanie inhales. "I'm sure I had it when we walked in." She opens up the 'find your phone' app on Becca's phone and puts in her details. The app thinks about it and then pin-points her phone's location. "It says it's metres away."

"Is this yours?" the bartender calls out from behind the bar.

"Yes! Thank God." Lanie rushes over and grabs it.

"Okay, now that that's settled," Becca says as she gulps down the last bit of her espresso martini, "I gotta get back to work. You going to be okay? Call me if you need anything." Before Lanie has a chance to respond, Becca continues. "And go easy on Aunty Susanne. She wanted to tell you. She really did." Becca double checks she's got everything, hugs Lanie and then turns to walk out, before Lanie remembers something.

"Oh! Becs! What did you need to tell me about

Thomas's case?"

"Shit. Of course. So, we can't actually go back to court until we try to resolve it in mediation."

"Which means what?"

"Which means we have to get in a room with Brett and his lawyer again."

"Great!" Lanie rolls her eyes. "When will that be?"

"Well there's no point dragging it out, so I can try and organise it for this time next week if that works for you?"

"Sure," Lanie says. "Just one more thing, if this evidence is as good as Jerome says it is, I want Thomas all to myself—let Brett see how it feels to go without seeing him for weeks at a time."

"Yep, I get it, Lanes."

"Right. Oh, and, Becs. When are you going to tell Brett, exactly?"

"I was going to call his lawyer now."

"Can it wait until after the weekend? I'm picking up Thomas from his house tomorrow, and I don't want it to ruin the weekend, especially now with everything that's going on with mum. I don't know if I have the energy to deal with everything at once."

"Sure thing. I'll wait until Monday to call his lawyer." Becca walks out the door, leaving Lanie by herself with her Fruitilicious tea.

FIFTEEN

LANIE IS KNOCKING around the department on Friday afternoon, doing some desk research, when she bumps into Mary. It's another overcast day and the rain is threatening, again. She's in the bullpen. There're ten cubicles with two desks facing each other. A small staff kitchen with free tea, coffee and an endless supply of Arnott's Family Favourites is off to one side, and the walls are plastered with cork boards and post-it notes.

Mary's at her desk leaning back on her chair, balancing on the two back legs, ostensibly working. She looks every bit the detective as she stares vacantly into space, rubbing a non-existent beard. Mary's kind of a weirdo. Lanie likes her.

"What are you thinking so hard about?" Lanie asks.

Mary looks over at Lanie, not sure when she entered the room. "I was thinking about postage letters with my name on them sitting in strangers' houses."

"What do you mean?"

"Well, I've moved houses a few times and each time I move, there's probably a mailing list I forgot to change, so my old place would still be receiving my mail."

Lanie stares at her with a yes-and look.

"So, now I'm picturing a stranger grabbing a stack of letters from their mailbox, carrying them inside, then finding an odd letter wedged in between their power bill and Ikea catalogue with a stranger's name on it, which is mine." She brings the front legs of her chair down with a thud. "My name—my identity—probably just sits there watching these strangers go about their lives, until they chuck it out. What if they're up to some weird kink stuff, and my name's in the room with them. It's wild, right?"

Lanie makes a sideways glance each way, double checking she's not on a reality TV show. "I once got a letter addressed to someone else," she says casually. "It sat on my kitchen table for over a month before I opened it."

"You opened someone else's mail?" Mary asks, aghast. "That's illegal, you know?"

"Well, yeah, I wanted to make sure it was nothing important."

Mary arches her eyebrows. "And?"

"And it was a $25 Myer gift card."

Mary leans forward. "What did you do with it?"

Lanie rubs her forearm. "I let it sit there for another month before putting it in my purse, where it sat for yet another month before I finally used it to buy..." Lanie stops and thinks back. "You know those nice wine glasses I got you for your birthday last year?"

"You got my birthday present with a voucher that was for someone else?" Mary feigns offence.

"Pretty good, right?" Lanie smirks, turning on her

computer.

"What are you working on?" Lanie changes the subject.

"Have you seen what they can do with deepfake technology now?" Mary asks.

Lanie shrugs. "I think I heard them talking about it on the news the other day, but I wasn't really paying attention. What's the deal?"

"Well apparently crims can now hack into CCTV and deepfake cover their face with someone else's. Only last week not-Donald-Trump stole a pair of pricey Balenciaga sneakers from a boutique in the city. I saw the video—it was pretty funny—it was just missing the Benny Hill music."

"Hmmm," Lanie murmurs, not finding the funny side. "That's going to complicate things."

"Relax, it's no worse than wearing a baklava, isn't it?"

Lanie looks at her. "No worse than a layered honey cake from Greece?" she teases.

"Haha—you know I can't say that word! Anyway, it's only an issue when people stop using their own eyes."

Lanie snickers. "It's not that far off, you know. People watch everything through their screens now. Jon made me go to that fundraising concert the other week, and the whole crowd was watching the show through their phones because they were filming it to share on their social media. They were literally there in real life, but were watching it through a screen."

"What a time to be alive," Mary adds, as they settle into their work. "Sorry, one more thing: you coming to Jon's girl's birthday party tomorrow?"

"Yeah, I'll be there."

"Steve's coming too you know?" Mary smirks.

Lanie's mouth opens to reply when the captain's door opens. He's been in a meeting. He steps out of his office and makes eye contact with Lanie. A man in a dark blue suit follows him out the door. It's Jerome Pitt. *What the fuck is he doing here.*

"Thanks for coming by, we're grateful," Lanie hears the captain say.

Jerome looks over and spots Lanie. "Detective," he says casually, "good to see you again."

Lanie stands up to meet him. "What are you doing here?" she asks bluntly. Too bluntly—paranoid he's undermining the case somehow.

Reading Lanie's chagrin, Jon jumps in. "Jerome is graciously upgrading the department's surveillance hardware for free—"

"It's really the least I can do—for Celeste," Jerome jumps in with a watery smile. "I saw the hardware you were using the other day at the hotel and thought you could use an upgrade, so I've just committed to supplying your team with all our latest tech."

Jon nods along like a brown-nosing bobblehead.

"Great." Lanie forces a smile.

"It's a total tax write-off for me, anyway, so no need to thank me," Jerome adds. "Anyway, I really must go. Jon it was good to see you again. And please let me know when you find out about the busker. It still breaks my heart that Celeste didn't come to me for help with her depression. She would have never been in such a precarious position if she'd gotten help sooner." He swallows the last word. "I just wish I knew it had gotten that bad, you know."

"Here, let me walk you out." Jon leads him to the door. "Goodbye, detective." Jerome winks as he leaves.

Lanie stares at the empty space the two men leave behind for a protracted moment, before getting back to work. When the captain returns, Lanie's looking for a file on her cluttered desktop.

"Lanie, with me," he says sharply. He looks as thrilled as usual, which is to say not at all. Lanie stands up and follows him to his office. Before she even sits down Jon asks, "what was that?"

"What was what?"

"You know what."

"Well, what if he did it, Jon? What if he's the killer?"

Jon rolls his neck. "Lanie, there are multiple people who saw him with Marco Vellis at the time of death. He was either at the bar still, or at Marco's apartment. As far as an alibi goes his is watertight. Besides, it's all above board. He's gotten it ticked off with the higher-ups. Anyway, I thought we had our guy. It's the busker, isn't it?"

"Maybe, but it's never that straight-forward." Lanie adjusts her t-shirt. "Anyway," she continues, wanting to cut the lecture short and get back to work. "I just want to thank you—"

"Huh?" Jon looks up, puzzled.

A smile creeps across Lanie's face. "I wouldn't learn nearly as much from someone who always agreed with me," she says with a healthy dose of facetiousness.

"Get out of here," he says. "I'll let you know when we find the busker."

Lanie returns to her desk. Mary's gone. She sits there in contemplative silence. Myriad half-thoughts marinate inside her head. The only thing she really knows to be true is that someone was in that hotel room with Celeste when she died. But who? Was it really the busker?

SIXTEEN

IT'S SATURDAY MORNING. Frost clings to the outside of the windows as Lanie pulls open her blinds. The Spring sun pours through her bedroom window, reflecting rainbows off the droplets of condensation. She slinks into a borrowed hotel dressing gown, tightening the rope around her waist as she steps into her living room, anticipating her first coffee of the day.

She has her morning routine down pat: she walks over to the couch, grabs the remote from the drawer and turns on the TV. The comforting drone of the breakfast show hosts fill the apartment with an agreeable hum. She shuffles over to the kitchen, fills up the kettle under the kitchen tap, returns it to its base and flicks it on—the bubbling sound warms up the apartment. She pivots right, opens the fridge and takes out a bag of English Muffins, which she picked up on her way home from work last night. She takes one, tears it apart and puts it in the toaster. She twirls the bag shut, and places it back in the fridge. While it's toasting, she grabs a mug down from the bench above the stove top, and heaps a teaspoon of Nescafe Blend 43 into it. The muffins bounce out of the toaster, she places them onto a waiting plate and spreads them with peanut butter, distributing it evenly across the cratered surface. The kettle whistles. She fills her mug with boiling water, grabs her muffin, and plants herself down at the kitchen bench. She brings up her phone in her right hand, flicking through the morning news, while the coffee and muffin take turns occupying her left hand. In a quarter of the time it took to make, she's done. She rinses her plate and mug and hops into the shower.

As she bathes, she can hear the news blaring from the TV. It's moved on from Celeste's case. From what she can hear, it's two talking heads arguing over climate change.

Talking head 1: Have you ever heard of a thing called climate change? The so-called warming of the earth?

Talking head 2: Ah, yes, of course I have heard of it, Jack. Yes, yes. That's why we're here, isn't it?

Talking head 1: Well, do you know what it is? Really?

Talking head 2: Well yes. It's the man-made increase of the earth's temperature.

Talking head 1: Ha that's what they want you to think. Do you realise that climate change is the most monstrously conceived and dangerous socialist plot we've ever had to face?

Talking head 2: That's simply not true. We thankfully deferred to experts during the pandemic, and millions of lives were saved. So, why are we still ignoring experts now?

Lanie shaves her legs, brushes her teeth, jumps out the shower, dries herself, gets dressed and is out the door and on the road in record time. It's her weekend with Thomas. She's organised to pick him up at 9 a.m. and refuses to be one minute late.

She pulls up out the front of Brett's, her ex-husband's townhouse, in Northcote. It's ground zero for Brighton spawn. All the privileged kids with old money moved out of their parent's mansions in Toorak and into Northcote. Classic gentrification. It drove the prices up and pushed the local families out, leaving the place a culture-less husk. Now it's full of entitled brats who listen to jazz music on vintage record players that they paid too much for at the local thrift store—the irony of which is not lost on Lanie, owning her own vintage record player.

She takes a deep breath, launches herself out of the car and slams the door shut behind her. She hates this bit. It always feels like she's borrowing her own son as if he was a library book, and she'd incur late fees and a nasty letter if she failed to return him on time. *It's bullshit, but hopefully not for much longer.* She walks over to the front door. Just as she's about to knock, it swings open and Thomas is there to meet her. He's been waiting.

"Hey little man!" she says cheerily. "You ready?"

"Yep." He bashfully wipes his nose with his sleeve and nods. Every fortnight it's the same—it takes him at least half an hour to warm up to her.

Lanie looks into the house. There's a hint of Brett's aftershave in the air. Just enough to trigger a flash flood of memories she thought she'd buried.

"Lanie," he says with a nod by way of hello, walking down the hallway throwing a blue and white tea towel over his left shoulder—one of those hospitality ones.

Brett isn't conventionally handsome, but he has a presence. He has brown hair with flourishes of silver, and a strong jawline, which push his eyes closer together.

When she sees him, she feels a pang of guilt about how she's about to blindside him for custody of Thomas, but she bottles it.

"Hello Brett. I'll have him back by 6 p.m. tomorrow." Lanie spots a young woman down the hallway. She's young—early twenties young. *Her body certainly doesn't look like it's been stretched six ways from Sunday by pregnancy*, Lanie thinks bitterly. She bites her tongue.

"Still driving that death trap?" Brett asks, eye-ing off Frankie, parked on the side of the road.

"What can I say? I hate change."

"Ha, that's the understatement of the year. Changing the bed sheets used to cause you anxiety!"

Lanie makes a pointing gesture with her thumb over her shoulder to Thomas to say let's go. "I can leave one of Thomas's alphabet books here if you like." She looks past Brett, down the hallway, as the young woman walks past again.

Brett ignores her and squats akimbo. "Be good for your mum." Thomas hugs him goodbye. "His inhaler is in the front pocket of his bag; there's some cash there, too, if he needs it."

Lanie grabs Thomas's hand. They walk over to the car. Thomas's plush monkey, Alan, drags on the driveway in his other hand. "We're going to Jessie's birthday party! What do you reckon about that?"

They hop in the car.

"Good."

"How's school?" Lanie asks as they drive down the highway.

"Good," he replies again—a master of one-word responses.

Lanie waves her hand in front of the air conditioner to make sure he's getting enough air. "What have you learned?" Thomas shrugs his shoulders. "Times tables?" She steals a glance over at him.

"No," he replies, staring out the window.

Lanie tries a different tact. "I have something for you." She motions to the back seat. Thomas twists his body to look. He spots the Sydney Airport shopping bag among the junk and reaches for it. He pulls it towards himself and excitedly plunges both hands inside. He pulls out a plush toy bird thing. His eyes brighten as he tilts his head, not sure if it's a bird or a dinosaur. Either way, he hugs it tightly.

"Thank you, mummy," he says in a way that needles her heart. He introduces it to Alan the monkey. "I'm going to call her Tracy."

Lanie's face tilts to one side. "Her?"

"Yeah, Alan needs a wife, if they're going to be a family," he says, knocking the wind out of Lanie's lungs. "Tracy meet Alan, Alan Tracy."

They pull into the Botanic Gardens. Other guests are just arriving too, carrying wrapped and ribboned presents. They get out of the car and follow the trail of colourful balloons. Verdant grass swishes underfoot as they wind their way through the gardens. The smell reminds Lanie of her dalliance with suburban life. They reach a clearing with an outdoor table, playground and BBQ, and lots of little swashbuckling pirates.

"Lanie!" Jon calls out, waving a pair of tongs, wearing an apron with a picture of a muscle-bound bodybuilder.

Thomas pulls at his mum's sleeve. "Mummy, where's my pirate costume?"

Lanie's eyes widen in horror. She completely forgot. She desperately looks around to see what's available for a make-shift outfit.

Jon calmly walks over. "Hey Thomas." He gets down on one knee. "Your mum asked me to bring your costume with me." He pulls out an eyepatch and bandana from behind his back. "Here you go matey," he says with a Captain Jack Sparrow slant. "Jessie is playing on the pirate ship over there. A little parrot told me she's looking for a salty sea dog to join her motley crew. Do you think you can help her out?"

Thomas's eyes light up. For a split second, Lanie

could glimpse the man he'll become.

He nods his head and runs off to the playground.

"Thanks for the save, Jon."

"Don't mention it. Now come help me cook the sausages."

Lanie grabs a diet coke from the Esky—where Mary seems lost in thought, trying to decide on what to drink—and joins Jon and the other guys from work around the BBQ. The captain pours his beer onto the complimentary hotplate and it hisses to life. The comforting sizzle of bulk-bought sausages and white onions warms the air.

"You look shithouse!" Steve says as she joins them. Saying the opposite of the obvious is Steve's go-to banter. Lanie has actually made an effort. She's swapped her weekday RM Williams for her weekend RM Williams, and her hair isn't in its default ponytail. Her chat with Susanne inspired her to have it down for once. And it's clean. Almost too clean. The sun bounces off its unusual shine, forcing Steve to use his left hand as a visor to block the glare.

If you saw Steve on the street you could tell he was a cop. There is just something about the way he carries himself that gives it away. It may have something to do with the cropped hair and goes-to-the-gym-regularly physique. Steve was razzing her up of course, because the police department has similar rules to the playground—or at least a similar inability to talk about emotions—and he quietly has a crush on her.

"Eat a dick, Steve," she replies as she tucks a loose

strand of hair behind her ear, and cracks open her can of Diet Coke.

"Shots fired!" Mary says as she and Sanjay walk over to join them.

Steve's actually a really good bloke and Lanie's not against his sophomoric flirting. But she'd never do anything with him. The truth is she's still struggling to overcome the sexual guilt drummed into her from her time at St Mary's catholic girls' school. *Bloody God-bothering, blue beaned bitches.* After everything that happened with Brett, she doesn't have the energy for anything serious. Thomas is the only man in her life now. She doesn't intend for it to be like that forever, but for the time being she's content. Plus, she's done the maths. If it takes half the time you were with someone to get over them, that would mean she still has another two years, one month and fifteen days to go until she seriously dates again. *But who's counting?*

"What were you thinking so hard about over at the Esky, Mary?" Lanie deflects the attention away from herself.

"Oh, you saw that?"

"Everyone saw that," Steve says.

"Hmmm, well I have a question for you all—"

"Oh, here we go!" Steve rubs his hands together. They all love when Mary has a question.

"Right," she says.

"Wait, wait," Steve interrupts. "Cap, get over here, Mary has a question."

Jon quickly turns over the last couple of sausages

and joins them.

"So, the bottle of wine you bring to a party as a gift, are you meant to drink it first or last? Because if it's a gift it feels rude to drink it first, doesn't it? It's like here's your gift, now give it back to me so I can drink it." She's getting animated with her hands. "But then it's also weird to drink it last, isn't it? Because then you're like: here's the wine I brought for the party, but I'm going to drink your wine first." She brings her hands up to her temples and makes a 'mind-blown' gesture. "Like, I am so conflicted, man."

"You drink it first!" Steve jumps in.

"No way, it's last, because then if it doesn't get drunk the host gets to keep it as an actual gift," Jon says. "Who in this case, would be me!"

"Thoughts, Lanie?" Mary asks.

"I suppose the question is, is it a gift to the party, or a gift to the host? Answer that, and you've got your answer," Lanie adds her two cents.

"You know what," Mary begins. "I think I might just start bringing two bottles of wine to every party."

"Yep, that'll work," they all say together.

"You're a real problem solver, Mary!" Steve adds.

Lanie grabs a handful of cheese and onion crisps from the table. "How are you Sanjay—how's the family?" she asks, before shoving them into her mouth.

"Not bad," he says, shaking his head, and taking a swig of some colourful-canned craft beer. Sanjay had his first child a few months ago. "Just happy to get out of the house for a bit to be honest."

"Jesus, you look a little wound up, mate," Steve says.

"Haha, yeah, you would be too if the closest thing you got to intimacy was folding your wife's underwear."

"Offt," Steve replies. He raises both hands. "Not going near that with a ten-foot pole."

"How's the Celeste Simone case coming along? Jon was telling us it may not have been an accident?" Mary asks, turning to Lanie.

"Hmm," Lanie begins, "well, the short answer is that she gave a random busker the key card to her room, and he followed her back to her hotel, drugged her and then tried to make it look like a suicide."

"Any signs of struggle?" Sanjay asks.

"Nope—zero."

"Sexual abuse?" Mary asks.

"None."

"Anything stolen?" Steve pipes in.

"Not that we know—her computer, phone and wallet were all still there—but it's impossible to tell as no one except Celeste really knows what she packed," Lanie replies. "Anyway, we're waiting for CCTV footage to put him in the hotel at the time of her death, so we can get a warrant to go turn his place upside down."

"Pfft, how the fuck does someone accidently give their key card to a stranger?" Mary responds.

"She got in a tiff with her husband, Jerome —the bloke that is so generously outfitting the department with his tech—over another woman, so gave away his fancy, two thousand-dollar, Gucci jacket to the busker, not realising the key card was in it."

"Oh shit," Mary says. "Yep, that'll do it."

Jon wanders back to the barbeque to check on the meat.

"He's lucky he only lost a jacket," Steve moans. "I had to split everything down the middle with my ex, fifty-fifty. So she ended up selling my new BMW X5 for one dollar. One. Lousy. Dollar."

"What did you do with your 50 cents?" Lanie asks.

"I told her to keep it. She reckons she bought a scratchy ticket with it and won thousands, too! Damn, I fucking loved that car, though."

"Language, Steve," the captain says from the hot plate. "Think of the children!"

"Won't somebody think of the children!" Steve, Sanjay and Mary all sing out together.

"And what's the long answer?" Steve asks.

"Huh?" Lanie utters.

"Well, you said that the busker was the short answer, so what's the long answer?"

Lanie puts her can of Diet Coke down on the green, wooden picnic table. "Well, I just can't shake the idea that it was somebody close to her—that she let them into her room. You guys said it, right: no struggle, nothing missing—"

"The husband? It's always the husband. Do you know that four women a month are killed by their husbands in Australia?" Mary says, her tone not quite matching the severity of the statistic.

"Firstly," Lanie starts, "of course we know Mary, we're the ones that have to catch the bastards. And second: I don't know, but there was some serious love-triangle shit going on with that group. Shit, maybe for once the obvious answer is the answer."

There's a moment's pause before, "Yeah, nah," they all chuckle simultaneously.

"Do you know I once had this dream where Steve—"

"I'll stop you there," Lanie interjects.

"No, not that kind of dream—gross. So, I had this dream where Steve solved this case, and I woke up and I was so annoyed that Steve solved it and I didn't, but then I realised it was my dream! So I'd actually solved it, not Steve!"

"Okay," Lanie says, elongating the 'o', while picking up her drink again and taking a sip. "But, what's your point?"

"I dunno, it just popped in my mind."

"Grub's up!" the captain calls out, putting an end to Mary's trademark tangent. The kids respond to Jon's call like he's the pied piper.

"Auntie Lanie!" Jessie, the captain's daughter, cries out.

"Happy birthday, kiddo!" Lanie digs into her bag and pulls out a small unwrapped box. It's a small robot-hand STEM science kit. She gives it to Jessie.

"This is for you."

Jessie takes it and her eyes light up. "This is freakin' awesome!" she screams. "Dad, look!" Jon looks over at the quintessentially Lanie gift. "Oh cool! What do you say to Auntie Lanie?"

"Thanks, Auntie Lanie. This is the best!" She runs off and adds it to the pile of pink Barbie dolls and tea sets.

"Don't mention it," Lanie says.

The kids grab their snags-in-a-blanket and run off together, leaving the adults sitting around the park bench. The captain's phone rings. Every one of the detectives at the table come to a complete, nosy silence.

"Captain Bailey, here." He puts one hand over the receiver to relieve them of their curiosity. "It's news about the busker," he mouths, then returns to the call. "Yep. Yep. Aha. Did he? And what time was that? Okay. Yep, thanks for that. I will. She's here with me. I'll tell her now. Thanks. Bye." He hangs up the phone.

He looks up to be met by four sets of eager eyes. He turns to Lanie. "It wasn't the busker."

"I knew it." Lanie kisses her teeth.

"The surveillance team stitched together the personal footage of the beat cops with the CCTV footage to track his movements and he didn't enter The Grand Theatre at all. The closest he got was the McDonald's on the corner of Russel and Bourke. There's restaurant video footage of him buying a dollar cheeseburger and coffee at midnight, the time of Celeste's death; then sitting in the restaurant to eat it. From there he walked to Central Station and caught the train home to Richmond, where, it turns out, he owns a comfortable two bedroom flat."

"And the key card? Lanie inquires.

"Nothing. He didn't use it."

The news washes over Lanie. "Hmmm, well someone was in the room with her," she says, rubbing her tongue on her front teeth.

"Well, luckily, we have our best detective on the case," Jon replies.

Steve quickly swallows his food and adds, "but I thought Lanie was on the case?"

The table laughs; Lanie rolls her eyes.

"Who's ready for cake?" The captain asks as he gets up, walks over to the cooler and pulls out a cake he'd been working on until the early hours of the morning.

"What's with the KISS cake—is that Gene Simmons?" Mary asks.

Jon stares at her. "It's a bloody pirate," he says, daring the next person to criticise his laborious creation.

"It looks great, boss," Steve says, smartly.

"Cake time!" Jon yells out, calling the kids back with the same effect as last time.

"Also, language, Jon," Steve says into his beer.

SEVENTEEN

THE SUN IS still up, but barely. Thomas and Jessie are the last two left on the playground. All the other kids and grown-ups have gone home. It's an impressive playground. There's a giant pirate ship with two long blue slides, a rope ladder, climbing nets, cubby holes, a steering wheel, gangplank, and cannons to shoot the landlubbers in the sandpit. Plus, a yellow-haired mermaid with a scaly tailfin, resting on the bow of the ship, for luck.

While the two kids take turns walking the plank, searching for hidden treasure, and swashbuckling the Dread Pirate Roberts, Lanie silently helps the Captain clean up.

"You alright—is this about the busker?" Jon asks.

"Nah, of course not. I knew it was too easy."

"What is it then?"

"I suppose you know about mum?"

"Oh, thank God she finally told you."

"She actually didn't."

"Hmm, I guess she was never going to keep it a secret for too long from a detective as a daughter…"

Lanie slides the dirty paper plates from the table into a large dark green garbage bag. "I wouldn't be so sure. Becca let it slip the other day," Lanie sighs. "I've been so sorry for myself about the divorce and about losing Thomas, that I kinda put the rest of my life on hold."

The captain shrugs empathetically. "Happens to the best of us," he says. "Lanie, I've known you for a long time, and listen to me when I tell you this: you've got to stop being so hard on yourself." He puts one hand on her shoulder and looks her in the eyes. "Trust me, that's what other people in this world are for."

Lanie's face creases; her eyes squint as she processes the classic Jon-ism.

"Your mum will be fine, Lanie. They've caught it early."

"So everyone keeps telling me."

"Fair enough," Jon says, knowing it was time to change the topic. "Now, tell me, what's going on with the Celeste Simone case. Now we know it's not the busker, I can tell you right now, I'm going to have trouble keeping the investigation alive—with the pressure Jerome's applying. So, what do you got? Leads?"

Lanie appreciates the pivot. Not the reminder that she's now working against the clock, but happy to not be talking about her mum. "I just don't know, Jon."

Jon pushes on his lower back with his two hands, stretching. "You think Jerome is crazy enough to bring us in when he did it?"

She looks up. "Honestly, maybe," she says. "You know he visited me at my apartment the other night, telling me to drop the case?"

Jon stops and looks up at Lanie. "Did he now?"

"Yeah, he's worried about her image—the 'optics' as he put it—now that she's not around to defend herself, he wants it out of the news cycle asap—you know how rich people are about that stuff."

Jon bends over to pick up some rogue wrapping paper.

"Jon there is one other thing I've been meaning to tell you..."

Jon looks up at Lanie.

"Jerome, he's, um..." *Just tell him. He'll understand. But what if he doesn't? Then I'll never get Thomas back.*

"He's what?" Jon leans forward.

"He's very generous, outfitting us with the latest hardware," Lanie finally says.

"Well, you've certainly changed your tune!" he chuckles.

"Anyway. Tell me more about the witnesses—are they helpful? If you told me twenty years ago that we'd be interviewing people as eyewitnesses who were watching a crime virtually; I would've laughed in your face!"

Lanie chuckles. She thinks before she answers. "These witnesses—Celeste's followers—they all streamed the exact same thing, yet they're bringing so much of their own baggage to what they saw. It's hard to filter through to the truth."

The two of them admire their tidying up, then take a seat at the park bench.

"Have I ever told you about the Robinson family

case I worked on?" Jon asks, who loves talking about the good ol' days after a few drinks. "The one with the kids in the basement?"

"You haven't but I get the feeling you're about to," Lanie says, grabbing the bridge of her nose.

"The two kids, little Ollie and Clementine were their names, they—"

'Bzzzzt' Lanie's phone vibrates, interrupting him. It's Pimm from Sydney. Lanie presses the side button to silence it. She'll call him back later.

"Ahem," Jon clears his throat. Jon's a bit of a dinosaur when it comes to people's attention and their devices.

"Sorry," Lanie says as she shoves her phone in her back pocket, "go on."

"The two kids were held in their basement by their father for the first ten years of their life—it was tragic. There wasn't even a window. But, what that bastard did was basically manipulate how they saw the world. And, among other things, all he ever showed them of us, the police, was news coverage and videos of violence and brutality. All they ever saw was the worst of us. Can you imagine? So when we found them, to save them, they didn't want to be rescued—they were terrified. Of us, the police!?" He shakes his head. "Their reality was puppeteered by their father—he pulled the strings of their truth, so they'd be too afraid to leave him."

Lanie hates the phrase 'my truth' or 'their truth'. It's an oxymoron. It rankles every sinew in her detective's body, whose basic job description is to find the 'truth'. Subjectivity is superfluous in her line of work.

"Lanie!" Jon snaps her out of her tangent.

"Sorry, I'm listening," she replies sheepishly.

"As I was saying, their reality was created by their sicko father," he belabours the point this time. "And while this is extreme, it's actually the same for all of us—except it's not transparent who the father is—who's manipulating what we see. You get me?"

"Yeah, I get it, Jon." Lanie idly peels off some green paint from the bench.

"Our environment—which we have limited control over—creates the lens we see the world through," he adds.

Lanie thinks about it for a minute, rubbing her right temple. "No wonder nobody can agree on what they see, if we're all seeing it through a different lens!"

"Precisely."

"You're too smart for your own good sometimes," Lanie says as Jon sits there pleased, seeing himself through her eyes.

"Are you going to be okay?"

"Always am."

"Good. So, hit me with it: other ideas; theories?"

"Hmmm," she goes to respond but stops. "I do have the beginning of one, I think…" She scratches her shoulder. "Sam's hiding something. I just know it. And Abbie—she still hasn't called me back, which is becoming more and more suspicious. But, to be honest, Jon, I've still got one last witness to talk to first, before pointing fingers."

Jon makes a circle with his shoe in the dirt under the chair. "I'm actually happy to hear that, Lanie. You're no longer slavish to your first opinion, which is bloody hard, I know, because our detective brains scream for us to be consistent. But, don't forget, the clock's ticking."

"Just one more witness, Jon. That's all I need—buy me as much time as you can."

Jon nods and stands up. "I'll do my best. Just remember what I told you about the Robinson case: perception is reality." He stretches. "And the reality right now is that Celeste Simone died of a drug overdose." He tilts his wizened head in the direction of the kids by way of saying let's get these two ratbags home.

Lanie nods in agreement. "Thomas! C'mon time to go," she calls out. "Thanks Jon, or is it Mr Miyagi, now?"

Jon laughs, clasps his hands together and bows his head. "You're welcome Lanie-san."

EIGHTEEN

THOMAS IS ASLEEP in the spare room. All that swashbuckling pooped him out.

Lanie's lying on her couch. There's a wheat heat bag around her shoulder, helping relieve the tension headache that's been building ever since she caught up with Becca. The TV's switched off so she doesn't wake up Thomas. She's sitting in silence, scrolling through Facebook on her phone which she's holding above her face. The blue light illuminates her features. A mutual friend of hers and Brett's has posted some photos of a family holiday to Bali. She clicks the post and swipes through the images of their idyllic vacation. In the pictures they're all getting their hair braided together, even the dad. *Adorable.* Lanie clicks back and into the same friend's homepage. At the top of the screen, under the friend's section she sees Brett's profile.

"Don't do it. Don't do it. Don't do it," she says to herself, before doing it.

She clicks Brett's thumbnail. There's lots of pictures, mostly of him and Thomas, but there's also another woman—the one Lanie saw around his house yesterday—who appears to be in a lot of the newer posts.

"Why did I do it?" She starts to feel anxious, looking at Brett's perfect life without her. Lanie closes the app and places her phone on the floor next to the couch. Opting to stare blankly at the ceiling, instead, following the cracks along the cornicing. Now it's just Lanie alone with her thoughts. *Fucking Brett and his picture-perfect life. It's his fault I'm putting the whole damn investigation at risk by accepting Jerome's help to get Thomas back. Fuck. I really need to tell Jon.* A dark cloud eclipses her inner thoughts. All of a sudden: actual darkness. At that poetically perfect moment the power to her apartment goes out.

"Seriously!" she yells at a whisper, so as to not wake Thomas. She lays there for thirty long seconds, hoping it's just a momentary thing, before she admits to herself it's not.

She gets up, chucks the heat bag on the couch and walks out to the balcony to see if it's just her apartment or the whole building. She opens the sliding door and steps out onto the balcony. Mobile phone torch-lights flicker into the darkness from the apartments around her. She moves over to the rail and peeps her head over the edge.

Her neighbours had the same instinct. "You alright?" someone asks from the darkness.

"Never better," Lanie mutters. She heads back inside to search for some candles. Her phone buzzes. It's a message from Pimm. *Shit!* She's mad at herself for forgetting about his call earlier. She unlocks her phone and reads the message.

Hey detective. It's Pimm. Call me back when you can. I've got something you need to see.

She finds the candles and a pack of matches in the spare cupboard near the front door. She lights up a couple and strategically places them on the kitchen bench in the middle of the room. She returns to the couch and calls Pimm back.

"Hello," he answers.

"Hi Pimm, it's Detective Daniels. I'm returning your call."

"Detective Daniels," the muffled voice on the other end of the line says. "I think I've got something for you. I don't know if you noticed, but I have a pretty extensive security system set up at home, with a few motion censored Ring cameras that film when there's movement."

"I know how Ring security systems work, Pimm. Cut to the chase—what's up?"

"Well, on the morning of Celeste's death, I went outside for a cigarette and took my laptop with me, so I didn't miss anything, and my Ring camera captured some of Celeste's live stream."

"Really?" Lanie asks. "How much?"

"Only around 10-15 minutes. It's mostly Celeste and Sam checking-in to the hotel, but it also includes something very interesting about the key cards."

"The key cards, plural?" Lanie stands up and starts pacing around.

"Plural," Pimm echoes. "I just knew Sam Bateman

had something to do with it!"

Lanie ignores the accusation and inhales.

"Detective, are you still there?"

"I'm here," Lanie replies. "Hey Pimm?" she asks tentatively, looking out at the light show beyond the balcony. "How did you know about the key cards?"

There's a strained silence.

"I um, I ah," he stammers.

"What's going on, Pimm?"

"Oh, no, nothing bad. I, ah, um started a support group for grieving fans like me, and Paula Abbas joined and we got talking and realised you'd interviewed both of us, so she told me about the busker and the key card. I haven't got her in trouble have I?"

"No, that's okay—It's a free country. You guys can talk as much as you like," Lanie says. "Send it to me now; I'll take a look."

"Sure thing," Pimm replies. "It's done."

Lanie's phone vibrates in her hand. She pulls it away from her ear and checks her email. He's sent her a video file. She puts the phone back up to her ear. "Pimm, are you still there? Thanks for this—you've done good. I'm going to watch it now. I'll call you if I have any questions."

Lanie's just about to hang up, when she stops herself. "And, Pimm... how are you?" she asks with uncharacteristic compassion. She hears him swallow on the other end of the phone.

"Um, I, I'm getting there, detective. I started that support group and that's helped a lot."

"Nice one, Pimm. Sounds like you're going to be okay."

"I think I just might be. It's good to talk to people in real life. Different, but good. Thanks for asking."

"You're welcome. I'll be in touch if I need anything more from you." She hangs up.

Lanie sits back down on her couch, opens Pimm's video, presses play, and watches it in the flickering candlelight.

It opens on Pimm walking out into his courtyard—the security system is motion-sensored so his movement triggers the system to start recording. The time code says 8.31 a.m., Saturday morning. Pimm sits down at the small iron two-seater table and sets his laptop in front of him. The security camera is perched over his shoulder, capturing around 90% of the screen. There's no sound.

Celeste is sat in a moving car, her gaze fixated on the Melbourne wheel to her left. She pulls out her phone and shoots off a quick text before tucking it away and resuming her quiet contemplation of the passing scenery.

The car veers off the ring road and into the CBD. Sam is waiting on the curb out front of The Grand Theatre Hotel. Her car pulls up. Sam opens the door. They exchange greetings as the driver—*this must be Gary*—retrieves her luggage from the boot and carries it over to them. Sam takes it; then he and Celeste enter the hotel through the front entrance.

Inside the hotel, Celeste purchases a couple of hot

drinks from a busy café before joining Sam in line. She and Sam make their way to the front desk to check-in, where the concierge hands Sam an envelope with two key cards inside.

Lanie pauses the video and zooms in to the pixelated film. "Holy Fuck! There were two cards!"

They make their way up the elevator, down the hall and to her room. Sam reaches into his back pocket, fishes out the envelope containing the key-cards, takes out one of the cards, swipes it over the sensor, unlocking the door, and takes a step backwards for Celeste to enter. She walks inside into the dark, and turns back towards Sam as he places one card in the holder, and the other one in his pocket.

"What the actual, actual fuck," Lanie says out loud, hitting every syllable, forgetting about Thomas in the next room. She pauses the video and takes a moment to process what she just watched. She draws a deep breath; then hits play again.

Celeste marches over to the bay windows to open the blinds. Sunlight pours into the room, and then—
Pimm picks up his laptop, stubs out a cigarette and walks back inside. His tiny courtyard becomes still again, before the recording eventually stops.

"Sam had another card!" Lanie exclaims, as the power in her apartment comes back on in a blinding flash, as poetically as it had gone out.

NINETEEN

"WAKEY WAKEY EGGS and bakey," Lanie sings out, knocking on Thomas's door. It's a Sunday morning. In spite of the growing urgency, Lanie forces herself to compartmentalise the case to give Thomas the attention he deserves—and she deserves. She pushes his door open to find he's already awake.

"I love you," Tracy the ibis says to Alan the monkey. He's playing with his toys.

"C'mon buddy, time to get up."

Thomas rolls out of bed and trudges out to the family room. He plods over to the TV, changes the ABC News to Paw Patrol and climbs up onto the couch. Lanie looks over at the TV in astonishment—she thought the remote was broken.

"What do you want for brekky, little man?"

He shrugs.

"Weet-Bix?"

"Yeah, Weet-Bix."

Lanie makes him two Weet-Bix with milk and a sprinkle of cinnamon, and gives it to him on the couch. She really can't wait until he gets out of this shy stage. Lanie sits next to him on the couch with her coffee, and peanut butter muffin. They're quietly watching cartoons when Lanie's phone rings. She picks it up. It's Becca.

"Hey Becs! Shit...zle! You told him? Yep, okay, no worries. Thanks for the heads up."

A kernel of dread lodges itself in her throat, but she swallows it. She's not going to let it ruin her day with Thomas.

"Told who what?" Thomas asks, finding his voice at the most lamentable moment.

Lanie puts her arm around his shoulder. "What would you say about us seeing each other some more?"

"That would be okay, I guess."

"You guess, do you?" Lanie wipes some rogue Weet-Bix off his forehead.

"Yeah, I like seeing you mummy, but my room's at dad's place."

Lanie smiles, resisting the instinct to say something negative about Brett. "I get it, buddy."

He finishes his last mouthful of Weet-Bix.

"Alright, let's clean up brekky, get dressed and get going. We've got a big day ahead of us!"

An hour later they're walking through the glass doors of her mum's retirement home. She's taken Thomas to visit his nan. Fiona's at the front desk again. She looks down at Thomas as he approaches. He's got his eye-patch on from yesterday, a superman cape that Alan the monkey normally wears, a Star Wars t-shirt over a button up shirt, swimming shorts and a Canadian Club promo beanie with side flaps which he found in Lanie's closet—he dressed himself this morning.

"Who's this little superhero?" Fiona asks, as Lanie catches up to him at the desk. He hides behind her leg. "Hello love, here to visit Susanne?"

Lanie nods.

"Just sign in here again and then go through."

Lanie types her and Thomas's name into the check-in computer and then winds her way through the corridors to her mum's room. It's early so the hallways are half as action-packed as the last time she visited. She knocks on the door and enters.

"Nanna!" Thomas squeals as he runs ahead of Lanie and onto his nan's bed. She looks tired. Lanie knows why, but her mum doesn't know she knows, so she doesn't say anything.

"Tiny Tom! How's my beautiful grandson?" Thomas cuddles her. She looks up at Lanie. "Two times in one week! To what do I owe the pleasure?"

Their eyes lock. She knows. And she knows she knows. Their expressions remain imperceptibly still while a torrent of understanding transfers between the two of them. In that silent heartbeat everything that needs to be said is said.

Lanie smiles and untangles the knot in her stomach. "We were in the neighbourhood."

Thomas screws up his nose, exposing his mum's white-lie.

"Well, I can never see enough of this little spunky monkey." She pulls off the ridiculous hat he's wearing and ruffles his hat-hair.

Lanie helps her mum into her wheelchair and the three of them amble around the fecund grounds of the nursing home. The sun is shining; woolly white clouds hang in the sky.

"How's the case going?"

"It's certainly going," Lanie responds curtly.

Susanne can tell Lanie doesn't want to talk about it so moves on. Instead, she turns her focus to Thomas. "How's Alan enjoying school, Thomas?" she asks by way of asking how he's doing at school.

"He's going okay."

"Just okay?"

"Yeah, some of the kids aren't very nice to him."

"Really? Why? How?"

"Well, when we play chasey at recess, they always get Alan because of his asthma, and then Alan can't get any of them back, so he's 'it' the whole time, and it hurts his feelings, but I tell him not to let it get to him and just ignore them."

Lanie looks on in disbelief as Thomas opens up to his nan in a single streaming sentence.

"Well there's only one thing to do about it. Next time you—I mean Alan—gets tagged, kick your foot out like this," she flicks her foot out from her wheelchair, "and trip the little buggers up! Then they'll be easier to catch."

"Mum!" Lanie interjects as Thomas giggles at his nan's patently irresponsible suggestion.

"What? It's a nanna's job to give bad advice," she says. "The good kind of bad advice."

"You want a chocolate milk, buddy?" Lanie asks.

Thomas grins and nods emphatically.

"I think I saw one in the vending machine over there. Here, take my card and go grab one."

He looks at the card, confused, leaving her outstretched hand hanging. "I don't need the card, Nanna taught me a trick to get it for free."

Lanie turns to look at her mum, again. "Is that right?"

Susanne looks at her sheepishly. "It's his tiny hands, they're perfect… never mind. Take your mum's card Thomas and be a good boy."

He grabs it and runs off. The two women watch as he ducks and weaves around the throngs of old people who look like they've spent too long in the bath.

When he's out of earshot, Lanie turns to her mum. "So, when does the treatment start?"

"Got my first bout of chemo in a couple of weeks—the 15th, 9 a.m. at Saint Vincent's. It's funny they say 'bout', isn't it? I suppose because it's a fight—"

"I'll take you."

"Oh, I know you will, I already put your name down at the hospital."

Lanie's lips curl, knowingly.

"Enough about that, though. More importantly," Susanne starts, "did you call that thirst trap of a young man from the café? What was his name—?"

"Mum!"

Susanne holds her stare.

"What's a thirst trap?" Thomas asks, making sucky sounds, sipping his chocolate milk.

The rest of the day, Susanne teaches Thomas how to whistle using his thumb and forefinger—the big ear-piercing kind. It annoys the hell out of all the other residents. As the dinner bell rings, they wheel Susanne over to the dining room, where she's met by her gaggle of friends at the 'cool' table.

"Seeya nanny," Thomas says, giving her a quick cuddle.

"Seeya kiddo," she says, slipping him a fiver.

"Don't do that, mum."

"I will do what I like," she replies. "How does the saying go? If you raise your children, you can spoil your grandchildren. But if you spoil your children, you'll have to raise your grandchildren—and we both know I certainly did not spoil you," she chuckles.

"See you Tuesday week," Lanie says with a nod.

Lanie and Thomas turn and exit, past the abandoned front desk—Fiona must've already knocked off for the day.

TWENTY

LANIE PULLS UP to the front of Brett's house. The fierce tug of her flight instinct pulls at her. She desperately wants to avoid the confrontation that's about to follow. She conquers the urge to stay seated, unlocks the doors, and steps out of the car. She pops the trunk and grabs Thomas's backpack.

He scrambles out of his seat and meets her around the back of the car, a plush toy in each hand.

Lanie hears the click of the deadbolt of Brett's front door and looks up reflexively. Her tongue rubs aggressively on her front teeth. She meets Brett's gaze and an all too familiar look greets her. It's the same look she'd get when he used to withdraw inside himself after she did something to offend him, which he'd keep to himself, because of his hackneyed inability to talk about his feelings. They walk to the front door, where he's waiting.

"Hi Brett."

He ignores her and turns to Thomas. "Tommy gun!" he says. "You must be starving. Tracy's cooked you your favourite Spaghetti Bolognese for dinner."

"Did she use nutmeg?" Thomas asks, playing with his backpack's straps.

"Of course mate!"

Lanie watches the interaction, doing a terrible job at hiding her surprise. She had no idea Thomas liked Spag Bol, let alone with nutmeg. *What even is nutmeg?*

"Why don't you go wash your hands and I'll meet you inside at the table. I just need to speak to you mum for a minute."

The smell of cooking onions and buttery garlic bread wafts warmly from the house. The condensation caused by the boiling pot of pasta crawls along the windows. The scene almost makes Lanie feel wistful for her old life, but she shakes it off. Thomas adjusts his backpack, takes off his shoes and runs inside, forgetting to say goodbye.

"See ya buddy!" she sighs to the empty space where he'd been standing. Lanie lets it go, trying not to take it personally, and looks up at Brett.

"Anything I should know about?" Brett pokes the elephant in the room, or not. Lanie can't really tell.

"No, nothing. Except mum did teach him how to whistle, so there's that—you may want to invest in some earplugs."

Brett stares at her. "Okay," he says, "well, I guess I'll see you Thursday. Until then, take care, Lanie." He turns inside and shuts the door. Not a slam, but not softly either.

Lanie was left standing on his doorstep by herself. *Well that actually didn't go too badly.*

Lanie drives home, catching every green light on

the way, pulls into her underground car park, hops out and catches the lift upstairs to her apartment.

She unlocks her door and steps inside. Thomas's toys—the ones that stay at her place—are strewn everywhere. She kicks off her boots and picks up the bits and pieces, expertly side stepping the minefield of random Lego and Hot Wheels cars, chucking them in the makeshift toy box made from an empty biscuit tin.

Once all the toys are picked up and put away, she plonks herself down on the couch for a moment's peace. She remembers her fridge is empty, so pulls out her phone, opens the Uber Eats app and orders a small Hawaiian pizza and Diet Coke from the local pizza joint down the road. The kind that piles the ingredients on; that is highly offensive to Italians. Italians like the guy from the coffee shop her mum won't shut up about.

She chucks her phone to the other side of the couch, out of arm's reach, massages both temples with her fingers and rests her eyes momentarily.

The discordant sound of the alarm on her phone comes into stark focus as she gathers her wits. "Shit! What time is it!?" she asks no one in particular, disoriented by the screeching, which she sets as intentionally offensive, because of her penchant for sleeping through the more pleasant options.

She jumps up off the couch, fumbles around in the dark for her phone, finally finds it and swipes it off. It's 4:30 a.m. Her flight to Adelaide leaves in an hour and a half. She's on the red eye there, to interview the final witness, Irene. She orders a taxi to come in twenty minutes, groggily stumbles into the bathroom, showers and gets dressed, pulling on last week's clothes hanging off the back of the chair in her bedroom.

Her phone dings, notifying her that her driver is out the front. She grabs her satchel, and steps out the front door, stomping right onto the now-cold Hawaiian pizza. She lets out a big, resigned sigh, before kicking the pizza inside, grabbing the Diet Coke and leaving the building to meet her awaiting driver.

Lanie uses the trip to the airport to try a breathing exercise she learned from the ChillTime app on her phone, which she subscribed to for the free two-week trial and then forgot to unsubscribe until three months later.

She cups her right hand into her left with her thumbs lightly touching, straightens her back, relaxes her shoulders, and closes her eyes so just a slit of light filters through. She takes a deep breath, breathing in all the stress and negativity, which she has in surplus, as black smoke, and then breathes it out, picturing it as white smoke. She breathes in. And breathes out—

"Get out the fucking way!" her taxi driver yells, shouting at a grey Subaru Outback going 60 kms in an 80 zone. Lanie's eyes snap open. She runs her hands through her hair, cracks open her bottle of Diet Coke and takes a long swig.

"How's the temperature—too warm?" the driver asks, politely.

They pull up to the airport, Lanie jumps out, floats through check-in, anxiously walks over to her gate to confirm it exists; then walks back to the food area and grabs a coffee. She returns to the gate, boards using the e-ticket on her phone, gets on the plane and arrives in Adelaide a little over an hour later, where she catches an Uber from the airport to Irene's house in North Adelaide.

TWENTY ONE

'AN EXPLORATION INTO the social impact of the Vicarious Experience Identity Split' is the title of Irene's thesis, which is due in just under three months now. It's a real page-turner, too. Or, it would be if she could get it out of her head and onto paper. Irene is at the end of her PhD in Sociology at the University of Adelaide. She just got home from fika at East Taste Continental with her Swedish professor.

'Treat it like a sculpture,' he said. 'Get everything down on paper and then start chipping away until the masterpiece appears.'

Easy for him to say. He doesn't have the blank sheet mocking him. Everybody loves her. More than she loves herself. Irene is an overachiever; fiercely independent, while at the same time in desperate need of connection—her ex-boyfriends and girlfriends would call her needy.

Her childhood wasn't a bed of roses. Her dad used to always tell her, 'families should never air their dirty laundry', which in hindsight was a way for him to get away with physically and emotionally abusing her mum longer than he should have.

Her mum eventually stopped putting up with his shit and left him, running away from Melbourne with Irene and her older sister to their grandma's in Adelaide. Her dad never even tried to see them. No phone calls, no emails, no birthday cards. Nothing. And that was just the way Irene liked it.

Irene's fairly well-adapted considering her upbringing. But it damaged her sister a bit, because as an adult she takes no responsibility for anything she does, like stealing their mum's retirement money to buy designer handbags and first-class flights to LA. Her sister is right into the whole influencer thing. Irene gets it. Their lives were such a dumpster fire, that when presented with the opportunity to live in someone else's shoes, her sister grabbed it with both hands—or feet, so to speak. You could call her sister her muse for her thesis. She does.

Irene lives in a small one-bedroom, second-floor apartment on O'Connell street in North Adelaide, a ten-minute free bus ride from downtown Adelaide and the university. She's travelled a lot, mostly during a gap year that lasted for three. She's aggressively and sometimes self-righteously pragmatic; the kind of person who chooses experiences over things. She had an out of body experience one time while she was brushing her teeth, but in retrospect she was just staring at herself in the mirror—she smokes a lot of weed.

There's a knock at her door. She walks over and opens it. Standing there is a dishevelled half Asian woman wearing all shades of black.

"Irene Pappas?" the woman asks with not even a trace of an accent. "My name's Detective Lanie Daniels, we spoke on the phone?"

Irene smiles. "Of course, detective, please come in." She leads her through her small studio apartment, down a long hallway, past the bathroom—boasting the only door in the place—past a ladder that leads up to the loft and her bedroom, through the small galley kitchen, past the living room, featuring no TV and boxy Ikea shelves with books sorted by colour, and out onto the balcony.

"You've been shortlisted as a witness in the Celeste Simone investigation," Lanie begins as the two take a seat outside. "I need you to tell me what you saw through her eyes the day she passed." Lanie goes through the motions the same as she did with the first two witnesses.

The dry sun beats down on them like an oven grill. "Of course," Irene replies. She gets up, leaving Lanie staring at an empty white-tiled wall. "Let me just grab a cold drink," her voice rings out from the kitchen.

Irene is short. Shorter than Lanie even. She has dark brown hair that falls just beyond her shoulders, and she's skinny. A healthy, athletic kind of skinny. Her top's showing her midriff and as she gets up and walks back into her apartment, Lanie can't help but notice her back dimples. She has brown eyes, a slightly-too-big nose, and milky Mediterranean skin, underlining her Greek heritage.

She returns to the balcony and sits back down with a blue Powerade, putting it down next to Lanie's phone, facing upwards with the voice recorder app open on it.

"Big fan?" Lanie nods towards the broken heart tattoo, the same one Celeste had behind her ear, on Irene's wrist.

"Not quite," Irene chuckles, unable to contain her amusement. "It's a stick-on. It came in that magazine over there, which I bought for my research." She points to a Who Magazine with Celeste on the cover, resting on the coffee table inside—the same one Lanie saw in Celeste's hotel room. "I got a little boozy a few nights ago, and, yeah, now it's on my wrist. It's the first time in forever I've bought a paper magazine."

Lanie twitches. "Okay," she says, staring blankly at the tiny droplets of condensation forming on the sides of the Powerade bottle, wondering if Pimm's tattoo was fake, too.

"So, where do you want me to start?" Irene leans towards Lanie.

Lanie looks up at Irene; shifts her attention to her phone on the table and presses the record button. "Let's go from when Celeste arrives in Melbourne."

TWENTY TWO

CELESTE TURNED HER live stream on when the plane touched down. It was around 6:30 a.m. The flight from San Fran had arrived on time; maybe it was early. She disembarked the plane and walked through the duty free store on her way through customs, picking up a bottle of wine. A woman served her; she was basic. Celeste made small talk, placed the bottle into her bag, put on her sunnies, slumped her shoulders to disguise her posture, and sauntered out of the welcome gate. She was exhausted from the flight and didn't have the energy for any of the attention that comes with being a world-famous influencer.

 Not that any attention was forthcoming, because Abbie Benson-Wheeler was there, too. She's a streamer like Celeste. A storm of camera flashes followed Abbie through the terminal, almost bundling Celeste over. She looked around for Jerome but he wasn't there. He'd sent a driver to pick her up—too lazy to do it himself. She spotted a big dude holding a sign with her name on it. Celeste shrugged, used to this kind of treatment, and strode over to him. As she approached, a ripple of recognition crossed his face.

"Miss Simone?" he asked hesitantly.

"Yeah, that's me."

"Mr Pitt apologises, he's at work, so he sent me to pick you up," he recited as if he'd been practising for the last hour, because he probably had.

Lanie faked a frown. "And how do I know you aren't just some crazy fan trying to abduct me?"

"I'm not!"

"You're not a fan?" Lanie held her expression.

He dabbed the sweat forming on his forehead with a chequered hanky—the kind that comes in three packs around Father's Day. "Oh, no, I'm a huge fan, Miss Simone." He looked up and saw Celeste break into a big grin.

"Good to know," she stopped and read his name badge, "Gary."

His whole body relaxed. "Here, let me take your luggage."

"Sure, here you go, Gaz. I just need to quickly use the ladies, and then we can get going."

He stopped and swivelled.

"Roger that, Miss Simone. I'll be right here."

Celeste glanced sideways at the growing herd of sheep following Abbie. It triggered her anxiety so she took a quick—air-quotes—'bathroom' break—

"Why air quotes?" Lanie asks.

"What, you don't know? Celeste was addicted to benzos. They weren't just for the flight. She suffered from anxiety; depression. She had an aggressive case of 'analogy malady', always comparing herself to others, which is ironic because her portrayal of life is generally the benchmark for comparison among teenage girls. That's why I've been streaming her 24/7. It's part of my research for my PhD."

Lanie quietly notes it down in her notepad. Irene shrugs and continues.

Celeste returned to Gary and then followed him to his parked car. He packed her bag into the boot, opened the back door for her, and jumped into the driver's seat. The car pulled out and drove past Abbie, who was still fighting her way through even more followers to get to her new Tesla.

Celeste stared at Abbie through the window, drawn to her blonde hair. The same iconic blonde as her own. "You've got to be kidding me," Celeste muttered. She sat there with her mouth slightly ajar, staring in disbelief at her doppelganger, before swiftly looking away to avoid meeting eyes and getting caught staring.

Gary drove to the city on the freeway, past the decrepit Melbourne Wheel; Melbourne's lame attempt at the London Eye, but with literally nothing to look at when you reached the top. The ride was boring—It's the worst part of travel: the journey after the journey.

Celeste killed time flicking through her phone. She wrote her mum the obligatory text, telling her she'd arrived safely, before getting comfy and staring out the window.

She finally got to her hotel, where Sam Bateman—tech genius and world-renown milquetoast—met her out the front on the curb side.

"Miss Simone," he said, holding out his hand as if he were a character in an episode of Bridgerton, and Gary's car was, in fact, a horse drawn carriage.

"Mr Bateman." She matched his histrionics. Sam helped pull her out of the car before they made their way through the hotel's big sliding doors.

"Welcome to The Grand Theatre Hotel," the door woman—who had the easiest job in the world on account of the doors being automatic—greeted them.

The hotel lobby opened up before her eyes. It was buzzing. Guests were coming and going, and there was a tiny cafe that was going gangbusters with walk-ins off the street.

"I could really do with a coffee." Celeste turned to Sam, her feet carrying her in the direction of the cafe and the sweet smell of caffeine.

"Why don't we check-in first and then get them to bring you one up?"

"So keen to get me alone, Mr Bateman?"

"I, ah, um," he muttered as Celeste walked off towards the cafe.

"You line up, Sam. I'll be right back."

By the time Celeste got back with the coffees, Sam was at the front of the line. She handed him his drink as they walked up to the front desk in step.

"Miss Celeste Simone! It's a pleasure to have you back with us at The Grand Theatre." The concierge bowed. He typed frantically on the keyboard, checking her in, before looking up and handing an envelope with the room keys to Sam.

They walked around the front desk to the elevator, past a glass staircase that led up to the breakfast bar, that climbed past a majestic oak bookshelf, filled with dusty books, that was actually very intricate wallpaper.

They caught the elevator up to the 5th floor. They stood together silently. Celeste fixed her hair in the mirror while Sam leaned against the wall, crossing his ankles, quietly clicking his tongue along to the music—an uncomfortable love song.

The lift arrived at their floor, Sam waited for Celeste to exit, then followed her, dragging her bag behind him. They walked down the hallway side-by-side. Sam put his arm gently around Celeste's waist, pulling her out of the way of the room service lady, pushing her cart in the opposite direction.

"Morning," Sam said.

The room service lady looked down at her feet and scurried away.

They reached Celeste's room. Sam grabbed the key card from his back pocket, held it against the sensor, until he heard a click, then pushed open the heavy door, leaving room for Celeste to step inside.

Lanie clears her throat. "Do you remember what Sam did with the key cards after he opened the door?"

Irene takes a sip of her Powerade. "Yeah, he opened

the door and put that one in the hard-plastic thing that turns on the power in the room."

"And the other one?"

"Hmmm," Irene ponders, before re-living the moment in her mind. "The clerk put two cards in an envelope and handed them to Sam. He took them and put them in his back pocket with his wallet, before wheeling her luggage up to the room. When they got to the door, he only pulled out one of the cards from his pocket, meaning he must've kept the other card," she says, looking up at Lanie. Lanie nods, which Irene takes as her cue to continue.

The room was plush. Like something out of an episode of Grand Designs—if they did hotel rooms. And the mini-bar was stocked.

Sam wheeled Celeste's bag behind the bed and hoisted it up onto the desk. He couldn't get phone reception, so walked awkwardly around the room searching for bars. He found one at the window, before Celeste reminded him about the hotel's Wi-Fi. He grabbed the password from the mini-bar and joined her on the edge of the king-sized bed as he connected to the hotel's internet.

"So where's Jerome, really?"

Sam looked up at her. "Where do you reckon?" he sighed, knowing she could guess the answer.

"His one true love?"

"Right. Work."

The extra benzo from the airport was starting to kick in, so Celeste told Sam to leave, and he did.

"Seeya tonight, Cel!" He walked towards the door before remembering something. "Oh, one last thing," he said, "Abbie's coming!"

"Awesome." Celeste rolled her eyes.

Sam shuffled his feet.

"Well you know how Jerome feels when I cancel plans, so I guess I'll still see you there!" Celeste added.

Sam left, leaving Celeste alone in the room. She got up off the bed, walked over to the blinds, shut them completely, so not even a slither of light filtered through, and walked back over to her bed, diving into the pillows. Within minutes she was sound asleep; her live stream still broadcasting.

When she woke up, she went straight for the coffee machine. She was foggy from the pills and another hit of caffeine would help drag her back into the right-angles of reality. She hunted around for the coffee pods but couldn't find them anywhere, so she settled for a glass of water instead.

She hadn't eaten since the plane, so she walked back into the room, picked up the phone on the desk behind the bed, and dialled room service. As she waited for someone to pick up, she eyed the wardrobe, remembering Sam mentioned something about a bunch of dresses to try on.

"Room service?"

"Hey, can I get one tuna sandwich on dark rye." She licked her forefinger and turned the page of the menu. "And one Greek salad without olives, please."

She motioned to hang up before remembering, "and some coffee pods for the machine in the room also, please." She returned the phone to the receiver and stepped over to the wardrobe. She pulled open the doors before a kaleidoscope of colour spilled out —like a rainbow drank too many Vodka Cruisers and vomited on her. She slammed the doors shut, making it a problem for future Celeste; then jumped on the unmade bed to scroll through her phone.

Before long there was a knock at the door. It was the maid from earlier with her lunch.

"Come in!" Celeste sang out, loud enough to be heard on the other side of the thick door.

The room service lady wheeled in a cart with the sandwich, salad and Nespresso coffee pods, got Celeste to sign and left. She wasn't a big talker.

After lunch, Celeste tried on the dresses—she couldn't put it off any longer—getting her fans to vote on which one she should wear to the Cup and that night for dinner. "Hey guys, I need your help deciding what dress to wear tonight—"

"And blah blah blah," Irene says. "Obviously, fashion isn't really my thing." She makes her point by looking down at her yoga pants and crop top.

"No judgement here," Lanie says.

"I saw the first couple of dresses before I had to go to the bathroom," Irene continues, "when I came back, her live stream was switched off. A few hours later I got a notification telling me Celeste had logged-on again, so I did too."

When Celeste turned her stream back on, Jerome was in her room. He was grabbing a beer from the mini-bar, standing at the small fridge, staring blankly at the options, before choosing a Corona.

He poured Celeste a glass of the red wine she'd picked up from the airport and passed it to her. Jerome sat down at the small table next to the window, away from the bath, and watched Celeste finish getting ready.

"Go with the boots," he told her. He always told her what to wear. At home—the few times they were there together—he'd even go as far as laying out her clothes for her each morning. He would say the human brain is only capable of making a finite amount of decisions each day and he didn't want her to have to waste one on choosing what clothes to wear.

That's why Celeste got into the habit of asking her followers to help choose her outfits, just to wrestle back some agency. Even if ultimately she was just transferring her independence from one master to the other.

Celeste obediently placed the boots near the door and joined Jerome on the couch. She put her wine down next to her computer and took a quick selfie of the two of them to share.

"Thanks a lot for sending a driver this morning," she said flatly, fidgeting with the strap on her dress.

He ignores her. "Abbie said she saw you at the airport?"

"Did she?" Celeste replied. "I didn't see her," she lied. "If she saw me, she should have come and said hi. Why didn't she?"

Jerome took a long sip of his Corona, while picking up and swirling Celeste's wine with his free hand. Celeste reached for it, but he jerked away, keeping it out of arm's reach like the tall kid in the playground with an ironic name like 'Tiny Tim', who on account of his size was destined for bully-hood—not unlike Jerome.

"Not yet," Jerome lectured. "It's airing. It needs to oxidise." He raised the glass to his nose and sniffed the wine—looking every bit the conceited ass he was famous for. "Letting it breathe helps soften the tannins."

Celeste joined him on the couch. "Really—is that right?" She tilted her head. "I thought that's just for young wines?"

Jerome went silent.

"The tannins?" she pushed. "For young wines?"

He finally passed her the glass. "Well, yes—of course it's even more important for maturing wines."

Celeste smirked and sipped the wine, shutting her eyes briefly to enjoy the small win.

While they were closed Jerome pulled out a little teal coloured box from his jacket pocket.

"What's this?" Celeste asked as she opened her eyes again; wishing she hadn't. She went through the motions; untied the shiny ribbon and lifted the lid to find a pair of white-gold earrings from Tiffany.

She shifted her glance from the earrings to Jerome and back again. An entitled expression stared back at her, expecting a thank you. Celeste played her part. "I love them," she said, with all the enthusiasm of a bath plug. She didn't love them. Celeste hated generic brands, second only to generic gestures.

"Thought you might," Jerome said, in a self-congratulatory tone. "Abbie told me they're in fashion right now."

A shiver slivered its way up and down Celeste's spine as she took another sip of her wine to hide her revulsion.

"Put them on; let me see," he demanded. Celeste was still processing that last titbit of information. She did as she was told and modelled them for him. "They really do look good on you," he said, as if she needed his validation.

He stood up, walked over to the mini-bar and grabbed a second Corona. "I'd get you another glass of wine but red is full of calories." Celeste ignored him and poured one for herself as she wandered over to the mirror to see how the ear rings really looked.

"What were you doing this afternoon?" Jerome asked.

"You know what I was doing. I was trying on dresses." Celeste studied herself in the reflection, teasing a rogue strand of hair back into place.

"No, I mean after that. You were offline for three hours. I didn't know where you were. I tried calling a few times but you didn't pick up."

"A few!?" Celeste said. "I had over ten missed calls from you, Jerome."

"Okay, so maybe more than a few, but you're avoiding the question. What were you doing; why didn't you pick up?"

"I was doing nothing. Just hanging around here, waiting for you. And, not that I need an excuse, but my phone was charging in the bathroom—it has the only free socket in this place. Why, what's the big deal?"

"No big deal…"

Celeste knew why he was really asking, but she didn't have the energy to argue.

"I couldn't get a hold of Sam, either? Was he here with you?"

"Sam left here just before I had that nap." She walks into the bathroom. "I've got no idea what he was doing after. Why don't you ask him? He's your friend."

"Why was he asking?" Lanie interrupts, tapping her pen rhythmically on the wooden table.

"He's a control freak," Irene replies. "He wanted to know where she was every second of the day. Hell, it's probably why he invented the Umwelts in the first place—to keep tabs on his girlfriends."

Lanie forces her hand to stop moving.

"He's got two sets of rules: one set for him, and one for her. He says he can't stand being alone, but then he stays in a separate room, in a separate hotel? Gimme a break," Irene scoffs. "He says it was for her.

For her creative process, but I call bullshit. If you ask me, it's so he could do as he pleases without Celeste knowing. She was miserable. I don't blame her for taking the happy pills. I'd do the same if I was her!"

Lanie slowly puts down her pen. "Why didn't she just leave him then—If she was that miserable?"

Irene pushes her chair back as though she's about to get up, but doesn't. "Oh, she tried! He didn't let her," she pauses, "he loved the image of being with her more than her, herself."

"Okay," Lanie leans back.

"And," Irene continues, "he would have never let her embarrass him like that. He's not one to take an 'L', you know?"

Silence fills the space between them before Lanie catches herself tapping her pen again—not entirely sure when she'd picked it up. "Do you think Jerome thought Sam and her had something going on?"

"Maybe," Irene shrugs. "He was anally persistent in wanting to know what they were doing that afternoon."

Lanie wills her hand to stop fidgeting as she weighs up her next question… "Did you know they were pregnant—"

"Ha! No they weren't—who told you that?"

Lanie stays silent.

Irene looks her dead in the eyes. "Oh, you're being serious?" She pulls her hair off her shoulders. "I'm sorry detective, but that's impossible; Celeste was infertile." She leans forward. "Jerome and Celeste were trying for a baby with IVF for years; it never worked. Trust me, there's receipts. In fact, Jerome became obsessed with the idea of being a father. He said some pretty messed up shit to her when the IVF didn't work—called her a barren slut one time, if I remember correctly, which I do, because he's a philandering douchebag. Anyway, why would Celeste be drinking—why would she buy the wine—if she was pregnant? She's selfish, but not like that."

Lanie massages her temples. "Maybe she didn't know she was pregnant? Are you sure she was infertile?"

"Yeah, 100%. Her IVF journey is public knowledge—Google it. Have you been living under a rock or something?"

"Ha," Lanie scoffs; then shrugs. "You could say that. But, sorry. Keep going."

Celeste came back from the bathroom, crashing into Jerome who was waiting for her by the door, staring at his watch. Celeste put on her boots as Jerome corralled her out the door, grabbing the keycard; shutting off the power as they left.

They took the lift down to the lobby, then exited through the front doors to a shallow bow from the doorman. "We're walking—the restaurant's just around the corner," Jerome barked. He headed off, not waiting for a reply. Celeste followed. They navigated their way diagonally through a few blocks and the standard slew of slow walkers and window shoppers at the Paris end of Melbourne.

It only took ten minutes before they reached their

destination: a neon-lit Thai restaurant. There was a long line to get in—not that that meant anything to Jerome.

He walked straight up to the desk. "My name's Jerome Pitt," he said, arrogance seeping out of every syllable. "I'm meeting Marco Vellis. He's inside waiting for me." He looked over the greeter's shoulder, as if she was invisible.

"Of course, Mr Pitt." She turned around and motioned for them to follow her. They did. They weaved their way through the dining room to the back corner, where everyone was waiting for them.

Sam and Abbie were there, along with their host, a guy named Marco. He was a real unit. He had the look of someone who was picked on at school, so went to the gym for the next five years so he could treat people how he didn't want to be treated in some kind of twisted universal revenge.

Lanie raises her eyebrows. "I've had the pleasure of meeting Mr Vellis. He's, um, quite the charmer," she adds, before looking down at her notes by way of encouraging Irene to continue.

"Please, sit," Marco said, opening his palm towards the table.

Celeste stepped around the table and gave Abbie a kiss on the cheek, while staring at both her blonde hair and dress, which mirrored her own.

"Who wore it better, am I right, ladies!?" Marco snorted gratuitously, looking at the two women.

Sam got up and hugged Celeste before pulling out

her chair.

"Waiter, let's get some drinks over here," Marco shouted, twirling his index finger in the air, before launching into a self-indulgent story, waving his arms around as if he was conducting an orchestra.

Celeste smiled and timed her nods to perfection, expertly creating the illusion she cared. He was easy to hate: arrogant, loud and lizard-brained. The dim lighting helped conceal Celeste's repugnance.

The waiter finally returned with their drinks. Celeste poured herself a mojito, before offering Abbie one, who declined. She said it was too sweet for her. Celeste shrugged, ignoring the fact that mojitos aren't even sweet. She stirred her drink and quietly sipped at it as she was forced to listen to Marco drone on.

He was trying to get Jerome to invest in a race horse. His words were like a cheese grater. She chased every superfluous statement with a sip of her mojito. She was a balloon ready to pop. And then she did.

"What do you know about horses?" She levelled her eyes and words at Marco. "It's a fucked-up sport—if you can even call it that. I can't believe kids get a day off of school to watch animals get tortured for entertainment. It's barbaric. Humans, no, men are the real animals!"

Jerome's eyes almost burst out of his head; Sam's looked down as he fidgeted with his cutlery, and Abbie's darted around the table. Celeste didn't care. She abhorred horse racing—she wouldn't have even gone to the Cup if Jerome hadn't made her.

Marco's nostrils flared, doing his best to imitate a horse, before Abbie cleared her throat and thrust her glass in the air. "Cheers!" she said. "To something we can all agree on: men being animals."

Marco swallowed his tongue and pride, and clinked everyone's glasses in the middle of the table. They all took a long sip, and before they'd returned their glasses to the table the waitress appeared with their food.

Irene pauses and Lanie uses it as an opportunity to jump in. "What was Jerome doing at this point?"

"I think he was as shocked as the rest of us. It was a good speech. The screen lit up with floating love hearts and smiley face emojis. Jerome wasn't impressed, though. He hates when he's not in control of the narrative, and an inebriated Celeste is not an easy thing to control."

"Did he do anything?"

"Jerome? Nah nothing. Marco was the one I thought was going to kill her. He was wringing his hands. But what could he do with the world watching? I thought it was a good save by Abbie. She diffused the situation."

Lanie rubs her chin with her right hand and leans back in her chair, signalling for Irene to keep going.

Dinner was served. The spread was amazing. There were chicken spring rolls, beef pad seuw, fish curry, as well as tofu pad Thai and barbequed cauliflower for Celeste and Sam, who were vegetarian—well Celeste was more a flexitarian; she sometimes ate fish, like the tuna sandwich at lunch.

Sam enjoyed the pad Thai a little too much, slinging some onto his white shirt. Desserts followed: coconut panna cotta and trifle. They all enjoyed it, except Sam who didn't eat any of it because of his diabetes.

By the time they'd finished, Celeste's earlier outburst was forgotten. They all got up and left to go to The Hunting Lodge. Marco's car was waiting out the front. He and Jerome kicked the driver out and made him walk, so all five of them could fit in. Celeste wasn't happy, but it's not like she could do anything about it. Not that it was a long walk, anyway. It was literally around the corner.

"Why couldn't she do anything about it?" Lanie asks.

"Ha," Irene laughs. "Let's just say Jerome isn't the kind of man who takes no for an answer."

Lanie scoffs, "I can certainly testify to that."

Irene nods eagerly, not fully across the exposition. "He would always say, 'it's better to be a warrior in a garden, then a gardener in a war.' It's a Bruce Lee quote, I think. He was an intense business bro, that's for sure. But that's the problem, right? Relationships aren't business transactions. But we digress."

They pulled up out the front of The Hunting Lodge hardly five minutes later, and it only took that long because they got caught behind a tram.

They skipped the line, got their arms stamped and walked up five flights of stairs to the rooftop bar, where Marco had booked a private corner. They sat down on an outdoor lounge around a short glass table, laden with full bottles of la-di-da booze. Celeste found a spot in the corner and Abbie sat next to her.

"Celeste," she whispered, nodding towards the bathrooms, "do you need the lady's?"

Celeste promptly got up and they shuffled off to the bathroom together, before triggering an advert for the vodka they were drinking.

Celeste came back online around ten minutes later, talking a million miles an hour.

"But I always thought you hated me!" Abbie said.

"Oh I do!" Celeste replied, candidly. "But that's got nothing to do with you. It's me. If I'm being totally honest with you, which I never thought I would ever be. I'm just jealous."

Abbie almost choked on her drink. "Jealous!? Of me? That's ridiculous. You're my idol. When I hear people say I copy you, it really hurts—I feel like an imposter most of the time; the Wish version of Celeste Simone, you know? That's genuinely what trolls call me online."

Celeste looked at her. "I had no idea. We should hang out more often—we should ditch these assholes and go back to my hotel room—I've got wine!" she joked, as the two laughed light-heartedly together.

"Why the change of heart?" Lanie inquires.

"Now, I'm no detective, but I can only think of one

thing that would inspire two women who don't like each other to go to the bathroom together; then come out of said bathroom BFF's. Celeste even did a backflip with Marco, thanking for his 'hospitality', which I assume is the same thing that magically turned Abbie and Celeste into buddies." Irene takes another sip of her Powerade.

"You're saying they went to the bathroom to do drugs?"

"You said it, not me," Irene responds. "Although, to be totally honest, it seemed to have hit Celeste a lot harder than Abbie. But, then again, Abbie is pretty much always bubbly, so it was hard to tell."

Lanie makes a note; then looks up. "Okay. What happened next?"

Abbie walked off, leaving Celeste with Marco and his buddies at the bar. After a few more drinks, including a shot of half yellow half green Chartreuse, Celeste needed some water.
Sam saw her struggling, so joined her at the bar, poured her a glass and helped her outside to their private table. It was a cool night. Celeste found Jerome's grey jacket hanging over a chair, so she grabbed it and slung it around her shoulders.

"You alright Cel?"

Celeste pursed her lips. "I'll be right," she said in a slightly defensive tone. She knew how to take care of herself. "Have you seen Jerome?" She was slowly regaining lucidity.

Sam rubbed the pad Thai stain on his shirt. "Last I

saw him, he was on level three—or maybe it was two—with Abbie." He was oblivious to how triggering that was to Celeste.

"That bitch!"

"Cel, stay right here. Don't do anything stupid," Sam said, still focussing on the stain. Celeste sat there for a brief eternity, before Sam stood up. "I'm just going to go get some more soda water for this stain. I'll be right back. Stay here."

Celeste nodded, watching as he disappeared into the crowd. As soon as she lost sight of him, she jumped up and went looking for Jerome and Abbie.

She searched every inch of the club before finding the two of them in a corner on the third floor. Jerome's forefinger was gently brushing Abbie's cheek. Abbie was flicking her hair and giggling like a schoolgirl—the Pornhub kind. Their mouths were close—close enough for Celeste to get the wrong idea. Or, the right one.

She rolled her shoulders back and marched over to them, fuelled by both booze and bags. Her fists clenched involuntarily. Her eyes shot lasers. "How could you do this to me!" she screamed.

"Do what?" Jerome replied, projecting innocence with that smarmy smile of his.

"And you!" She turned to Abbie and stared directly into her eyes. "I knew I couldn't trust you, bitch!" The music changed tracks on cue, just as 'bitch' left her mouth, so everyone could hear it.

Before Abbie could respond, Jerome grabbed Celeste's arm and pulled her to the side. "Celeste, calm down, will you. We were just talking—you're acting jealous."

"Her ears aren't in her mouth, you liar!"

Jerome kissed his teeth. "Celeste, stop. Why are you being so crazy?" A crowd had gathered, including Sam and Marco. "Listen to me," he clenched her arm, "nothing is happening."

"Nothing!?" Celeste shrugged free of his grip and crossed her arms.

"It's all in your head. You're being hysterical."

Celeste wasn't falling for his gaslighting. Not this time. She wasn't blind. In fact, the opposite. Thousands of fans saw it, clear as day. She drew a long breath and willed her hands to stop shaking. "I hate you!" she wailed as she turned and left.

"Wait!" Sam called after her. "Let me walk you back to the hotel." Jerome stood in his way.

"Let her go. It's all a big show for her followers, anyway." He turned his back on her, forcing Sam to do the same.

Marco put his arm around Sam's shoulders. "Don't worry about it, she's nuts—all women are," he said, before putting his other arm around Jerome's shoulders and turning them both towards the bar and calling out, "shots!"

Celeste was a hot mess. And she was pissed—drunk and angry. Although, the adrenaline was processing the booze in her system faster than Sam offered his shoulder to cry on. She forced her way out of The Hunting Lodge and stumbled down Bourke street past a crowd or drunks, spilling out of KFC with family sized buckets on their heads. It was late and it was a full moon; the freaks were out. Celeste shouldn't have been walking alone, not in Melbourne. Although, she wasn't really alone as all her followers were there with her.

She bounded down Bourke street, headed for the hotel, when a busker began singing to her. He was singing some boomer song about her boots. The ones Jerome made her wear—he probably put him up to it somehow. She walked over and stopped in front of him to catch her breath.

The busker was an old guy with dreads, which he was constantly tucking behind his ears in between vigorous guitar strums and long drags of his rolled tobacco cigarettes. It was hard to tell whether he was homeless or hipster.

Celeste searched her pockets for cash to give him but couldn't find any. Plot twist: she unbuttoned Jerome's garish grey jacket and dropped it in the hat he'd set aside for donations.

There's no way the busker would ever wear it, but it was a brand name so he could sell it on Marketplace. Celeste gave him a complicit grin, walked off, turned the corner and dashed to her hotel, hugging her arms from the cold.

She got to the hotel, walked straight past the concierge and caught the elevator up to her room. The elevator doors slid open to reveal a giant abstract painting of a demonic looking elephant's face, which dominated the hallway.

Lanie pinballed from wall to wall down the

corridor. She made it to her door, reached into her clutch for the key card, and just when she thought that her night couldn't get any worse, she remembered Jerome had it.

She took a deep breath, mustering all her strength to head back downstairs to ask for a new card, when the lovely room service lady from earlier came to her rescue.

"Are you okay Miss Simone?" she asked in that warm-hug kind of voice, only grandmothers have. "It's okay love. I can open the door for you."

"Thank you," Celeste said in between sobs.

The woman opened the door, folded up a 'do not disturb' sign from her cart and shoved it into the empty card slot so the power would turn on.

"Thank you," Celeste said again, "I'm good now." She walked into her room, shivering from the cold and immediately put the other 'do not disturb' sign —the one from her own room—on the outside door knob.

She walked back into the room and over to the table, poured herself a glass of wine and then turned the heater up full bore.

She turned to the mirror again, like she'd done earlier in the day when she was trying on the dresses.

"Well, it's been another eventful night in the life of Celeste Simone. Thanks for streaming my bin-fire of a day. If it wasn't for you guys, there's no doubt I'd be cancelled, so I just want you to all know: I appreciate you! Love you all!" she said before switching off her live stream for the last time.

TWENTY THREE

"AND THAT'S IT. That's everything I saw."

"Thank you, Irene." Lanie leans back in her chair and cranes her body to one side to stretch out a kink in her neck.

"But just to confirm: you're saying that Jerome was abusive towards Celeste. That he gaslit her?"

Irene leans forward. "Yeah, that's right. It was obvious wasn't it?"

Lanie scratches the back of her head.

"I just hope Celeste doesn't become another statistic, you know." Irene grabs the now-empty bottle of Powerade and stands up. "I'm not saying Jerome fired the proverbial gun, but he was definitely the one holding it, if you know what I mean? He drove her to depression and to drugs, and if they're what lead to her death, well that's on him, isn't it?"

Lanie squints. "We'll see." Her tongue rubs against her front teeth as she packs up her stuff and heads towards the door, cordially escorted out by Irene. "Thanks again."

Lanie walks down the stairs and out the front gate onto the sidewalk. It's a busy tree-lined street with a row of boutique shops, hole-in-the-wall cafes and run-of-the-mill restaurants. She's got some time to kill before her flight so decides to wander around for a bit before ordering an Uber. The only other time Lanie visited Adelaide was with Brett. They came for Thomas's baby moon, spending a week up in the McLaren Vale. They had massages. Lanie got a facial and it was delightful. Brett's full body massage not so much. He got a big oafish man as his masseuse who breathed through his mouth the whole time. He couldn't wait to get out of there. In hindsight visiting a region known for wine and cheese wasn't the best idea for a pregnant person. It was beautiful though; probably the last time she and Brett were ever really, truly happy together.

Lanie walks down the street and ducks into the first cafe she crosses. It's a typical Italian joint, decorated in Ferrari paraphernalia, with pictures of the old Adelaide Formula One Grand Prix proudly hung on the wall. It's just past 11 a.m., and the tables are starting to fill up with people, grabbing an early lunch. The salivating smell of pizza permeates the air.

Lanie steps up to the counter. "One long black please, take away."

The barista rings up her order; she pays and finds a spot out of the way of the busied waiters and waitresses marching in and out of the kitchen with baskets of herb bread and deep bowls of pasta.

Abbie still hasn't phoned me back. Lanie's now past the point of thinking she's intentionally avoiding her. She calls her while she waits for her coffee. The phone rings out yet again, going to message bank. *Fuck me—she's on the run.* Lanie's unable to abate the suspicion that comes with Abbie's absence. She leaves another message—not mincing her words this time.

"Hey Abbie, Detective Daniels here. You need to call me back immediately."

She sighs and runs her hand through her hair. "I need to tell Jon about this, get him to file a missing person's—"
"Long black for Lanie!"
"Yep!" Lanie raises her hand and grabs it from him. As she does her phone vibrates. It's a message from Abbie.

Sorry I keep missing you detective. I've been on a digital detox. Call you back in ten.

Nothing to worry about. Lanie inhales. She puts her phone back in her pocket and leaves the cafe. She turns left down a side street, past a charming old movie theatre, advertising movies that are decades old, looking for a quiet place to take the call.
The street conveniently leads to a large, grassy public square. She crosses the road and finds a shady spot under a tree, clearing away a bunch of empty cream charger bulbs and putting them in the bin, which belie the big, fancy houses that border the perimeter.
Lanie sits and waits, leaning against a giant

eucalyptus tree, taking tiny sips of her piping hot coffee.

Ten minutes pass and nothing.

University students pass by, backpacks hanging low, wearing them like she used to when she was their age.

Fifteen minutes; still nothing.

A few people in suits, who must work nearby, find comfy spots on the grass, sit cross-legged, open up their Tupperware containers and tuck into last night's spaghetti leftovers.

Twenty minutes now.

That's enough time. Lanie brings her phone up to her face to video call Abbie. It rings. And rings. And just as she's about to cancel the call, Abbie picks up.

"I'm here, detective, I'm here!"

"Abbie, hello. Good to finally catch you." Lanie's caught a little off guard that she finally picked up. "Sorry, I couldn't wait any longer. I have a plane to catch back to Melbourne soon," Lanie apologises, without needing to.

"No problem, detective."

"Does your camera work?" Lanie asks, staring at an unmoving thumbnail image of Abbie, along with her own talking face in the top right corner. Abbie has brown hair in the image, but even with brown hair she and Celeste could pass as sisters. Lanie could only imagine what she'd look like with blonde hair.

"Wait, let me try." Nothing happens. "There, did that work?"

"It didn't." Lanie stares at the inanimate thumbnail. "I still don't see you."

"Hmm, I'm not sure, then. I think there's something wrong with my camera. We can still voice chat, though, can't we—is that okay?"

Lanie nods her head. "It'll have to be."

"Great. How can I help you, detective? Sorry I've taken so long to call you back. I've been on this digital detox, only an hour out of Melbourne, up in Daylesford since last Monday. I needed to get away after what happened. It is just tragic what happened to Celeste—I hope you're able to find that busker who did it!" she rambles before Lanie even gets a word in.

How does she know about the busker? "You're right. It is, and I just have a few questions about that night. I believe you were with her the night of her death—"

"Yes."

"Right, so you, along with Jerome Pitt, Sam Bateman and Marco Vellis were all out to dinner together, followed by drinks at The Hunting Lodge, correct?"

"That's correct. We all went out for dinner to a Thai restaurant and then to The Hunting Lodge afterwards."

"And when was the last time you saw Celeste?"

"She was having a psychotic episode, running out of The Hunting Lodge, just after she caught me and Jerome together."

Lanie sips her now-luke-warm long black.

"You still there, detective?"

Lanie swallows and clears her throat. "Yes, still here, sorry, I was just taking a sip of my coffee."

"How would you describe your and Celeste's relationship?"

"We, um, we, you could say we were colleagues. The media liked to present us as enemies, or whatever, and we may not have been best friends per se, but we were, yeah, professional acquaintances—let's call it that."

Lanie chews the insides of her cheeks. "Was she threatened by your rising popularity—you almost have as many followers as her now, don't you?"

"Celeste Simone? Threatened?" Abbie scoffs in disbelief. "No, I don't think so. Plus, I think she still has hundreds of thousands more fans, so I don't think she's too worried—or that I was even close."

"Okay," Lanie replies, moving on. "I've got multiple witnesses telling me you and Celeste frequented the bathrooms together many times at The Hunting Lodge, is that right?"

"I don't know, did we? We may have. I don't remember going to the bathroom any more than usual on a night out." She sounds skittish.

"Sure, but, did you always go together?"

"Yeah, I don't know about every time, but definitely sometimes."

"And was there any partaking of illegal substances that I should know about?" Lanie cuts to the chase.

Silence.

"Need I remind you that if you lie you could be charged for perjury?"

"I understand." There's another brief pause. "We were doing cocaine in the bathroom. It was her idea."

Lanie draws a deep breath. "And where'd you get it from?"

"I don't know, detective, it was Celeste's. I assume she got it from Marco, though."

Lanie taps her free hand's forefinger against her cheek.

"Okay, and you're sure the last time you saw Celeste was at the bar. She didn't invite you back to her hotel?"

"What!? Where'd you get that idea? I would never invite her back to my hotel!"

"Right, but did she invite you back to hers?"

Abbie clears her throat. "Not that I recall," she answers nervously. "Even if she had, why would I go back there, after the way she spoke to me?"

"Okay. So, what did you do after Celeste left The Hunting Lodge, then?"

"Nothing, really. I left the boys and went home to my hotel, the Hilton; said goodnight to my fans, then took a long, hot shower before going to bed."

"And these rumours about you and Jerome having an affair," Lanie continues, "were they true—is there any substance to them?"

It was Abbie's turn to go quiet.

"Abbie, are you still there?"

"They're true," Abbie sighs. "It was evident, wasn't it?"

Lanie finishes her coffee and nestles the empty cup

into the grass. "Evident, how? By all accounts Jerome kept it secret from Celeste."

"Yeah, but she wasn't stupid. She knew. Shit, I dyed my hair blonde just like hers for Jerome—because he told me to; that's what he likes. Talk about a dead give-away."

Lanie leans back against the tree, rubbing her jaw. "Did you love Jerome?"

There's another long silence.

"I guess I did," Abbie finally concedes. "But I don't anymore."

Lanie ignores the qualification. "And when Jerome didn't come to your defence at The Hunting Lodge, how did that make you feel?"

"It doesn't matter, does it? What matters is how Celeste felt. She was the one who just found out her husband was cheating on her, which drove her to suicide—even if it was by the hand of a random busker."

"Sure, but it must have made you feel something?" Abbie takes short, rapid breaths.

"Did Jerome promise you he'd break up with Celeste?" Lanie's seen this narrative play out a million times before.

"No, never! This isn't some crime novel, detective, and I'm not some jilted lover."

"No?" Lanie leans forward. "Then tell me, if you've been on a digital detox since Monday, how do you know about the busker?"

There is another long pause. Lanie thinks Abbie's going to hang up.

"Sam told me."

"Sam!?"

"Yeah, he left me a message. I listened to it just before I sent you that text before."

"I didn't know you and Sam were friends?"

"No, I guess we're not. But he thought I should know, considering we were the last people to see Celeste alive."

Lanie throws her head back. "Did Sam like her?"

"Of course he did—everyone did."

Lanie re-phrases the question. "Yes, but was he in love with her, then?"

"I, ah, I maybe," Abbie scrambles.

"Okay Abbie, I'm going to need you to come back to town for me, just in case we need to talk again. Can you do that?"

"I honestly just want to leave this mess behind me, detective—it has nothing do to with me."

"And you can, as soon as the investigation is over," Lanie says. "I can send a police car to pick you up if you need?"

"That won't be necessary. I can make my own way back to the city."

"Great, thank you. I look forward to talking to you again in real life."

As she's about to hang up, Abbie stops her. "Wait! If you think Sam had anything to do with anything, you're wrong. He wouldn't hurt a fly—he's a good man," she says. "You may not believe this, detective, but Celeste and I, we're not that different—we're both victims here. I'm just lucky Jerome didn't drive me to the places he drove Celeste! At the end of the day, that prick played both of us."

"Maybe," Lanie says. "Let me know when you're back in town."

Lanie presses the disconnect button, navigates to her Uber app and orders a car to take her back to the airport—it'll be there in 5 minutes.

In the meantime, she brings her phone up again, types The Hunting Lodge into a google search and calls them. "Time to see this place for myself."

TWENTY FOUR

LANIE ARRIVES BACK in Melbourne around 4 p.m. and catches an Uber to The Hunting Lodge. She has a hunch she wants to investigate. Her phone rings. It's Jon. She picks up. "Hey Jon, what's up?"

"Lanie," he replies by way of hello. "Any trouble at the airport?"

"Ha, nah, not this time. It only seems to happen in Sydney," Lanie replies, referring to the stolen identity thing.

"That's good to hear," Jon says. "But, tell me, how'd the last witness go, what's her name?"

"Her name's Irene, and her take was… enlightening. Would you believe Jerome and Celeste may not have had the fairy tale relationship he lets on?"

Jon clears his throat. "You're saying he could've done it?"

"Maybe. I'm still not sure I'd go that far, but I'm definitely getting closer to the truth. I finally got a hold of Abbie Benson-Wheeler, too. Turns out she and Jerome were having an affair behind Celeste's back." Lanie stares out the window of her Uber at the Melbourne Eye.

"Figures," he says. "Just a friendly reminder that

time's almost up. I need you to wrap this case up 'yesterday', because Jerome's got some powerful friends putting pressure on me to call it an accidental OD and be done with it, which without any hard evidence to the contrary does sound like it's the likely situation."

"No evidence? The hell, Jon!" Lanie scoffs. "Didn't you just hear me—Jerome and Abbie were having an affair?"

The captain clears his throat. "That doesn't exactly mean he murdered his wife."

"No, but maybe she did!"

Silence.

"Find me proof, then, and stat."

"Fuck," Lanie says away from the phone, before putting it back on her ear. "Just one more day, Jon! I'm so close—I can feel it. Bateman's got something to do with this, as well. There was another key card, and he had it!"

"Alright, alright," Jon says. "One more day; then that's it."

Lanie hangs up, just as the Uber pulls up out the front of The Hunting Lodge. The logo above the door matches the washed-out stamp she saw on Celeste's wrist.

"Thanks," Lanie says to the driver as she shuffles out of the back seat.

"No worries, have a good day," he replies. The prices were surging, so he's chuffed with the fare. Lanie would be livid paying the $130 if she wasn't charging it back to the department. If the captain approves it, that is.

She gets out, walks through the unlocked front door and up the stairs to the first floor, where there's a familiar looking bartender polishing glasses.

"Hi," Lanie begins, "I'm detective Lanie Daniels of the Victorian Police. I called earlier asking if I could poke around. It's in relation to the Celeste Simone investigation."

The bartender nods. He's in his early twenties, middle part, wearing baggy jeans and a corduroy shirt. "Yep, I know, no worries. Do you need anything from me?" he asks. "You want a drink or something?"

Lanie nods. "Yeah, a glass of still water would be good," she says, opening and shutting her mouth widely, trying to pop her ears from the flight.

The bartender grabs a freshly polished highball glass, spins it around against the palm of his right hand so it's the right way up, grabs the soda gun and pours her a glass of water. The two of them watch the water trickle out slowly. When the glass is three quarters full the bartender scoops up some ice from the well and slings it in, before slapping it on the drink mat on the bar and squeezing a fresh lime into it.

"Thanks." Lanie reaches for it and takes a sip. "Also, can I go upstairs to the rooftop bar?"

"Yep, one sec, let me take you." He grabs a lanyard of keys hanging off a bent nail in the doorway that leads behind the bar. "This way, follow me." He walks around the bar and Lanie follows. They climb another couple of flights of stairs, and come out on the fifth floor. The bartender leads her past an empty bar and over to a glass door, which he unlocks, pushes open and wedges a handful of bar coasters under so it stays that way. "There you go," he says. "I'll be downstairs if you need me."

"Thanks." Lanie steps outside, covering her eyes with her left hand from the sharp glare bouncing off the monotone city buildings. She steps out and finds herself standing on the rooftop of the bar, which she was looking down on from Celeste's room last week. Her hunch was correct. That's also why the bartender looked familiar. He was the one out here cleaning the bar mats.

"I knew it!" She looks up at The Grand Theatre Hotel and pulls her phone out to call them.

After a few rings the concierge picks up. "Grand Theatre Hotel Melbourne, my name's Simon, how can I help you?"

"Hello, this is Detective Daniels, I'm leading the Celeste Simone investigation."

"Hello detective—I know who you are, we met last week. How can I help?"

"This is a weird request, but can you please send someone up to Celeste's room, and get them to swing the curtains backwards and forwards for me?"

The concierge pauses, wondering whether to ask why or skip the small talk because he really doesn't care. He opts for the latter. "Of course; I'll do it myself. When do you need that done by?"

"Right now!"

Pause.

"So you want me to go up to her room and swing the curtains backwards and forwards?"

"You got it!" Lanie replies. "Call me back on this number to let me know when you're about to do it, please."

"Okay, give me five minutes."

"Thank you, Simon—I'll see you shortly."

"See me? Never mind." He hangs up.

"Detective Daniels," Sam Bateman calls out tentatively from behind her.

"Fuck!" Lanie jumps in the air, making a kung-fu motion with her hands, despite never having done kung-fu in her life. "Seriously. You scared the living bejesus out of me!" she says. "You need to wear a cat bell or something. Far out, man."

"I'm sorry Detective, I didn't mean to—"

Lanie catches her breath and calms her nerves. "It's fine. Don't worry about it." She shakes it off. "What are you even doing here, Mr Bateman?"

"I lost my glasses, so thought I'd come and check here." He's looking behind a big pot plant. "But it doesn't look like they're here."

"You don't mean the glasses currently on your face, do you?"

Sam chuckles. "No, detective, these are a spare pair."

"Okay. It's good that you're here actually. I had some questions for you. Do you mind if I can get half an hour of your time now, after you've looked for your glasses, to save a trip later?"

He checks his smart watch. "Yeah, that should be fine." He brings his hand up to cover his eyes from the glare, like Lanie. "Would it be easier if we went inside?"

Lanie's phone rings.

"Simon?" She pulls it to her ear.

"Yep, it's me. I'm in the room."

"Great, now I want you to go over to the blinds and just swing them back and forward."

Lanie turns and addresses Sam. "We will; I just want to see something first."

Sam follows her gaze and looks up to the adjacent building. Both their eyes are drawn to a room with the blinds being vigorously swung back and forward. Celeste's room. The person doing the swinging stops and spots both Sam and Lanie looking up at him, hands shielding their eyes.

"Is that you, down there?"

"Sure is. Thanks for doing that."

He waves to them with his free hand, then turns away from the window. "No worries. Is that all you need?"

"It is. Thanks again," Lanie says before remembering something. "Actually wait! I do have one more question for you: what time did you say Celeste got back to the hotel, again?"

He stops and thinks. "From memory, it was around 10 p.m. Why?"

"When we last spoke, you said it was eleven?"

Silence.

"If I said eleven, it must've been eleven, then."

"Alright," Lanie says. "And you definitely talked to her?"

"Yep. Definitely—hundred percent."

"And it was definitely her?"

"Well, yeah, unless there was another blonde in a yellow dress that looked just like her, I'd say it was her!"

Abbie! Lanie thinks. *Shit—there's your proof, Jon!* "Okay. Well, thanks again for going up to her room for me just now—appreciate it." Lanie hangs up the phone and files the Abbie revelation for later.

Sam's still staring up at the window. "Interesting, isn't it?" Lanie says. "While you were all down here partying, Celeste was just there," Lanie points, "all alone, having a heart attack." She turns towards the door. "Now, let's go inside, out of this damn sun."

Sam wipes his spare pair of glasses on his shirt, turns and follows her back down to the second floor where the bartender's now re-stocking the fridges. Lanie walks over to the bar and grabs her water.

"You don't mind if we sit here for twenty to thirty minutes, do you?" Lanie asks him, leaning over while pointing to the booths to the right of the bar.

"Go for it," he says, as he punches an empty Corona box and folds it in on itself.

They take a seat at one of the booths. The bar doubles as an American Diner during the week, so the table is set with placemat menus and mismatched cutlery.

"Thanks for sending that shortlist last week, too, by the way. The witnesses have shed a tonne of light on what happened that day, and the dynamics of your friendship group."

"Glad I could help." Sam slides into the booth and sits directly opposite Lanie.

"One of them doesn't like you, that's for sure. If I didn't know any better, I'd say he was even jealous of you and your relationship with Celeste." Lanie's trying to elicit a reaction, but failing.

"I don't think anyone is jealous of me, detective."

"Hmm, maybe not," Lanie shrugs.

"It must be hard for you to be back here?"

"It is."

"Because?"

"Because here is the last place I saw Celeste alive." He passes her little 'gotcha' test.

"That is despite having a key to her room?"

Sam's mouth twitches.

"And Sam, and this doesn't look good for you, I know exactly where Jerome and Marco were at the time of Celeste's death, but I just can't seem to place you."

He draws a deep breath, then leans forward. "Well, unlike Jerome and his new best friend, Marco, I didn't quite feel up to partying after what happened, so I went back to my room, alone. That's the truth." His voice shakes. "And the key?" he asks. "Well, I thought the busker had the key, didn't he?"

"That's true," Lanie says. "The busker had one of the keys, but I believe you kept a second one after helping Celeste check-in?"

Sam straightens the placemat in front of himself

so it's perfectly symmetrical to the table. "Oh, I, ah," he stammers. His brain scrambles for an answer. "You know, I think you're right. I'm replaying it in my head and the concierge did put two keys in the envelope when we checked-in, but I completely forgot about the second one. It's probably still in my pocket," he says. "But I never went back there after I left her in the morning," he stumbles over his words. "Here, or just downstairs, is the last time I saw Celeste alive. I swear."

Lanie shifts in her seat, trying to get comfy. "I've got a statement saying it was you who called the police from the hotel?" Lanie's head nods towards the adjacent building.

"Yeah, that's correct."

"So, what were you doing there that morning, Mr Bateman?"

"I was there to see if Celeste was okay," he says defensively. "I'd tried calling the whole day before. When she didn't pick up, I thought it was because she was mad at me. But after another night passed and I still hadn't heard from her, and she hadn't posted anything on social media, I thought I'd check up on her." He bites his bottom lip.

"And then?"

"And then I got there and the concierge remembered me from when we checked-in, so agreed to take me up to her room. We went upstairs, I knocked on the door; there was no response, and then the smell hit us," he says, swallowing hard. "The smell." His face suddenly goes pale. "I'll never forget the smell." He draws a deep breath. "We knocked again before the concierge used his master key to open the door; then I walked in, and I saw her in the bath," he says. "It didn't even look like her. I mean, it was her—they made me ID her—but it hardly looked like her. The water it made her look different."

Lanie looks at him, her thoughts oscillating between empathy and suspicion.

"That's when I called triple zero and the police and paramedics came, but it was too late. We'd found her too late." He's breathing through his teeth.

"Will you excuse me for a moment, I need to use the bathroom." He slides out of the booth, standing up and pacing to the bathroom—not waiting for permission.

"Sure." Lanie leans back in her cushioned chair. While he's gone Lanie opens her emails on her phone and absently marks all the spam emails as read.

Sam returns a few minutes later with the look of someone who's splashed water on their face.

"Do you need more time?" Lanie offers.

"Thank you, but I'm okay. Let's keep going; get it over with," he says, holding his cool hand over his flushed cheek.

"If you're sure." Lanie sips her water, giving him some time, anyway, before she clears her throat. "Okay, so, I've got witnesses saying that you went to chase after Celeste after her and Jerome's altercation, is that right?"

"Yeah I did," Sam confirms. "But I think chase is a strong word; I offered to walk her back to her hotel—that's all." He looks down at the table, instinctively lining up the knife and fork in front of him. "But she didn't want that; so, I let her go by herself, thinking it would help clear her head—I wish I didn't. I really wish I didn't."

"Did Jerome actually physically stop you from following her?"

"Yes. He, he, um, can be—"

"Don't mind me," the bartender says, putting an unlit tea light candle in the middle of their table, before doing the same with the next table and then the next, setting up for the night's service.

Lanie turns back to Sam. "What kind of relationship did you and Celeste have, Mr Bateman?"

"We were friends," he replies. "I would see her a lot because I would see Jerome a lot."

"Just friends?" Lanie pulls the lime wedge out of her glass and squeezes it again.

Sam's breathing becomes shorter. "Sorry, detective," he says. "Just give me a second to gather my thoughts so I can give you the answers you deserve."

He looks down at the table and then back up at Lanie. "Celeste and I were just friends, but sometimes I would see us as maybe more, but I never acted on it. And let's be honest, she was out of my league." His phone rings. He looks down at the name on his screen and his eyes widen. "Sorry, I need to take this, just give me two minutes." He gets up and walks over to the window.

While he's gone, Lanie quickly reaches over to his cutlery and messes them around a bit, before sitting back in her chair again.

Sam finishes his call, comes back and sits down.

"How about you and Jerome? Would you say you were friends?"

"Yes, of course," Sam scoffs nervously.

"Even though he purchased your share of Umwelt before it sold for millions?"

Sam looks up at Lanie and meets her eyes for the first time. "I know where this is going, detective. I've read the articles: that Jerome had already made a deal to sell the business before buying me out. But the truth is even if that was true, if it wasn't for him, I wouldn't have gotten the money together in time for my mum's treatment. By buying me out, he literally helped save my mum's life. So, even if he profited a little more—"

"A lot more!"

"Sure," Sam says. "Even if he made all the money in the world, I wouldn't change a thing. I wouldn't swap my mum's life for anything, let alone money. So, yes, I know Jerome's an opportunist—he always has been. And I could be mad at him, so raving mad that I'd murder his wife—if I'm picking up what you're implying—but I'm not. I'm grateful. My mum's alive because of him." He looks down and straightens up the cutlery again.

Good speech. But he's hiding something. Lanie picks up her glass of water. "Did Celeste ever tell you she was on the antidepressant, Mirtazapine?"

"Mirtazapine?" Sam repeats uneasily. An unease that betrays his ignorance.

"That's right." Lanie places her glass back down without taking a sip. "What aren't you telling me, Sam?" She uses his first name.

Sam's eyes dart around looking for refuge. "Celeste was on a lot of different drugs for her depression; I'm not sure I remember that one in particular, though," he confesses, despite his body language saying otherwise.

"And what about Abbie?"

"Abbie?" Sam covers his mouth. "What about her?" Something in his voice proves Lanie had pulled the right thread.

"Jerome told me she went to him for help with her own depression. Do you know what medication she was on?"

Sam thinks before he answers. "Ah! I knew I'd heard that name before! You're right, detective. Abbie was on Mirtazapine, not Celeste."

"You're sure?"

"Yes, I'm sure. She went to Jerome for help. He got her a doctor and the doctor prescribed them to her." He swallows. "I know because Jerome got me to fill the script so the media wouldn't find out."

Shit shit shit! Lanie's mind is spinning. *Abbie's antidepressants were in Celeste's body and Sam had a script for them!*

"Are you and Abbie friends, Mr Bateman?"

Sam looks at Lanie quizzically. "Not really. I only

know about her depression because Jerome told me. Otherwise I've never really spoken to her. I mean, apart from small talk at parties like the other night, but otherwise, nope, I really wouldn't call us friends."

"So you didn't contact her the other day to let her know about the busker?"

Sam screws up his face. "No," he says. "I haven't seen her since the night we all went to dinner. Jerome said she's gone off grid on a digital detox, or something—can't blame her, really. I wouldn't be surprised if we never see her again."

"Okay." Lanie rubs her chin.

Sam's phone rings again.

"Sorry detective." Sam stands up, checking his watch. "Do you have any more questions, because I really need to get back to work now."

Lanie looks up at Sam. "No, that's all for now, Mr Bateman. But please keep your phone close in case any more comes to mind."

"Of course. And I'll see you tomorrow, anyway, detective."

"Huh?" Lanie squints.

"At the mediation with your ex-husband for the custody of your son," Sam qualifies. "Jerome's got me coming along with the new evidence."

Lanie finishes her water with a loud gulp. "Oh, yes. I almost forgot," she says. *Too late to tell Jon now.* "What even is this evidence I keep hearing about? It'd be nice to know before tomorrow—not a huge fan of being left in the dark."

"I wish I could tell you more, but Jerome's told me not to say anything until the meeting. If nothing else, he's a showman. But I will tell you this: it will get your son back."

TWENTY FIVE

IT'S TUESDAY AFTERNOON, just over a week after Celeste's death; the day of the mediation. If it was Jerome and Sam's intention to draw Lanie's attention away from the case, then this is about the only thing in the world that would do it. As Lanie pulls up to the courthouse, she sees Thomas waiting out the front with Brett. *What's he doing here? He should be at school.* Thomas spots her, untangles himself from his dad's tight grip, and runs over.

She climbs out of her car and hugs him.

Brett takes a step to follow Thomas before realising he's headed towards Lanie. Their eyes meet.

"Brett," she says, by way of a hello. He's wearing a light grey suit with a white shirt and blue tie. He's probably come from work. He's a financial advisor. Him and his private school buddies all are. Whenever Lanie asked them what they actually do, she was invariably met with a string of words that barely made sense in the order they were spoken. In the end she simply rationalised it as a bunch of old-school-tie boys creating obnoxiously fictional jobs, as a way to pass around their old money while appearing to be active members of society.

Every Sunday afternoon he and his buddies would stand by the barbeque chatting incessantly about the stock market, or crypto, while she entertained their trophy wives. *Don't miss those days.* The stock market: straight white man's astrology, her mum calls it.

He's standing next to his lawyer. She's young-ish, brunette, wearing a dark blue power suit. A Birkin bag hangs nonchalantly off her shoulder. She's the total package. *Brett has probably fucked her.* She offers Lanie her hand, along with a wave of heady perfume.

"Tracy," she says. The name comes as a sucker-punch to Lanie. He has fucked her. It's the same girl that was around his house at the weekend, and in all the photos on Facebook. Lanie forces a smile and takes her hand. She's shook. Brett doesn't offer the same courtesy. In fact, after his initial hello he hasn't looked at her. He's not happy about being back here. She can't blame him.

Lanie picks up Thomas who's still holding onto her leg, and the four of them make their way inside. A receptionist is waiting.

"Hey little man. Do you like colouring in?" she asks Thomas. He nods shyly, still half hidden behind Lanie's leg. The receptionist pulls out a brand-new Spider-Man colouring-in pack and hands it to him. "I bet you can't stay within the lines," she challenges him, as she leads him to the corner of the waiting room. Thomas rips open the pack and gets stuck in. "Now, if you'd like to follow me," she says to the three grown-ups. She shows them through to a small boardroom, where Becca's waiting.

"What are we doing here, Lanie?" Brett asks sharply, making no effort to hide his contempt. He takes a seat on one side of a long, rectangular table.

Lanie takes her seat on the other side, directly opposite him. The seating arrangement is intentionally confrontational. The room is modest, bordering on claustrophobic. but that may be due to the context. It smells like a year seven classroom, and looks the same. There's a single open window, and a white board with legalese scribbled all over it.

"Seriously, what the hell am I doing here?" Brett asks frankly, the palms of his hands facing upwards. "She," he points at Lanie, "picked my son up from school in that old car of hers, drunk. So, unless that piece of shit car has magically become a time machine and you've used it to stop yourself from getting loaded and putting my son in danger, I don't see what's changed."

Lanie looks over to Becs searchingly. The truth is she doesn't actually know what's changed either. And she was beginning to have deep regrets about accepting Jerome's help. *Too late to turn back now.* But she'd do anything to get Thomas back, even if that means making a deal with the devil—which it probably has. *How does the saying go? Ask forgiveness not permission. Jon will understand. It's all for Thomas.* Lanie's tongue starts rubbing nervously against her front teeth.

There's a knock at the door. The receptionist's head

pokes through the gap. "Mr Jerome Pitt is here."

"Who?" Brett snaps.

Jerome strides through the door with his trademark swagger, and Sam in tow. "Sorry I'm late," he says as he walks inside and takes a seat on Lanie's side of the table. Jerome's entrance is impressive, like always. The room does a double take of Sam. They look at him then at Brett. Then at him. Then at Brett. Brett looks like Sam, if Sam went on a reality show and had one of those make-overs. He's the Clark Kent to Brett's Superman.

Becca cups her mouth and whispers, "no wonder you've got it in for him." Up until now, Lanie had hardly noticed the resemblance. *Sure, maybe if you squint.*

"What I miss?" Jerome asks, with his easy charm.

Tracy clears her throat. "My client wants to know what has changed since the last time this went to arbitration," she says evenly. "Miss Daniels here," she motions towards Lanie with an open hand, "unequivocally demonstrated her inability to take care of a child when she was caught driving under the influence with her son in the car. Putting it bluntly: she's an alcoholic. And a danger to that little boy out there." She points to Thomas in the other room, busy colouring-in a picture of Spider-Gwen.

"Recovering!" Lanie interjects. "And we didn't crash. It was just a little bump; no harm came to Thomas."

Jerome stands up. "Looks like our timing is impeccable." He looks at Sam, giving him an actionable nod. Sam nods back and pulls out his laptop.

"We have obtained Umwelt footage I think we should all watch together."

Lanie cocks her head sideways, looking at Becca.

"Some of it will look familiar, as it's the same footage Brett showed during the initial hearing, except he conveniently edited some parts out. Didn't you, Brett?" Jerome looks right at him. "And," he continues, "before Sam plays it, I must apologise to everyone for not sharing it sooner. We only just managed to secure it last night."

Sam rotates his laptop so everyone can see the screen. He hits the spacebar and the video plays.

The video is grainy. It's not exactly original. It's from Brett's point of view—Lanie had always wondered why he'd conveniently been recording that day. There's a time code in the corner. It's the day Lanie was caught drink-driving with Thomas in the car. Brett is looking at Lanie who is at the kitchen bench reading some case files.

"Fast forward for me Sam," Jerome asks. Sam reaches his arms around and fast forwards a few minutes.

Lanie walks over to Brett and gives him a kiss on the cheek. "I'll pick up Thomas today," she says, before walking out of the room. Brett springs to action. He darts around the bench to the pantry, pulls out a bottle of Smirnoff vodka and tops up Lanie's drink with it. We hear a toilet flush; Brett quickly returns the vodka to the pantry and runs around, reaching his side of the bench just as Lanie returns.

Jerome leans over and stops the video.

Lanie is trembling. The blood has drained from her face. "What. did. you. do!?" She's breathing rapidly through her teeth.

Brett looks up at Jerome. "What the fuck is this? This never happened." He turns and faces Lanie. "Lanie, look at me. You know me. You may hate me right now, but you know I would never do this. Never."

His lawyer intervenes, stopping him before he can say any more.

Lanie's seething—she wills both hands to stop shaking, but they refuse. "What did you do?" she repeats. "You, you, psychopath!"

Becca puts her arm around Lanie. "Easy, Lanes," she says. Jerome sits back down while Sam nervously avoids eye contact, fastidiously making sure his laptop is lined up with the desk.

"Wait," Brett says suddenly, turning to Jerome. "I thought your company doesn't save videos, let alone access them without permission. Where's all that talk about privacy now, you lying son of a bitch?"

Jerome was expecting this response. "This is obviously not original Umwelt footage." He straightens his tie. "You weren't running the latest security software which made it easy for hackers to tap into your account, and sell your archived videos on the dark web." Jerome stops and takes a long sip of water, letting his statement linger. "Nothing is ever truly deleted with the blockchain," he adds. "This is why we recommend turning on two-factor authentication, which our records clearly show you didn't." He sits down, pulling together the two lapels of his suit jacket.

"I think that's enough for one day," Brett's lawyer addresses the room but is looking squarely at Jerome.

"Agreed," he says, returning her stare. She flushes under his gaze, looks down and tucks her hair behind her right ear, before gathering her folder and making her way out with Brett close behind.

Lanie was silent, except for her continued short, sharp breathing. Her tongue was furiously making circles against her front teeth. She couldn't believe it. This whole time she'd blamed herself; punished herself, and it was Brett's doing all along. At least ten minutes pass as Lanie sits there in shock. "Where's Thomas?" She sits up straight.

"Brett took him home," Becs replies. "Probably for the last time."

Becs gets out of her chair and kneels down in front of Lanie, resting her hands on her knees. "Lanie, with this new footage, you're not just going to see Thomas more. You're going to see him all the time. This'll get you sole custody. In fact, Brett may be looking at jail time for what he did. Unlikely, based on who his friends are—he'll probably buy his way out of it—but you never know—God knows he should!"

Lanie looks up at Jerome, who'd stepped over to the window. "Mr Pitt. I don't know what to say."

"Call me Jerome for a start," he says. "Mr Pitt's my father. Plus, after all we've been through, I think we can use each other's first names."

"Yes, of course, Jerome. Thank you. Thank you. How can I ever repay you?"

Jerome turns to her. "It's my pleasure Lanie—and you don't need to repay me. It's been a long week for both of us. Thank you for letting me help you with this. If only Celeste had let me help her, maybe she'd still be alive—"

Knock knock.

He's cut-off by a gentle rapping at the door.

It's the receptionist. She walks in with drinks and a tray of Turkish Delights from the Persian cafe across the road. "Here are your coffees." She steps towards Jerome and Sam. They ordered them on their way in. "One double ristretto for Jerome," she says, holding up the disposable cup to the light and twisting it, reading his name on the side written in Sharpie. "And a flat white for Sam with Equal sugar."

She turns to Lanie. "Miss Daniels, can I get you a coffee?"

Lanie freezes before forcing herself to respond. "No nothing for me." Her mind's racing at the mention of Equal sugar. She draws a deep breath. *It was Sam's Equal. His diabetes! It was right there all along. He was the other person in that room.*

"How's the case going? Jerome asks. "Jon tells me your investigation is done?"

"Ah, yeah, yep..." Lanie replies, wanting to get out of there. "Actually, we have a new suspect."

She catches Jerome off guard. "What? Is that right? I thought we'd all agreed it was an OD?"

"No, I mean, yes, we do have a new suspect. Now if you'll excuse me, I've got to get back to it, actually. But thank you again, Mr Pitt. Really." She gets up to leave, avoiding Sam's gaze. "Thanks for all this." Her eyes dart around the room.

"Are you okay, you've turned white as a ghost?" Jerome asks.

"Yep, it's just all this stuff with Brett. It's a lot to process." She looks over at Becca. "Hey, Becs!"

Becca pauses the video, which she'd gone over to watch again, and looks up.

"Can you walk me to my car, please?" Lanie wants to get her away from Sam.

"Sure," Becca shrugs her shoulders.

"Thanks again," Lanie says to Jerome, as she and Becca walk out of the room.

"Seeya guys," Becca says cheerily, giving them two thumbs up. "Top work with that video!"

"You're welcome." Jerome smiles a lop-sided smile, picking up on the change of energy.

They exit the room, Lanie grabs Becca's arm and drags her out of the building.

"Lanes! What are you doing—what's up with you?"

"It's Sam. He murdered Celeste Simone."

"He what? How do you know?"

"Long story, that I don't have time to tell you right now. Just trust me. I need to get back to the station and tell Jon, and I don't want you anywhere near those two."

"Of course. I trust you."

"Alright, good—I'll call you later." Lanie dashes over to her car. She slides in, dials Captain Bailey's number, and puts him on speaker. She pulls out and starts driving to the station. He picks up. "Jon! I know who murdered Celeste Simone."

TWENTY SIX

"SAMUEL BATEMAN." LANIE declares triumphantly, as she weaves in and out of traffic. "And I've got proof."
"Motive?"
"Yep, he had it—big time. I'm on my way, I'll tell you everything in ten minutes, maybe fifteen—fucking traffic."
"Are you sure?"
"I've never been so sure in my life. Fuck! I knew from the moment I met him. I should've trusted my gut. I've just left him and Jerome at the courthouse. Get the arrest warrant and meet me downstairs, we'll bring him in together."
"What were you doing at the Courthouse with them?"
Lanie pauses. *Fuck.* "Long story, Jon. I'll tell you everything when I see you."
She frustratingly navigates her way through roadworks. "C'mon, c'mon, c'mon!" She stupidly has 'avoid tolls' set to default on her maps, so now's stuck going at a snails-pace on a one-lane road in the middle of suburbia. She practices those breathing exercises again to bide her time.
Around 40 minutes later she finally pulls into the

underground car park at the station. She's craning her neck, looking for Jon.

"Where are you, Jon?" she mumbles urgently. He's not there. She pulls into a park and catches the lift upstairs to his office. The doors slide open to the bullpen. Jon is there, waiting.

Sam and Jerome are there too.

"What the fuck?" *Fucking traffic.*

"Detective Daniels, good to see you again so soon."

Lanie groans. "Didn't I just leave you two?"

Hmmm, you did, but what can I say? You're exceptional company."

Sam is standing behind Jerome like a child hides behind a parent when they're in trouble.

Lanie notices the skin around his cuticles are chewed raw. "Jon, we got our guy!" Lanie storms over to Sam. "Samuel Bateman you are under arres—"

"That won't be necessary, detective," Jon interrupts.

She meets his eyes, then turns back to Sam. "You are under arrest, anything you do or say—"

"Detective Daniels, stop it right now. That's an order."

"Jon, what the hell is going on?"

"He didn't do it. C'mon let's go to my office."

Lanie wonders if he's being deliberately obtuse. The four of them walk through the mostly empty bullpen—besides Mary and Sanjay who are making themselves scarce—and into his office. The desk is solid oak. It's immaculate, apart from a purple-polka-dotted giraffe statue that Jessie, his daughter, made for him out of play-dough. The walls are stereotypically adorned with newspaper clippings and framed certificates. In the centre of the wall is his prized-possession—albeit more than a touch twee: a clipping of the very first case he solved.

"Okay everyone take a seat," Jon says.

Jerome and Sam shuffle into their seats, while Lanie remains standing. She moves over to the side and just in front of Jon, who's in his raised chair.

Lanie doesn't wait for permission to start. "Someone was in the hotel room with Celeste when she died, Jon." She walks over to Jon's Aldi Nescafe rip-off, places the mug on the stand, puts a pod in and presses the start button. It growls discordantly. As it rumbles, Lanie continues, "we know this, because they got sloppy and didn't clean up the extra glass of red wine they'd used." Lanie turns to Jerome. "Now, you don't like red wine, do you Mr Pitt?"

"No, not really." He shakes his head

"No, beer is more your style—tasteless Mexican beer to be precise. But the same can't be said for you, can it Mr Bateman?" She looks over at Sam. "You love red wine, don't you—it's better for a certain condition of yours?" The final drabs sputter out the coffee machine and into the cup. Lanie grabs it, places it on the bench and starts scooping tea-spoon after tea-spoon of sugar into it. "I have footage and witness testimony saying they saw you, Mr Bateman, hold on to one of the two key cards that granted access to Celeste's room." Lanie picks up the coffee, walks over to Sam and puts it down in front of him.

"Plus, nobody seems to know where you were at the

time of her death—you left Jerome and Marco to be alone, didn't you?" Lanie stirs the hot coffee with one of Jon's pens she finds on the desk. "And, Mr Bateman, would you care to take a sip of this coffee for me?" She slides it in front of him on Jon's desk.

"No, thank you." He scratches his forearm.

"No? Why not?"

"I don't feel like a coffee right now, especially one that's been stirred with a biro."

He looks up at Jon and then Jerome, with an expression that asks whether Lanie is crazy.

"Is that right?" Lanie presses. "It's got nothing to do with your diabetes, then?"

"My diabetes?"

"Yes, Mr Bateman. Your diabetes. Now what if it was Equal sugar I'd put in this mug. Would you drink it, then?"

Sam's confused—she saw him only forty-five minutes ago drinking a coffee with Equal. He's not sure what the connection is. "Yeah, even if it was Equal I still don't feel like a coffee right now."

Lanie sits down. "When I investigated the hotel room, the morning of Celeste's murder, along with the extra red wine glass, there was also a screwed up empty sachet of Equal sugar that had been dropped by the foot of the bath." She pulls out her phone and shows them all a photo. *Got you, you bastard.*

Sam scoffs nervously. "Yeah? I was there earlier in the day, so what?"

Lanie chuckles. "That's true, you were, but you didn't have a coffee then, did you, because there were no pods at that time. Celeste had to ask the room service lady for more when she got her lunch—hours after you had left her." Lanie brings her hands together at her fingertips. She bounces them off each other. "So, what did you do, you sick fuck? Fill her with drugs and then have a glass of wine to settle the nerves?"

Sam sits there emotionless. Jerome's face creases at the eyes as he flinches at every word. "And as for motive: well, was it pay-back on Jerome for him taking your part of the company just before it sold for billions? You told me you don't care, but I think you do—who wouldn't? Or was it because of your unrequited love of Celeste? If you couldn't have her, then nobody could, isn't that right?" Lanie draws a deep breath and turns to Captain Bailey. "Oh, and I want an APB out on Abbie Benson-Wheeler. She has something to do with this too, which I'm sure Sam will reveal when we interrogate him. So, can I arrest him now?"

For finding out his friend murdered the so-called love of his life, Jerome is eerily unperturbed.

"What do you have to say for yourself, Sam?" Jerome asks.

Sam adjusts his glasses and clears his throat. "I'm sorry but it wasn't me—I told you yesterday."

Jon looks over at Lanie, sharply.

"Well, how do you explain the red wine, and the Equal sugar, and the key card?" Lanie inhales. "And I almost forgot. Don't forget your OCD—the drugs in that bathroom were lined up perfectly, just like the cutlery yesterday." She clenches her jaw.

Sam interlocks his ankles and leans forward. "Like I already told you about the key card," he says, reaching into his pocket and pulling it out, "I totally forgot there were two until you mentioned it, so I went home and checked the pockets of the pants I was wearing that morning and it was still there. Look, here it is." He hands it to her. "I was going to show you back at the courthouse, but you ran off. And as far as the wine goes. What can I say? I'm not the only person in the world who drinks red wine. It wasn't mine, DNA test the glass if you have to. Take a sample of my DNA right now! I want you to if it clears my name in your eyes. And the same goes for the Equal. I think I can explain that too. See, Celeste would drink Equal when she was trying to lose weight, which was pretty much always—came with the job. Also, are you saying that I had wine and a coffee? It just doesn't make sense."

Lanie goes to protest, but Jerome cuts her off. "I think that's enough," he says. "You've done some good detective work, but you just got it wrong this time—it's all circumstantial. I told you when I saw you the night of the Melbourne Cup that Sam's innocent, you should've listened to me then, instead of wasting your time. I've said it before, but the real culprit is her depression. Not Sam or Abbie or a random busker. It's the malady of the social media age. It's insidious. Haven't you read the papers?"

Captain Bailey lifts himself out of his chair. "We are sorry, Mr Bateman and Mr Pitt. It appears it was an accident, after all," Captain Bailey apologises. "We are truly sorry, aren't we Lanie?"

Lanie's shoulders slump; she sighs, knowing she's lost this battle, despite every sinew in her body wanting to arrest Sam, and slap that shit-eating grin off of Jerome's face. "Sure," she says, vacantly looking at the purple play-dough giraffe.

Sam's about to respond but Jerome jumps in. "Don't worry about it, and just so you know, I don't intend to take this any further. You're only human; you made an honest mistake—your job can't be easy. C'mon Sam, let's go."

Jon walks them out, continuing to apologise, leaving Lanie by herself in his office. "That patronising motherfucker," she seethes, picking up the giraffe and ditching it at the closed door with an almighty thud. It sticks for a moment and then drops to the floor.

Jon returns solemnly. He steps over the giraffe then looks up and gives her a look. A what-the-shit-was-that look.

"Jon, he was there, I know he was in that room when Celeste died."

"Sit down!" he orders. She can hear the strain in his voice. *He's already moved on from anger and onto the disappointment stage.*

Lanie sits and straightens her shirt. "Jon! I'm telling you—"

"Why didn't you tell me Jerome was helping you with Thomas' custody case?"

Lanie's whole body slumps. "I—"

"It's a gross conflict of interest, Lanie. Do you understand how serious that is? You might lose your job! I thought you were better than this."

"I'm sorry, Jon. I didn't ask for his help, and I wanted to tell you, but—"

"Just go home. I'll tell them it was the news about your mum, that it turned you upside down. Don't come back until I work this out—if I even can. You should of told me Lanie."

"I know—I just thought. Fuck, I don't know what I thought. It was dumb. I am sorry Jon." She stands up to leave. "And tell Jessie I'm sorry about the giraffe." Jon can't even look at her. She walks out his office and over to the elevator.

She paces back and forward in the lift like a caged animal as it descends down to the car park. The doors pull open, she storms over to Frankie, jumps in and slams the door shut. The sound echoes off every crevice of the empty concrete car park. She sits in her car, takes a couple of deep breaths and then smacks both hands back and forth against the steering wheel in a wild flurry, to a chorus of half-honks. She puts the old Fiesta into gear and screeches off, leaving a little bit of rubber on the polished, oil-stained cement.

TWENTY SEVEN

SCREW IT! SHE thinks as she makes her way out of the underground car park and to a dive bar around the corner. Not the cool Hollywood movie variety, but an actual run-down, derelict pub. The kind where old men order ponies and pay in pennies.

She parks badly in a no standing zone out the front, spills out and charges through the front door. It's dire; perfect. There's a pokies room to Lanie's left, past a cigarette machine and glowing, ribbed condom dispenser. The soul-sucking, monotone, 8-bit melodies float obnoxiously into the main bar. Keno plays on multiple boxy, 32-inch TV screens, bolted to every corner. A pool table sits off to the right. The green felt is white in places from wear. The beer stained carpets reek of stale stories and drunken brawls started over nothing in particular.

The bartender is wearing a plain black apron over a pin-striped shirt featuring a peeling iron-on of the pub's name: The Earl of Leicester. The bartender's old. She smells of a combination of shampoo and rolling tobacco. She's skinny and wrinkled and looks like she's smoked enough cigarettes to last several life-times—non-smoker lifetimes. She leans over and opens the glass washer. Steam swallows her. The water highlights the I've-given-up look etched into every line on her face.

Lanie walks over and orders, "two shots of tequila," making a backwards peace sign with her middle and forefinger.

The lady stops polishing a schooner glass and wordlessly reaches under the bar, pulls out two fluorescent plastic shot glasses and slams them onto the counter with a clunk clunk. She pivots and grabs the Coyote house tequila from next to the ice well.

Lanie's mouth begins to salivate, but not in a good way. She swallows the lump in her throat, trying to talk her out of it—she hasn't drunk since Thomas's accident. *Brett, that motherfucker.*

The bartender pours the shots, splashing tequila over the bar mat. She puts the bottle back and turns to the cash register.

While the lady's back is turned, Lanie shoots one and then the other—bang bang. It tastes like ass and it burns like one the morning after dodgy Mexican. She keeps swallowing, stopping herself from chucking it up. She shakes her head, and complements it with a tiny grunt.

"Gin and soda, with fresh lime, if you've got it," she says chewing on her tongue.

"Only got lime cordial, darl."

"Whatever, fine," Lanie says. "Here, put my card behind the bar. It's gonna be a long night."

The bartender makes Lanie her gin and soda and plonks it down in front of her. Lanie slugs it back.

"Another."

The old woman obliges, and Lanie does the same.

"You might wanna slow down there," the woman rasps half-heartedly.

Lanie stares back at her. A keep-your-advice-to-yourself stare. "Another."

The lady pours another.

"Thank you." Lanie reaches across the bar, grabs a straw and shoots it into her glass. *I know he was there, I just know it. Everything points to Sam Bateman being in that room with her.* She's starts to feel warm. The Asian blush begins to powder her cheeks. *And Jerome, that bastard, he set me up this whole time.* Her heart's racing. *And Brett! That asshole spiked my drink.* She picks up her glass and takes another sip of gin and soda. She puts the glass back on the bar, miscalculating the distance, so slamming it down as if it was closer; spilling half of its contents. *Fuck my life.* Lanie picks up her drink, trudges into the pokies room and takes a seat in front of a machine. She stares at it blankly, pressing the button on autopilot, like the drinking bird Homer Simpson uses in that episode where he wears a moo moo. She sits there for who knows how long, mindlessly spinning pixels. She doesn't care if she wins. That's not the point. She hopes she loses. Anything to numb her from how she's feeling.

"Hey sweetheart," an older man that smells like piss and peanut butter says as he walks past. She could tell he was married, despite not wearing a ring, because his left jean pocket was scuffed white from where his wedding ring would catch, from years of pulling his hand in and out. Lanie ignores him.

"I said, hello darling," Lanie rolls her eyes and keeps pressing the pokie machine button. "A smile wouldn't kill ya, would it!" Lanie's left eyelid twitches. She turns around and punches the asshole right in the throat.

His thorax crunches and shifts under the force of her fist. His hands grab at his neck, as he desperately tries to suck in air. "That bitch hit me," he croaks, not loud enough for anyone to hear—not that they'd care if they could.

Lanie coolly turns back to the pokies, pushes the button, watches the colourful graphics on the screen spin around and around, and loses again.

"Lanie!" Becca calls out. "What are you doing?"

Lanie turns to Becca. "Becs! What's happenin'? Let me get you an espresso martini!" Lanie says as she stands up and quickly down again. "When did gravity get so heavy?" she slurs. "And can someone please change this fucking music—I've been listening to this song for hours!" she yells to the bartender, referring to the music coming from the pokie machine.

"Sorry. Sorry," Becca says to the bartender, with open palms. "I'll take care of it."

The guy clasping his throat comes over. "This bitch your friend? Tell her she's gonna hear from my lawyer," he says, hoarsely.

Becca looks up at him. "Your lawyer, huh? Well, here's my card, tell them to call me. Now get lost!"

Lanie laughs a little maniacally.

"Lanes, look at me. Lanes, how much have you drunk?"

"Umm, only seven drinks," Lanie says, counting them on one hand.

"Let's get you out of here." Becca helps Lanie up and drags her outside. "Is this about Sam and Jerome, or Brett? It's evil what Brett did to you, spiking your drink like that. Looks like you were right about him all along."

Lanie scoffs. "I told you so," she says, but it felt hollow.

"Looks like Frankie's staying here tonight," Becca says as they walk past him out the front of the pub. "I'm driving you home."

"The captain didn't believe me about Sam," Lanie says. "He sided with them over me."

Becca looks sideways at Lanie. "I'm sure he had his reasons, Lanes," Becca remarks, as she carts Lanie out with her arm around her shoulder—thanking the heavens that she's small. They reach Becca's car—a new silver Mercedes coupe—and jump in.

"Did you know they call poison the woman's weapon?" Lanie goes off on a tangent, thinking about Celeste laying lifeless in the bathtub.

Becca starts the car and keys Lanie's address into Maps. "You need to eat." She turns back to the navigation and revises the route to go via a McDonald's.

"If I was gonna murder someone, I wouldn't poison them. I'd look them in the eye and strangle the life out of them." She's wringing a make-believe neck in her hands.

"Big yikes! That's dark, Lanes."

Lanie shrugs. "Just saying."

The two friends sit there quietly as the blurry, street lights zip by.

"Fucking Jon," Lanie breaks the silence. "He's meant to have my back, but looks like I'm wrong about that, as well." She looks out the window. "How'd you find me, by the way?"

"Jon—who most definitely does have your back—called me. He said you could use a friend." Becca lets that sit with Lanie for a moment before continuing. "Then I logged back into the 'find my phone' app, which you used on my mobile at the pub the other day, and it led me straight to you."

Lanie smiled. "You detectived me!"

"Yep, detectived the detective! Just don't think you could do my job," she teases.

"Oh no, I'm far too honest for that," Lanie snorts, thinking she's hilarious.

The car pulls into the McDonald's drive-thru.

"Welcome to McDonald's, can I take your order?" the Macca's girl asks through the speaker.

Lanie leans over Becca. "I'll get one large cheeseburger meal, no pickles, with a coke, six nuggets, and an apple pie and some of those animal crackers."

"Will that be all?"

Lanie turns to Becca who shakes her head.

"Yep, that's all."

"Thank you. Drive to the first window please."

Lanie holds her gaze on Becca, waiting for an explanation.

"I'm not eating that shit."

TWENTY EIGHT

BECCA DROPS HER off out front of her apartment building. "You going to be alright, Lanes?"

"Yeah, don't worry—nothing this…" she holds up her bag of Macca's, now translucent in some spots, "and a Berocca won't fix." Lanie turns to walk inside, but stops. "Hey, thanks Becs. I owe you one."

"Ha, more than one!" Becca replies. "But who's counting?" She waves goodbye with a quick salute; then drives off, leaving Lanie alone on the sidewalk.

Lanie stumbles over to the front door of her apartment block, searching for her beeper to let her in. Someone's at the door. *It's probably just an Uber Eats driver*. She edges closer. The guy's face is illuminated by his mobile phone. He looks familiar, but Lanie can't place him. He finishes whatever he's doing on his phone and reaches for the doorbell.

Lanie's phone buzzes. With her free hand she pulls it out of her jacket pocket. It's a message from a Piero. *Do I know a Piero?* She opens it, the stranger's voice calls out from the doors,

"Lanie?"

Oh shiiiit. Piero from the cafe! "What are you doing here?" She swiftly hides the bag of Macca's behind her back.

"You texted me." He holds up his phone screen with a quizzical look on his face.

Hey comeovr and fuck me... 52/432 Murray road, Preston. Its out-of-your-league Lanie.

Lanie squints at the screen before her eyes widen in horror, and not just at the spelling mistakes and bad grammar. She has no recollection of sending it. Zero, zilch, zip. *Bloody tequila!* She re-reads it, just to make sure it was her. It was—of course it was.

"I sent that two hours ago. Have you been waiting here the whole time?" she asks incredulously, not inviting him up, but also not turning him away.

He looks at least ten years younger than her. His cropped black hair cuts into his sharp hairline. He's taller than Lanie, but who isn't? The yellow street light bounces off his creamy Mediterranean skin. Lanie bites her bottom lip and rubs her forearm.

"This was a bad idea," Piero concedes, noticing a slight sway to Lanie's swagger, realising she's had a few drinks. He starts heading towards the street. "I should go." He brushes past her.

She's overcome with a wave of bar soap and testosterone. Not the brutish body gel smell you'd find in a high school locker room, but soap. Delicate and clean.

She puts her arm out. "This way," she says, as she opens the glass doors. Piero nods obediently and follows her inside. They enter the lift. Lanie hits the button and they stand silently for anywhere between twenty seconds and forever. They're inches apart, but feel connected by the atoms between them.

When did I shave last? Lanie wonders. *Shut up!* The lift door opens. *For Christ's sake don't sabotage yourself.*

An old lady in a violet parachute tracksuit enters with her Pomeranian. She places herself uncomfortably between them. The dog sniffs at the Macca's bag still in Lanie's hand. The unfortunate waft of a cheeseburger and nuggets grows as she smells it through Piero's nose.

How old does he think I am? The doors open and the lady and her dog exit, leaving the two of them alone again. Lanie captures her reflection in the mirrors, the fluorescent down-lights forcing her to look away. *Ignore it, you look fine—it's the lights.*

They travel up one more floor. The doors pull apart. Lanie leads Piero into the hallway. He follows her to her front door. A lump has formed in her throat. It's been a long time since she's had someone over. Her nerves reach fever pitch as she anticipates what comes next. She fumbles through her key ring, finds the front door key and unlocks the door. The jingling sound of the keys is heightened by the otherwise noiseless apartment. They step through the threshold. He immediately pins her against the wall with exhilarating force. They kiss, a long, intentioned kiss. The kind she's rehearsed in her head countless times with faceless men. She drops the bag of food by the door and shoves him in the direction of her bedroom. A bread crumb trail of clothing follows them: shoes, socks, jackets, t-shirt and jeans. Lanie grabs Piero's right bicep, then rests one hand on his sculptured abs. She pushes him onto the bed. As they tumble down, he spins her around. He deftly clicks off her bra. She unthreads it from her arms. He crawls up to her, his fingertips gently caress her milky skin, making figure-eights down her thighs. Their eyes meet and he kisses her on the lips, gently biting down on the lower one. He tickles his tongue across the roof of her mouth, sending shivers euphorically recoiling up and down her body.

"Wait, wait!" Lanie says. "Do you mind, just, um..." She starts to blush.

Piero looks at her quizzically. "What is it?"

Lanie leans forward and whispers, "do you mind brushing your teeth before we, you know?"

Piero looks down and smiles before letting out a gentle laugh. "Of course," he says, dragging his right leg off of her and onto the floor next to the bed. "But I didn't bring a toothbrush."

Lanie chuckles nervously. "I have spares," she says. "Oh shit. This is weird isn't it? I've killed the mood, haven't I?"

Piero just laughs again. "It's no problem," he says easily. "Just tell me where a toothbrush is and I'll be right back." He walks towards the small en suite.

"They're in the second drawer under the sink. You can't miss them." Lanie pulls the covers over herself.

"Got it!" Piero calls out, over the sound of crunching

plastic toothbrush packaging. Piero dutifully brushes his teeth, even borrowing some of Lanie's mouthwash. He places the used toothbrush in the holder next to Lanie's, holds his cupped hand over his mouth and breathes out to check his breath—minty.

He leaves the bathroom and switches off the lights. He inches back into Lanie's bedroom, and towards her under the covers. The quilt rises and falls with each gentle breath. He steps towards the bed and just as he's about to dive back in, he discovers Lanie's fast asleep. She's passed out. He smiles, grabs a pillow and makes himself comfortable on the couch in the living room.

TWENTY NINE

IT'S WEDNESDAY MORNING. Lanie wakes up. The sunlight filters in through the cracks in her venetian blinds. Her head is pounding; her stomach's screaming and her mouth feels like it's stuffed with cotton balls.

What happened? she thinks, before it all comes rushing back to her. *Shit!* She nervously reaches behind with her arm, blindly prodding the white bedsheets around the space behind her back. It's empty. It was all a dream.

"Morning," Piero says, walking into the room, drying his hair with a towel, with another towel wrapped around his waist.

Oh fuck! It wasn't a dream.

Seeing the horror on Lanie's face, Piero reassures her. "Don't worry," he says, "nothing happened."

Lanie rubs her eyes.

"So, what do you want to do today?" he asks, as if they'd been here a million times.

Lanie sits up, pulling the doona with her, covering her chest. "I ah…" she searches for the right words; her brain scrambles to invent a story. "I have to, um…" her foggy head isn't doing her any favours. "I um, you have to leave. I've got to work."

Piero screws up his face. "I thought you said you have the rest of the week off?"

Lanie closes her eyes and inhales, trying to focus. "I did, did I? Well, I just got an email this morning, I've been called in." She jumps out of bed, somehow wrapping the quilt all the way around her. She follows the trail of clothes, picking up her top and jeans and taking them into the bathroom.

Meanwhile Piero gets dressed and casually makes his way over to her kitchen. "Nescafe? Seriously?" he says, professionally offended, studying the commercial-sized tin. "Do you really think this is the forty third blend? I don't remember the forty second blend, do you? And why did they stop at forty-three? Surely they should've kept going? I mean have they tasted it?" His incessant prattling makes Lanie feel nauseous. "Let's get out of here and grab a real coffee," Piero suggests.

Lanie answers from the bathroom, "I would love to, but honestly..." She walks out the bathroom fully dressed, droplets of water giving away that she splashed her face a few times. "I really do have stuff to do." Piero looks in the empty fridge.

"Oh, I see what's going on here," he says, his lips curling into a grin, turning to face her. "You used me."

Lanie's brain works in overtime, trying to come up with an excuse.

Piero laughs. "Relax! I'm messing with you, but I can take a hint." He moves over to Lanie. "Thanks for last night," he says as he hugs her.

Her reticence belies how she sees herself. She shakes it off and assertively kisses him on the lips. Hard. "I'll call you," she says.

"Si," he replies, smiling. He grabs his jacket from the floor and makes his exit, smirking at the bag of cold McDonald's on the way out. "Ciao bella."

Lanie walks over to the TV, grabs the remote and then puts it back down, without turning it on. She doesn't need the noise this morning. She wanders back into the kitchen and over to the yellow medicine basket above the fridge. She reaches up on her tippy-toes and teases a box of Panadol over the side of the basket. It falls down into her cupped hands. She grabs a glass from the drying rack next to the sink, fills it with tap water and swallows two pills. She fills the glass up twice more, trying desperately to rehydrate herself, then steps over to the fridge and looks inside. She stares blankly into the white void, finally grabbing the lonely, weeks-old broccolini and chucking it in the trash on the way out the door to the nearby cafe and heavenly egg and bacon roll.

Lanie takes the lift down to her underground car park, where she's assaulted by screeching tyres, bouncing around the basement and her brain. As she turns the corner to her car spot, she discovers Frankie's not there. *Someone's stolen my car!* She pulls out her phone from her back pocket, unlocks it and sees a message from Becca.

Frankie's at The Earl of Leicester xxx

Lanie looks around to see if Becca's hiding somewhere. She's not. She just knows her too well. Lanie's struck with a new wave of nausea. She covers her mouth with her right hand. *Offt! It's probably for the best, anyway.*

She takes the lift back up and walks out the front door. The daylight smacks her mercilessly. Her brain pulsates in pain. *Why tequila!* Her pupils dilate. She bends over akimbo to suck in some deep breaths.

"This is gonna suck," she mutters. She steels herself and starts walking in the direction of the cafe. There's a dull ache in every muscle. She stops and rests on a retaining wall not twenty metres from where she started. She pulls out her phone and orders an Uber. She swallows the nausea, quietly hoping a huge crack in the Earth would open up and swallow her likewise. The Uber arrives five minutes later. She climbs in and greedily drinks the free bottle of water. The tinted windows and air-conditioned cabin provide sweet relief. The news is playing on the radio.

Today the world mourns Celeste Simone's tragic death. Her memorial is being held in her hometown of Melbourne at the St Patrick's Cathedral. She leaves behind her loving husband, Jerome Pitt, and millions of grieving fans around the world. The memorial will be live streamed and is expected to be virtually attended en masse by people from all over the globe. After a comprehensive investigation Captain Jon Bailey of the Victorian Police has officially declared her death a tragic accident.

The news only heaps on Lanie's misery.

"Would you prefer some music?" the old, messenger-hat-wearing, retiree Uber driver asks with a lopsided grin, seeing the struggle written in her face.

"Yes, sure," Lanie replies, swallowing another pang of nausea.

The driver swiftly turns down the volume, clears his throat and, "I don't wanna wait for our lives to be over…" he recites the opening bars to the Dawson's Creek theme song.

Brilliant, I've got the one Uber Driver in Melbourne with a sense of humour—just what I need right now.

The Uber pulls up at a cafe—the same red-tiled cafe she abandoned when this all began—and she jumps out, feeling partially better. "Don't forget to give me five stars," she hears the driver's voice trail behind her.

She walks in and finds a seat inside. It's a minimalist space with clean white walls, white countertops and white tables and chairs, polished concrete floors and black geometric light fittings. The menu is written on the wall in a non-permanent marker. Lanie sees her egg and bacon roll up there. A familiar waitress walks over and places a brown serviette, cutlery and recycled Herradura bottle filled with tap water on her table.

"Do you need to see the menu?"

"Nope, I know what I want: a bacon and egg roll and a black coffee, please," Lanie orders—looking forward to finally eating a whole one without being interrupted. A dainty orange tea cake, like the one Pimm shared with her caught her eye when she walked in, too, but the booze in her belly was crying out for oily food. *Maybe next time.*

"No worries," the waitress replies, turning towards the kitchen.

While Lanie waits for her order, she settles in and does everything she can to shrug-off that nagging feeling of unease that Sam did it, and put the case behind her. She's feeling cold, so puts her headphones in to help warm up with some lofi hip hop. The waitress brings over her coffee.

"Your roll won't be a minute," she reassures Lanie, whose stomach is grumbling.

"No worries," she mouths back as she looks around for the WiFi password. "Sorry, excuse me," Lanie pulls out her left headphone, "can I grab the WiFi password from you again?" Lanie unlocks her phone, ready for the girl to tell her. She swipes down to the WiFi screen and discovers she's already logged-in. "Oh, never mind, it's already connected."

The girl rubs the triangle tattoo on her forearm. "Yeah, the network remembers you." A bell dings from inside the kitchen, and Lanie's head. "That'll be your food." She turns to go collect it.

Lanie freezes. Her mouth drops. "You idiot Lanie," she berates herself out loud. She raises her phone and finds Frank Farmer's contact—the so-called citizen journalist—and calls him. He picks up straight away. "Frank, I need your help," she says. "I need you to get the network history of The Grand Theatre Hotel and cross reference it with Sam Bateman's mobile to see if his phone connected to the network between 11 p.m. and 3 a.m. on the night of Celeste's murder," she whispers the last word as the waitress returns with her egg wrap. "If he was in the room his phone's IP address should show up on the WiFi network—all three witnesses told me he connected to the WiFi that morning."

There's silence on the other end of the phone. "It was a murder then?" Frank finally says.

"What did I just say?"

"You do realise, detective, what you're asking me to do is illegal?" A conspiratorial smile evident in his tone.

"Just do it Frank. And quickly."

"You got it, detective," he says, to the soundscape of his keyboard clacking. "Why don't you get your cyber security guys onto it?" he asks, guessing Lanie's gotten herself in trouble again, which is the only time she contacts him.

Lanie's running out of patience. "The captain benched me, I'm cut off from police resources."

"Again?" Frank chortles.

"Don't worry about that, just do this for me, Frank."

"Oh, I've already done it."

"What! Well what did you find?"

Frank clears his throat for dramatic effect. "Sam

Bateman was there. In fact, he wasn't just in the hotel, he was connected to the room's Wi-Fi."

"I fucking knew it!" Lanie slams the table with her free hand, disturbing the old couple, sitting side by side in silence, reading separate newspapers, eating a long brunch next to her.

The waitress looks over from behind the coffee machine, shaking her head.

"Sam Bateman you fucking fuck!" Lanie whispers. "I fucking got you!"

"Woah."

"Thanks Frank! You know if you ever need a real job, we'd take you in a heartbeat, right?"

"Ha! I'd never sell-out to the cops. Besides, I'm not sure how far a referral from you would even get me."

Lanie chuckles. "You're probably right. Thanks Frank, I owe you one."

"Ha! Heard that before," he replies. "Wait! wait!" he says, before she hangs up.

"What is it?"

"While you were trying to recruit me to your fascist regime, I thought I'd check whether anyone else from that gang of weirdos was there, and it turns out it wasn't just Sam Bateman who visited The Grand Theatre that night…"

Lanie holds her breath. She knows what's coming next.

"Abbie Benson-Wheeler was there as well.

"Fuck! I knew it!"

"Anyway, good luck, detective. I'll be watching!" He hangs up.

Lanie looks down at her plate; at the greasy egg wrap. *One of these days I'll get to eat you*, she laments. She takes a big bite, followed by another and another until her mouth is full. She chases it with a big sip of coffee, gets up and strides out of the cafe. She's got a memorial to attend.

THIRTY

THE SUDDEN JOLT of adrenaline sharpens the rusty edges of her hungover. She checks her watch. The memorial starts in forty-five minutes. Frankie's not that far away. It'll be quicker to run there than wait for an Uber.

Her phone buzzes. It's an email from Frank. He's sent over the WiFi logs from the hotel, with Sam's and Abbie's mobile's IP addresses clearly highlighted. *Bloody legend.* She takes off, reading a note at the top of the email.

I know you're probably on your way to the memorial so just an FYI: you've been blacklisted from attending. I'd hazard a guess and say it's Jerome Pitt's doing. The facial recognition software on the security's Umwelt Lenses will spot you from a mile away. Be careful.

"When do us Daniels women ever do things the easy way!" she says out loud, quoting her mum.

She pounds the pavement, doubling her effort. Tequila and gin seep out of every pore. Her loose black tee-shirt clings to her back. She's holding her jacket in one hand, while the other swings metronomically back and forward. The brisk Spring air inflates her lungs as she inhales deeper, faster. With each heavy thud, the weight of her own body shoots up her ankle, shin, knee and hips. She's out of shape, but her single mindedness drowns out any physical pain. She rounds the final bend; skids on dry leaves, and feels her feet fall from under her in slow-motion. A passer-by rubber-necks her tumble and takes a step towards her to help. "I'm good," she says, warding him off with a freshly-grazed palm. He shrugs his shoulders and saunters off. "My bones broke the fall," she adds sarcastically, through gritted teeth. She pulls herself off the pavement and limps the rest of the way.

Frankie the Fiesta is there, parked out front of a dingy old pub. *What was I thinking?* As she approaches she sees a parking inspector writing her a ticket. "Hey! Stop, I'm a detective!" she calls out in between deep gasps of breath.

The parking inspector languidly raises his eyes to meet hers. "Yeah, and?"

"And... stop writing me a fucking ticket!"

The parking inspector shrugs, prints the ticket and slaps it onto her windshield to join two others. He glibly tips his hat and ambles away. "Detective."

Lanie doesn't have the capacity to care right now. She grabs the tickets, unlocks the door and chucks them in the backseat with all the other junk. She takes a breath before turning on the car. The cold sweat on her t-shirt brushes against her skin, making her shiver. She pulls it off over her head and uses it to dry her armpits, before grabbing a cleaner but not clean one from underneath the tickets in the backseat. She puts it on and ties her hair back.

"Now, let's go get this bastard." She presses the ignition button and the engine sputters to life, along with the radio. It's her song.

Rollin', rollin', rollin'. Rollin', rollin', rollin'. Rollin', rollin', rollin'. Rollin', rollin', rollin'. Raaaaaawhide.

"Nice to have you along for the ride, dad." She pats the dashboard and steals a glance towards the heavens. She hits the accelerator. The torque pushes her body back in the seat.

Rollin', rollin', rollin'. Though the streams are swollen. Keep them doggies rollin'. Raaaaaawhide.

She burns down Nicholson street, the automatic gears shift soundlessly. She's travelling south, darting through traffic, gazing straight ahead, only half-aware of the outside world. Her thumb taps at the steering wheel to the music.

Move 'em on, head 'em up. Head 'em up, move 'em on. Move 'em on, head 'em up. Raaaaaawhide.

She speeds up at an amber light, pulls the wheel, and takes a sharp left down Albert street, then a right down Gisbourne.

Cut 'em out, ride 'em in. Ride 'em in, cut 'em out. Cut 'em out, ride 'em in.

She pulls over in front of the St Patrick's Cathedral

as her song reaches its final, epic crescendo.

Raaaaaawhide.

She jumps out. The place is packed. There must be thousands of people there, huddled in the shadows of three giant spires, waiting for the service to start. She impatiently moves through the crowd at a snails-pace. A 19th century gothic-revival cathedral towers above her. She's approaching it from the south, along the Pilgrim Path. Water cascades down a channel that divides the two sides of the stepped pathway.

"Sorry," she says as she bumps into a woman in a black hoodie.

"Detective Daniels!?" a familiar woman's voice calls out from behind her. Lanie turns her attention in the direction of the voice, losing the hooded person in the crowd for the second time that fortnight.

"It's so good to see you again." It's Paula. She's wearing the mustard Alice McCall dress.

"Paula," Lanie finally responds, looking past her. "It's good to see you too, Paula, but I'm actually in a bit of a hurry."

"Oh, okay. No problem, maybe I'll see you inside—I can save you a seat if you like?"

"Sure." Lanie forces a smile, nods and pushes past her.

She climbs upwards, ducking and dancing past groups of Simoners. Within the channel of water there's a number of blue stone tablets laid down with the water flowing over them. The tablets are inscribed with gold-inlaid quotes. Lanie reads one as she continues her climb upwards.

> *Incarnate Word,*
> *in whom all nature lives,*
> *Cast flame upon the earth:*
> *raise up contemplatives*
> *Among us, men who*
> *walk within the fire.*

That's all she can make out. The rest has been slowly devoured by water. It reminds her of something Jon would always say: 'run towards the fire'. *Which is exactly what I'm doing right now, Jon.* She reaches the top of the stairs. *It's just too bad you're not here with me.* She's met by a giant bronze bowl, which shoots water in three directions onto the seven stepped structure below. She heads towards the west doors, under the gaze of two bronze statues with an undeniably Italian theme: St Francis of Assisi, and St Catherine of Siena. *You were listening in religion class—the sisters would be proud.* She makes a hard right, following the perimeter of the basilica, searching for a back door. She blindly turns left and crashes headfirst into a security guard. Their eyes meet. The jig is up. The facial recognition software programmed into the security guard's camera is going to set off an alarm and alert Jerome she's there.

But nothing happens.

His stare oscillates between her and his screen.

"Are you okay Ms Dzunka Juric?"

It's about time a bit of luck falls my way. "Sorry, yes. I'm fine." She hurries away. "Thank you, Jesus!" she says, under the gaze of his colourful geometric likeness in the giant stained-glass window above her.

She tracks around the wall looking for a way in. She comes across a stout wooden door with cast iron hinges. It's the priests' living quarters. The doors creak open. She sneaks inside, careful not to draw attention. The place is deserted. She makes her way down a hallway. The soft, linoleum floor helps conceal her footsteps. The muffled sound of a door closing somewhere up ahead inoculates her with adrenaline. An image of the Virgin Mary hangs on the wall. Her sad, maternal eyes follow Lanie as she edges down the hallway. There're small bedrooms on both sides: boxy, sanitised rooms with single beds and terse white sheets, smelling like a mix of starch and frankincense. The hallway opens up into a kitchenette opposite a small living space. Lanie freezes as she spots an elderly man on a cane lounge watching an old TV with bent rabbit-ear antennas. Presumably an off-duty priest with an unironic friar tuck haircut. He's leaning into the TV, his back to Lanie. She holds her breath and steps behind him. She sneaks towards an ornate door, etched with a depiction of Christ's crucifixion. *This has got to lead to the church.* She turns the oversized brass knob. The door's hinges screech open to reveal she's in the sacristy, just behind the altar. There's someone else in there. A male. His back is facing her. It's Samuel

CHRISTOPHER OTT

Bateman. *Got him.*

THIRTY ONE

"HOLD IT RIGHT there!" Lanie says. Sam's back stiffens. He slowly raises his hands in the air as if he was in some cops and robber's movie. Lanie steps sideways trying to get a better angle on him as he turns around slowly.

"You think you're so smart, don't you, Mr Bateman? But I got you, you lying prick! Take a wild guess whose phone puts him in Celeste's hotel room at the time of her death?"

Sam's face contorts. His hands shake like the leaves on the trees outside. "You don't understand." He's facing her now, hands lowered but still open. He's scared; terrified.

Lanie steps towards him, beginning to read him his rights. "Samuel Bateman, you are under arrest for the murder of Celeste Simone. Anything you say or do will be used against you—"

Sam's eyes dart over Lanie's shoulder. There's someone there. Lanie jerks around. "Hold it!" she says. The person freezes. It's a woman. She's wearing the black Nirvana hoodie.

"Samuel didn't kill anyone," a familiar voice says from under the hood. "Abbie!" Lanie faces her. Abbie slowly pulls the hood back on her jumper. *Holy fuck.* It's not Abbie. It's Celeste Simone. She's alive.

"What the actual fuck!?" Lanie blinks to make sure her eyes don't deceive her. She opens them again and Celeste Simone is still there—in the flesh. Lanie's attention darts back and forth between her and Sam. "Celeste!? You shouldn't have come back," Sam says.

Celeste takes a single step towards them. "I couldn't let you take the fall for something you didn't do, Sam."

"Hold it!" Lanie says again. Celeste freezes. "Someone want to explain to me what the fuck is going on? You're meant to be dead!"

"Celeste, you're alive—it's a miracle!" Jerome's stentorian voice steers him through the other door that leads out to the altar.

Lanie takes a guarded half step back. "You stay right there, Mr Pitt. Don't come any closer." She holds out both hands.

"Celeste," Jerome continues. "I thought I'd lost you," he says, putting down the notes he'd written for her eulogy on a nearby table and stepping towards her.

"No you don't—I said stay there," Lanie says, desperation seeping into her voice. She backs into the only corner left in the room, resting against a bench, not far from Celeste.

"And you would have if Sam killed me, like you told him to!" Celeste howls.

Jerome turns to his old friend. "I what!?"

"Stop it! Stop lying! I know it's true. You wanted him to kill me so you and Abbie could be together. Sam recorded everything—I've got it right here!" She holds up her mobile phone, pushing it in Lanie's direction.

"Celeste, look at me. I don't know what he told you, but I never—"

"Stop lying. It's all here on my phone." Celeste looks down at her phone screen, presses a few buttons and then looks up again. "And now the world will know the truth, Jerome!"

Audio starts playing. It's Jerome. "I want her gone, Sam," he says. "Make it look like an OD and no one will ask any questions."

Jerome's jaw clenches. His eyes ignite.

Celeste continues. "It doesn't matter, anyway. There will be no happily ever after for you now."

"Wait, what!?" Lanie finally puts it all together.

Celeste turns to her. "Jerome told me that if I left him, he would ruin me, that he'd ruin my career—he'd take my life from me. Death was the only way out, so when an opportunity to fake it presented itself, I took it. Who wouldn't?"

"That's enough!" Jerome snarls. He turns to Sam. "You had one job, Sam. One fucking job. But you just had to save her, didn't you? Didn't you! You ungrateful nobody. I gave you everything, and this is how you repay me. By helping this useless slut!?" He points at Celeste. "She played you Sam. You fucking idiot!"

Sam rolls back his shoulders. "You don't give a shit

about me! Or Celeste. You never have."

"Ha," Jerome scoffs. "Don't be naive Sam. I was doing this for her." He shifts his gaze back to Celeste. "I wasn't going to give you any drugs you weren't already taking on your own." He turns back to Lanie. "No one was going to question anything—especially not some washed-up alcoholic detective like you. Even you should've been able to piece together the bleeding obvious. I fucking laid it up for you: clinically depressed social influencer couldn't cope with the bright lights and unattainable standards and blah blah blah, but you had to keep digging, even when I told you to stop."

"You arrogant piece of shit!" Celeste screams before Lanie can respond. "Why wouldn't you just let me leave you?" She clenches her fists. "Why wouldn't you just let me go!" Tears start to stream down her face.

"Let you go—why would I let you go?" Jerome scoffs. "I made you. You would be nothing without me. You are mine."

"You're fucking nuts," she screams. "That's why I had to do it!" She turns back to Lanie. "It was my only way out of this nightmare!" She rubs her eyes vigorously, forcing her inactive Umwelt Lens to pop out.

Lanie takes a step towards Celeste.

"I don't think so," Jerome says, pulling out a gun from the back of his pants, and pointing it at her. Lanie flinches, covering her face. *Where the fuck did that come from.*

"It didn't have to be this way," Jerome says icily, turning back to Sam. "If you had just done what you were told, Sam, then this would all be over. The world would be celebrating the short but bright life of Celeste Simone, and Abbie and I could have finally been together, happy."

Lanie's tongue involuntarily rubs against her front teeth in furious little figure eights. She inches imperceptibly towards Celeste, or more accurately towards the loose Umwelt Lens on the floor, stealing unnoticed millimetres at a time.

Jerome swings his gun in Lanie's direction. "What are you doing?" he barks. Lanie feigns another flinch, dropping to one knee.

Jerome turns back to Sam. "It didn't have to be this hard."

Lanie slowly reaches down, grabs Celeste's Umwelt Lens, puts it in and turns them on.

At his small two-bedroom terrace house, decorated in too much Tibetan art, in Redfern in Sydney, a notification pops up in the upper right-hand side of Pimm's screen, who's taken the day off to watch Celeste's memorial.

In a big, grandiose, empty house in Brighton the same notification appears on Paula's computer, which her husband with the turmeric beard notices as he walks past the empty study. After checking no one's around, he sits down and watches it—his guilty pleasure.

And in a small one-bedroom apartment in

Adelaide, a notification distracts Irene from putting the final punctuation mark on the first chapter of her thesis, which she's finally started.

All three witnesses click the notification and stream Celeste's point of view for the first time in over a week.

"There's just one thing I still don't fully understand," Lanie says, standing up, drawing Jerome's attention. "Why would you want to murder Celeste Simone?"

Jerome looks down, then back up at Lanie, Sam and Celeste—in that order. He weighs up whether to invent a story or tell the truth. He opts for the truth—no one will believe them anyway. "Because I'm pregnant," he spits out. "I'm having a boy." The confession hangs in the air. "It was the only way." He looks over at Celeste's ashen face. "Did you hear me, Celeste? I'm finally going to have a son. Can you believe it? You should be happy for me?" he continues, "it's all I ever wanted, you know that."

Lanie follows Jerome's gaze to Celeste, who's fallen to the floor, sobbing uncontrollably. "It's Abbie, isn't it—the mother of your child?" Lanie asks.

"Well done, detective," Jerome says, throwing his head back. "I suppose even a clock's right twice a day."

Lanie grimaces.

Jerome continues. "So you finally got a hold of Abbie on that damned digital detox of hers, did you? And she told you?"

Lanie looks across at Celeste. "No, I never did."

"Abbie was pregnant?" Celeste asks weakly, looking at Lanie rather than Jerome for confirmation.

"Abbie *is* pregnant," Jerome says, correcting the tense. "Why are you asking her?"

"Celeste," Sam interrupts, gasping for air, "what did we do?"

The cold-blooded truth slowly crawls its way across Jerome's face, as he realises what Lanie had figured out minutes earlier. "Done? Wait. Whose body is that out there?" He points his gun to the altar.

Lanie takes a step towards Jerome, her palms open. "Jerome, listen to me. The girl in the hotel room. The girl out there, it isn't Celeste. It was never Celeste. It's Abbie," she says. "Celeste murdered Abbie."

His muscles constrict; his face turns whiter than the Holy Sacrament wafers, sitting on the nearby table. "You," he starts, swallowing each word, "killed, my, son!?" He points his gun at Celeste's fractured figure on the red-carpeted floor.

"I didn't mean to, I swear," Celeste wails, resting her face in her hands, before rallying. "I didn't know—how could I know she was pregnant? She came to my hotel after the fight; she wanted to talk about it—that stupid, naive little girl. I didn't want her to, but she insisted—she just came around anyway." Celeste wipes her eyes with her sleeve. "So, I thought it'd be fun to put something in her drink. That moron, Marco, had got us some coke at the club, but Abbie—sweet, perfect, innocent Abbie—wouldn't have any, and she lorded it over me!" She sits up. "And I had my Xanax from the flight. But Jesus Christ! I never thought it'd kill her. I'd been taking them all day; I was fine! But then she had a heart attack. I didn't know what to do, so I called Sam." She turns to him.

"It was Sam's idea to put her body in the bath." She points at him, before stopping herself. "No, it wasn't. What am I saying? I'm lying," she admits. "It was mine; I made him do it." She rests her face in her hands again. "I got him to put the stick-on tattoo from the magazine behind her ear, so that everyone would think it was me. And I was the one who got him to lay out the drugs in the bathroom, making it look like an OD—good loyal Sam," she continues, looking away from him. "People always said Abbie and I looked alike, especially after she dyed her hair." She turns to Jerome. "It's what drew you to her in the first place, isn't it Jerome! You found a younger version of me—you wanted to replace me!"

"Shut up!" Jerome barks. "Shut up! You're going to pay for this. You both are!" He wheels around, flashing his gun at each of them in turn.

"Fuck you!" Sam screams, throwing caution and care to the wind. "You're fucking pathological!" He's trembling.

"And you're unhinged! Both of you!" He turns to Jerome, then Celeste. "You use people—you used me!" He looks squarely up at Jerome. "You took my life's work and claimed it as your own," he says. "Then you thought you could order me around like I was nothing more than your dog!" He swallows. "And you!" he continues, facing Celeste now. "You said you loved me—told me that we'd be together! But it was all one big lie so I would help you cover up a murder, and I was stupid enough to believe it." He's angry at himself. "I was always just a pawn in your psychotic little games." Sam looks down at his hands, inspecting them as if they didn't belong to him. "And now an innocent person is dead. Two. And I'm an accessory."

Sam breaths heavily, exhausting years of pent up anger.

Jerome looks over at his old friend and meets his gaze. The same friend who he'd grown up with; who he'd started Umwelt with in his parents' garage. "Sam," he says, with eerie serenity. "You're right." He swings the gun upwards and points it at himself, placing the barrel under his chin.

"Wait!" Lanie yells, lunging towards him.

"And I am truly sorry."

Bang. The shattering sound of a gunshot echoes throughout the church, reverberating around the world to thousands of viewers streaming at home.

THIRTY TWO

SMOKE RISES FROM Captain Jon Bailey's gun. Jerome curls over; blood crawling along his white cotton shirt.

"Lanie, are you okay?" Jon asks as the room swiftly fills with police.

Lanie's muscles finally relax. She turns off Celeste's live stream. "I'm fine, Jon. These fucking people—I told you!"

"Yeah, yeah," he replies. "You can 'tell me so' all you want later. Let's get this mess cleaned up first."

They look over at Jerome's contorted body, laying on the floor. The shot went clean through his shoulder. It'd hurt a lot, but it won't kill him. Jon always was a good shot.

He groans in agony as he's hoisted onto a gurney while being arrested for conspiracy to murder. "My son!" he repeats over and over, a shadow of the man that had forced his way into Lanie's elevator over a week ago.

"Wait a second," Lanie says to the paramedics as they're wheeling him out. She steps over to Jerome. "Not bad for some washed-up alcoholic, hey, Jerome?" She pats him on his gun-shot shoulder.

"See you in jail, pal."

Mary and Sanjay pick up Celeste's crumpled body from the floor, cuff her and read her her rights as they drag her limp body out of the church and to the back of a police car, past a shook crowd of Simoners, who thought they'd be attending Celeste's memorial today, celebrating her life, but got so much more than they'd bargained for.

There's already a crowd of Carters there, too, fighting for the best angle, streaming their point of view to the rest of the world. Frank's there also, sucking on another iced latte; he's somehow found his way past the police tape, again.

"What do we do with this guy," Steve asks, holding Sam's hands behind his back, ready to handcuff him, and drag him off with Jerome and Celeste.

Lanie walks over to him. "Mr Bateman, helping to cover up a murder is a very serious crime. You destroyed evidence, you obstructed justice and God knows what else." She meets his eyes.

"I'm sorry," he says. "I didn't want to, but Celeste… Actually, no. Celeste didn't make me do anything. It was me. I'm ready to be held accountable for what I've done."

"You didn't let me finish," Lanie says. "But considering the only evidence you did any of that stuff is the word of an actual murderer, who psychologically coerced you into doing all of these things, I think I may have difficulty getting any of it to stick, so," she says, looking over at Steve, "let him go."

Steve thinks about protesting but instead shrugs, lets him go and walks away.

"Are you serious?" Sam massages his wrists. His body is still shaking from the adrenaline.

Lanie nods.

"But I thought you hated me?"

"I never hated you, Mr Bateman. I hate bad guys, and, it turns out, you're not actually one of them."

Sam fixes his glasses. "Thank you, detective."

"Oh and Sam, there's just one more thing I can't work out," Lanie says. "Why would Jerome get the police involved, when he's the one who wanted Celeste killed?"

Sam lets out a nervous laugh. "You met him, right? He thinks he's smarter than everyone—even the police. He thought the closer he kept you, the more he could control you. But he got that wrong—he had no idea you'd be so persistent."

Lanie shakes her head. "That's one way to put it," she says. "Oh, and also, the evidence you showed with Brett, I suppose it's fabricated?"

Sam winces. "It was Jerome's idea, I swear. He wanted leverage over you. He recreated the whole scene in one of his studios, then applied your faces over the actors using deepfake technology—that's the insane lengths he'd go to own people."

Lanie grimaces. "Thought so."

"How'd you know?"

"Brett never really spiked my drink. I've been lying to myself about how much I drank that day. I know it was too much, and it's time I finally took responsibility for it. I'm not perfect. None of us are. And that's okay."

THIRTY THREE

"SO WHAT ARE you going to do with the video?" Susanne asks Lanie as she reclines on the hospital chair in the chemo infusion area, with an intravenous drip hanging off her left arm, reluctantly pumping a stress ball in the same hand.

The room feels orange: the walls, the recliners, the monitors, even the medication that Susanne's getting injected into her arm is on the same orange spectrum. There're five other recliners in the room, with only two being used by other patients, who are absently watching the TVs hanging from the ceiling, and the news reports of Abbie Benson-Wheeler's murder.

Susanne's wearing a violet fancy dinner dress with her favourite pearl necklace. They told her to wear something comfy, like a tracksuit, but she refused—that's not her style. She's also wearing a Swarovski turban. She made the choice to shave her hair last week, so she didn't have to watch it fall out. In fact the whole nursing home did it for her, including the front desk woman, Fiona, and Raymond—that old pervert.

"Well, it's obvious, isn't it?" Lanie says. "I can't use

it, can I?"

"Of course you can't," Susanne cackles, interrupting the sombre mood of the place. "But there was a time there, where you would have seriously thought about it."

Lanie smiles. A light, unburdened smile. "What can I say, I'm growing as a person."

Susanne mirrors her grin. "Well, I guess it's never too late."

"Actually, I already had Becca contact his lawyer and call the whole thing off."

Susanne straightens her arms, trying to get comfy. "Too bad, it would have been good to see Thomas some more."

"Yeah it would have, but I see things through Brett's eyes now, and he has every right to be pissed at me for what I did. Hell, I'm pissed at me for what I did. In fact, I've kinda come to the realisation that all that time I spent being angry at Brett, was actually me just being angry at myself. He's a good man. It just never worked out between us, and now it's my job to make sure that impacts Thomas as little as possible."

"I'm proud of you!" Susanne says. "Even if that does mean I'll have to pay for the vending machine now I won't have his little hands to help!"

Lanie chuckles. "I'm sure Brett will still bring him around for visits, mum," she says as the equipment starts beeping.

A nurse rushes over and presses a button to stop the incessant wail. "You're all done, love." She takes out the needle.

"So, what's next?" Susanne asks, as she shakes her arm and rolls down her sleeve. Lanie walks behind her mum and helps her up out of the recliner and into her wheelchair.

"You know what?" she says, as she starts wheeling her out of the room. "I might take a break. I've got lots of days in lieu built up."

"Haha," Susanne laughs. "You? Take a break? Pull the other leg why don't ya." She grabs the front collar of her dress and shakes it to let air in and dry up the sweat. They exit out of the hospital's front doors.

"Nanna!" Thomas yells excitedly.

"Tommy Gun!" she calls back with as much enthusiasm as she can muster, disguising her exhaustion. "How'd you get here?"

"Dad brought me," Thomas replies, giving his nanna a big cuddle, as Brett finally catches up with him.

"What are you doing here, Brett?" Lanie asks, genuinely surprised.

"I, um, thought it'd be good for Susanne to see this little guy," he says. "Becca may have let slip about the cancer. Plus, I thought we could talk. I think it's about time Thomas sees his mum—sees you—more," he says. "When I was faced with the prospect of losing him, it changed my perspective a little bit." He looks up and meets Lanie's eyes. "But I mean, only if you want to?"

Lanie smiles. She's on the cusp of tears. "I do—I would love that."

"Good," he replies, nodding, before turning to

Susanne. "And how are you feeling Susanne?"

Susanne smiles. "It'll take more than a tiny bit of radiation to stop me," she says, ruffling Thomas's hair, before turning to Lanie and giving her a wink. "Besides, when do us Daniels women ever do things the easy way."

EPILOGUE

LANIE'S BACK AT the cafe, where she was sitting somewhere between a fortnight and a lifetime ago. The sun shines down into the courtyard as she scrolls through the morning news on her phone.

The waitress carries over an egg and bacon roll along with an empty glass and recycled Jack Daniels bottle full of tap water, and lays them out neatly in front of her on the bench. Lanie nods her head in thanks.

"Also," she starts, pointing to the counter, "can I please get some of that orange cake from the front window?" The waitress nods silently and walks back inside. Lanie expertly lifts the top of the bun, douses the insides in hot sauce, returns the crown and takes a big, greasy bite. A combination of sauce, egg yolk and oil drips out of the end and onto the floor, where there's an awaiting marmalade cat. Lanie pulls out a slither of bacon from her roll and shares it with him. The two sit there in companionable silence before her phone interrupts with an obnoxious dial tone that Thomas had set and she doesn't know how to change. It's Tod from the forensics team. Lanie picks it up.

"Well if it's not my favourite forensics guy! You're ringing to congratulate me on solving the case?"

"I heard—well done, detective," Tod says. "Listen, sorry to call you on your day off, but I just got back the results on the hair follicle, and thought you'd want to know them, you know, before you go sit on a quiet beach somewhere."

Lanie puts down her roll. "The hair follicle? I totally forgot about it. Whose is it, then?"

The name makes Lanie choke on her food. "Thanks," she says, in between fits of coughing, before hanging up.

She clears her throat, forces another quick bite of her breakfast, stands up and pours the remainder of her coffee into her keep cup. She makes her way out of the faded red-tiled roofed cafe to her red Ford Fiesta named Frankie, parked half a metre from the curb, dialling Captain Jon Bailey on her mobile phone. He picks up. Lanie doesn't let him say hello. "Jon, we need to find Paula Abbas."

CHRISTOPHER OTT

End.

CHRISTOPHER OTT

The worlds they perceive, their Umwelten, are all different.

- Jakob von Uexküll

CHRISTOPHER OTT

About the Author

In the footsteps of other authors, Christopher has been a copywriter for over a decade, winning awards for creativity across the globe, including the Cannes Festival for Advertising. From big shiny agencies with table tennis tables and open bars, to Twitch to the Walt Disney Company, Christopher has written for some of the biggest brands in the world, before choosing to finally write for himself with this his first novel. He normally talks in the first person (I swear) and goes by just 'Chris' (unless he's in trouble, of course), but since becoming an author, has decided to write in the third and use his full name—every three syllables of it—Christopher, as it sounds more author-y. Thank you for reading his/my novel; hope you liked it. Of course, if you did, please leave a nice review. And if you didn't, if you could keep that to yourself, that would be greatly appreciated.

CHRISTOPHER OTT

ELEPHANT IN THE DARK

CHRISTOPHER OTT

Manufactured by Amazon.ca
Acheson, AB